Copyright © 2020 by Shantel Tessier

All rights reserved.

No part of this book may be reproduced or transmitted in any form or by any means, electronic or mechanical, including photocopying, recording, or by any information storage and retrieval system without the written permission of the author, except for the use of brief quotations in a book review.

This book is a work of fiction. Names, characters, places, and incidents either are products of the author's imagination or are used fictitiously. Any resemblance to actual persons, living or dead, events, or locales is entirely coincidental.

For more information about the author and her books, visit her website- www.shanteltessierauthor.com.

Editor: Jenny Sims

Formatter: CP Smith

Photographer: Furious Fotog

Model: Alex Michael Turner

KINGDOM

TITAN

THE DARK KINGS

BESTSELLING AUTHOR
SHANTEL TESSIER

PROLOGUE

TITAN

I SIT BEHIND my desk, the dark curtains pulled closed to block out the early morning rays of the Las Vegas skyline. Taking a sip of my black coffee, I look up at the five women standing in my office. "Strip down to your bra and underwear," I order.

Four of them begin undressing without hesitation. They do this for a living, though it's usually under flashing lights, fog machines, and thundering music. And don't forget the money that comes with selling your body. But still, they're not shy. The last one on the right watches the others with wide green eyes as she nibbles on her bottom lip.

"Problem?" I ask.

She looks at me and swallows. "I … uh, I didn't know … I didn't wear a—"

"You don't have anything I haven't already seen," I interrupt her rambling.

"Here," Sandy chirps. "You can wear mine." She unclasps her black lace bra and holds it out to the blonde. Her rather new and perky looking paid for DDs are now fully on display.

"My boobs are too small for that!" the girl shrieks in horror.

Sandy drops it to the floor and shrugs. She slaps her palms down on her bare thighs and does a little hop in her six-inch heels.

Fuck! It's too early for this shit. I'm not a cheer coach gearing them up for a game. Rubbing my temples, I stare down at their paperwork that covers my black desk. "Megan, you didn't list your limits," I announce, glaring up at her through my lashes.

Her eyes drop to the floor, and I don't miss the fact she's still dressed. Her arms now hugging her small chest. "I didn't understand …"

"What a limit is?" I bark out.

She flinches and whispers, "I've never done anal …"

Jesus!

The other girls laugh. "It's more than just that," Sandy tells her with a smile on her face.

"What else could there be?" Megan asks wide-eyed.

Fuck me! This girl is sheltered, and I should have stayed in bed.

"Are you willing to do bondage?" Sandy fills her in, placing her hands on her wide hips. "And if so, do you mind being gagged, flogged?" Megan gasps. "If you enjoy being tied up, do you prefer rope, handcuffs, chains." The girl begins to tremble. "There's also fisting …"

Just then, my office door swings open, and the only woman I don't mind seeing enters the room.

I stand. "Ladies, this is GiGi. Think of her as your … house mom." Good enough. "She will take your measurements and record them for your files." The four half-naked women nod with excitement. "Once the fitting is over, Dr. Lane will see you."

"Doctor?" Megan swallows.

"Yes." Growling, I look at her. Has she not listened to a damn thing I've said? "All Queens are required to be on birth control. Ninety-five percent of our clients already have wives and children. They want to be guaranteed that there won't be any surprise babies or a Queen trying to get knocked up for blackmail money." We guarantee our clients' satisfaction. And unplanned pregnancies are not going to obtain that. And I'm not about to trust any woman with my reputation and dedication with my clients.

They all turn and bounce out. "Megan, have a seat." I stop her.

She falls into one of the black leather chairs across from my desk and looks up at me. Jesus, she has tears in her eyes.

I walk around my desk and lean up against it. "Why are you here?" I ask. Crossing my arms over my chest, I glare down at her.

She picks at a piece of nonexistent lint on her jeans. Her dirty blond hair shields her face from me. "I need money."

No surprise there. "What do you need money for?"

She heaves a heavy sigh, unable to meet my eyes. "My father is a druggie. My mother left us a year ago. Went to the store to buy a pack of cigarettes and never returned." She swallows. "I have a younger brother who's three. I want to get him away from our father, but I don't have that kind of cash. Not to give him what he needs."

"Your application stated that you're twenty-one."

"I lied," she whispers.

I already knew that. And I'm pretty sure she's a goddamn virgin. "How old are you?"

"Eighteen."

"Attending high school?"

She shakes her head. "I dropped out when my brother was born. I needed to stay home with him."

I run a hand down my face, that headache intensifying. "Being a Queen isn't a good fit for you." That's as nicely as I can put it.

Her head snaps up. Her green eyes narrow on me before she averts them and slumps her shoulders. "I know. I don't know what I was thinking." She pushes her hair behind her ear.

All types of women come and go from my office, and I can tell when someone is being neglected. Her cheeks are sunken in. Her eyes have circles under them. Her tank top keeps falling off her shoulders, and her collarbones are prominent. She probably makes sure her brother is fed before herself, and I respect that. "Are you quick on your feet?"

She nods once. "And I'm a fast learner."

"Have you ever been a waitress?"

"No."

I sigh. Just let her leave …

"But I can do it." She sits up straighter, eyes wide with hope. She doesn't wanna take her clothes off, but she's willing to carry drinks around in a tight mini skirt and halter top. Doesn't matter how you dress it up, sex equals money. The more you show, the more you'll make.

Maybe it's my fucking headache, or maybe I'm just in a giving mood. Doubtful, but I say, "Go to this address and give this to Mitch." I walk around my desk and sit down in my chair. I write as I speak. "Tell him I sent you, and he'll get you on the schedule." I tear off the Post-it and reach across the mahogany surface. She can't work in Kingdom. In the state of Nevada, you have to be at least twenty-one to even serve drinks. But I have hookups all over this town, including restaurants.

She grabs the note. "Thank you, Titan. Thank you so much."

I nod and hold up the paperwork. "I'll tear this up except for the NDA." She nods quickly. "What happened up here does not leave this room."

"Yes, sir."

I point at the door. "Get going."

She runs out of my office much faster than she had entered.

Opening the bottom drawer in my desk, I pop the top off the pill bottle and toss a couple into my mouth before washing them down with my coffee.

The girls re-enter my office with GiGi. "All done, Titan." The sixty-five-year-old lady smiles at me. She wears her bleach-blond hair up in a tight bun. It's not even eight a.m., and she has a full face of makeup topped off with fake eyelashes and red painted lips. She's always well put together and in a good mood.

The girls giggle, and Sandy picks up her bra and places her tits back in it.

"Thanks, GiGi. Send Dr. Lane in, will ya?"

She nods.

Sitting back in my chair, I fold my inked arms over my chest and look at the four women who stand before me.

The *Queens* of Kingdom.

Three of my best friends and I own a hotel and casino in the heart of Las Vegas. I oversee the Queens, our secret service. I have a list of men a mile long who want our girls. A couple of senators, a handful of movie stars, and even more rock stars. CEOs and some blue-collar hardworking dads who just want to blow off some steam before going home to their nagging wife and screaming kids. They fly in from all around the world.

They want a date for a work event, they call me. They want a woman to take on a trip to Maui, they call me. They want a woman for the night in one of our exclusive suites here at Kingdom, they call me.

I pull four cells out of my top drawer. "Here are your phones." I place them on the desk.

They had to hand them over when they arrived earlier. "I downloaded the Queens app on them. If at any time you feel uncomfortable or think it's getting out of hand, make the call. It calls me directly."

The brunette who hasn't said much over the past two hours looks at me. Her name on the NDA she signed says Maggie. She came with Sandy. "Do you have to end a date early often?"

I shake my head. "No. Our clients understand how it works, but I understand that sometimes things can go too far. You have too many drinks. He decides he wants more than what he pays for. You call me, and I'll take care of it."

"Have you had to do it before?"

I nod.

"And?" she asks.

"And I ended it." Simple as that. A girl has never been raped or beaten while on the clock. My clients understand what they sign up for when they request a girl. If they so much as break any rule on the contract, I will break their fucking necks. But I understand I can't be there with them a hundred percent of the time, so we make sure all bases are covered.

For the most part, everything always goes smoothly. The girls get to keep sixty percent of what I charge, and some have never even taken their clothes off. Getting naked and sucking dick aren't requirements to be a queen, but if that's what they want to do, then by all means. Plus, they keep a hundred percent of their tips off the books. That's between the client and the Queen to negotiate.

The cheerful blonde who answered every question on her application with hearts over her i's steps forward. Her name is Whitney. She places her hands on my desk and smiles down at me. I already know where this is going to go. "Do you sample the product? You know, rate it for your clients?"

"No." I don't shit where I work. The Kings and I have enough problems as it is. I don't need to add pussy to the mix.

She pushes her bottom lip out as her dark eyes roam over my inked arms. "That's too bad."

My door swings open so hard it hits the interior wall, and one of my best friends and business partners enters my office. His blue eyes are narrowed, and his chest bowed. He's pissed about something. And if I had to guess, I'd say it's regarding his brother, Grave, who is another friend of mine and business partner.

"Have you seen this?" he demands, storming over to my desk. He slaps a piece of paper on the surface. "This is bullshit!" He points at the headline. Bones is the only guy I know who will see an article on the internet and print it off to read over and over.

Instead of reading it, I watch Whitney stare at Bones like her next meal. I'm forgotten. She's already moved on. I smile to myself. I'm not going to tell her that she has better odds winning the lottery. Bones doesn't touch anyone associated with Kingdom. He flies out of the state to get his dick wet. His current flavor of the month is a five-foot-eleven runway model who lives in a six-thousand-square-foot penthouse in New York. She's already planning their wedding. He's just using her. Like we all do. Men like us don't fall in love. Not every King needs a Queen.

"Hi." She has her tits pushed up in the air.

Placing my elbow on the desk, I watch in amusement as she tries to seduce him. Like she has that skill.

"I'm Whitney." She jumps in front of him.

He ignores her as he begins to pace. "Titan!" he snaps.

"What?" I glance up at him.

His jaw is set in a hard line. He stops pacing and places his tatted knuckles on my desk. Leaning over, he speaks quietly to me. "Did you know about this?"

"And who are you?" Whitney asks, still going on.

He turns his head to look over at her, and her eyes widen as she takes a step back. Bones can have that effect on you. His fuck you attitude can turn anyone away.

I stand from behind my desk, grab her upper arm, and shove her out of the room as she protests. "Everyone out!" I order to the other three, who exit without argument. Slamming the door shut, I go back to my desk.

I pick up the paper and read over it. And sure enough, it's about Grave. *Kingdom heir arrested for DUI.* And then it shows his mugshot. "No surprise there," I say, tossing it back down.

Bones pushes off my desk. "I'm going to fucking kill him myself."

I wouldn't put it past him.

"We need to do something. I will not let him throw away his life." He shakes his head. "Not like …"

"As much as I hate it, there's nothing you can do," I tell him regretfully.

His younger brother has a death wish. Been that way since we were kids. And the man isn't going to change now. He loves the drugs, the women, and the booze. Not to mention his addiction to fighting and gambling. "He's an adult—"

"I don't care what he is," he interrupts me. "What I care is how he drags Kingdom's name through the mud." He sighs. "One day, I'm gonna get a call to identify his body."

"In Grave's defense, that could happen to any of us." The four of us are not careful with our lives. One of our best friends is Luca Bianchi—the son of a Don and head of the mafia here in Vegas. We recently helped him kill and bury several bodies.

"Really?" he snaps at me. "When was the last time you were arrested?"

"Let me talk to him," I offer, ignoring his question.

He snorts.

I sit back down in my seat. "Seriously. I'll take him out this weekend. Just feel him out." I gesture at the paper on my desk. "You know how reporters lie about shit. Maybe what is written and what actually happened are two different things." Doubtful, but it was worth a try. I'll have to ask Cross if he was there with him. And if he wasn't, then that's who Grave would have called to bail him out.

He snatches the paper off my desk. Wads it up and tosses it into my trash. "Fine. But if you don't talk some sense into him, my fists are going to."

My cell rings, and I pick it up. "Hello?" I ask as Bones plops down in the chair across from my desk, letting out an annoyed sigh.

"Titan. I have something you might want to know," the man says in greeting.

"What is it?" I ask, closing my eyes, wishing this damn day was over. The bitch just started.

"Nick York passed away."

They pop open. "When?" I demand, and Bones sits up straight, noticing the change in my voice.

"Last week. Heart attack."

I hang up.

"What was that about?" he asks.

I set my phone on the desk and lean back in my seat. "Nick York passed away. Heart attack."

His brows rise. "Interesting."

That is interesting, considering that Bones used to fuck his only daughter. And the fact that his business partner owes us five hundred thousand dollars.

That is very interesting. I pick up my phone and make another call.

EMILEE

STANDING AT THE floor-to-ceiling window that overlooks the Las Vegas Strip, I don't see the casinos or tourists that walk the streets with their phones out, taking picture after picture. Instead, all I see are my blue puffy eyes and runny nose. I quickly wipe the tears away that silently continue to come no matter how much I try to stop them.

My body is heavy. My chest tight, and my heart is shattered.

Two months ago, I found out that my mother was sick. *She is going to die*; the doctor had said. *There is nothing we can do*, he had added. I've spent the past two months trying to prepare myself to tell her good-bye. To find a way to be at peace that her suffering will end, and she will no longer be in pain.

But I could have never prepared myself for this.

Two days ago

Sitting on the floor in the middle of my Chicago apartment with boxes surrounding me, I have one open between my legs. I'm shoving scarfs into it when I hear my phone ring in the other room.

I let out a long breath, blowing the loose strands from my ponytail off my face as I debate whether I want to answer it or not.

I've been avoiding my friends and their endless questions that will come when I answer. I went home to Vegas a couple of months ago and was told that my mother is dying. My time is limited. I had to come back to get a few things in order and pack up my apartment while putting it up for sale. While I was there, one of my best friends, Jasmine, had called me, and I told her what happened. I should have kept my mouth shut, but it was like vomit. I was unable to hold in the emotions that flooded me. I told her. I know she's spoken to our other best friend Haven by now. She's been blowing up my phone, but I just don't have the words. I don't have the energy to talk about it.

It quits, and I feel relieved. But then it immediately starts up again. Getting to my feet, I step over a few tubs full of clothes and make my way down the hallway to my bedroom at the end. I pick up my phone off my queen-size bed and frown when I see the number.

It's my father's business partner. "Hello?" I answer.

"Emilee ..." He sighs, and my heart begins to pound.

"Is my mom okay?" I rush out. Maybe my father had to take her to the hospital, and that's why he didn't call me himself.

"It's not her," he says quietly, and a knot forms in my throat. "You need to get home. Something has happened."

My father had died.

That was the *something*. In the middle of a meeting, he stood from his chair and fell to his knees, then went down face-first from a massive heart attack.

"Emilee?"

I jump back from the glass and drop my phone. "Yes?" I sniff, wiping my face once again. Turning around, I see my father's assistant standing before me. She can't even give me a smile to comfort me. What little makeup she wore today is smeared across her face. She has worked for my father for over twenty-five years. She took the news as bad as I did because he was like a brother to her.

"He's ready for you," she says before turning her back to me and walks over to her desk.

"Thank you," I mumble so low I'm not even sure if she can hear me. I kneel, picking up my phone off the white marble floor where I had dropped it and bite my bottom lip, trying to calm my breathing. Nervously, I run my hands over my hair. I have it up in a tight bun, and my stomach growls as a result of not eating since ... I don't know when. Food has been the last thing on my mind. And what little I have eaten; I can't keep down. My nerves keep getting the best of me.

The fear.

The sadness.

The deep fucking hole in my chest.

It's all too much.

I'm not a stranger to death. My mother's mom died when I was eight, and I remember her service. How my mom was too weak to stand. My father had to practically carry her back to our car. She couldn't get out of bed for weeks.

Nanny's death crippled our family. Literally. My grandpa died three months later, and my mother swore it was from a broken heart. And it put her back in bed for longer than when she lost her mother. Both of her parents were gone, and she had no one else. She was an only child. Nanny and Pappa had her when they were in their mid-forties, so all her aunts and uncles were already gone. All she had left was my dad and me. But at times, I didn't think we were enough. She never seemed to have recovered from the loss.

The older I got, the more family members passed away. My father's parents died when I was sixteen in a fiery car crash. But he didn't crumple like my mother did when she lost her parents. No, he didn't miss a beat. He went on with his life as though nothing ever happened. He was strong; the exact opposite of my mother and me.

"Emilee?" Mrs. Williams asks, noticing my hesitation.

Nodding, I turn, walking down the long hallway past the photos of my father and his business partner that hang on the wall. They own a construction company and have built more structures than I can count over the years here in Las Vegas.

I try to calm my heavy breathing as my heels clap on the floor. Pulling my shoulders back, I grab the door handle and push it open. Stepping into the office, I pause. *It's empty.* "I thought you said he was waiting for me?" I manage to get out, poking my head out of the room.

"He is." I hear her voice travel to me from the front. "He's in your father's office."

My head whips around. "He's what?" This time, she doesn't respond.

Shutting the door, I walk to the next one and shove it open. "Why are you ...?"

"Here she is." George stands from my father's seat, and my heart stops to see him there.

My father wanted this office for the view. He loved Las Vegas. It's on the corner of the building, on the thirty-fifth floor. Fifty percent of the large room has floor-to-ceiling windows. He said there was not a better view in Nevada. When he would have to work late, my mother would bring him dinner. We'd have a picnic on his office floor as we watched the city light up the sky, and he would show us where his next project was going to be.

This was his space. His home away from home. And now George is going to take it over as if it were always his.

That's what makes me so nervous about this meeting. George insisted that I come here after the service. He said he needed to see me, and that it was important. "Mr. Yan, this is Emilee York." He introduces me to my father's attorney.

The man stands from his chair and reaches out his right hand, and I take it in mine. "I'm sorry we have to meet under these circumstances," he offers. His dark eyes seem saddened by the situation, but I don't trust him.

I had just met him at the funeral. We didn't speak, but I knew who he was because George had pointed him out to me. I didn't pay much attention to him then, but now, as I take in his Armani suit and welcoming smile, I don't like him. If he's my father's attorney, why am I just now meeting him?

I give him the weakest smile I can muster and take the seat across from the desk, pushing my black dress farther down my legs. It's not short by any means. It falls just to my knees in this position, but sitting here with both of them makes me uncomfortable. Too exposed. Or maybe it's the fact that I'm in this room, knowing my father won't be walking in anytime soon. To hug me. To hold me. To love me.

I do a quick scan of his desk and see all his pictures of my mom and me are gone. The few boxes over in the corner give me an idea of what happened to them.

I blink, trying to hold the tears that sting my tired eyes at bay.

George's creamy brown eyes look over my face, lingering on my lips, and I shuffle in my seat. Wanting to get the hell out of here, I clear my throat. "You needed to see me?"

Yan hands me a piece of paper, and I read it over. It's all bullshit words that I can't even pronounce let alone know the meaning of. It's in fucking attorney lingo. I blink. "I don't understand."

George sits back in his seat. "It's simple, Emilee. Your father had a will. Well, a trust."

I nod. "Okay." I'm not surprised. My father was always preparing for the unexpected, and he understood that death was a part of life. He wanted my mother and me to be taken care of. "Are we going to have a get-together for a reading of the will?" That's what we did when my father's parents passed. They were billionaires and had two kids, my father and my uncle Jack. We had to fly to Texas and meet with their attorney, and he named off every asset that they had left to their children. It did not go over well. They left my father over seventy-five percent of their fortune. My uncle was pissed. I haven't seen him since.

"That's what this is." George points at the papers that I still hold.

"I don't understand." I look back down at it. I don't see my mom or me mentioned anywhere on it.

"He has made me the executor," George announces.

"And?" I lick my dry lips.

"And I'm in charge of everything."

I swallow the lump that forms in my throat. "What do you mean? Everything?"

"We were fifty-fifty partners in York and Wilton Construction. We started it together right out of college," he rambles.

Yeah, with my father's money. He acts like I don't know him. "The house?" That's what I care about. Making sure my mother has a place to stay is the most important part.

George looks over at Mr. Yan and then back at me. "Also mine."

I stand. "I don't see how it can be *yours*," I growl, getting pissy. "It's in my father's name." He built her that house five years ago. It was exactly what she always wanted. She designed everything from the mosaic tiles and the crystal chandeliers to the color of paint in the closets. She had rugs flown in from Paris that she designed, for God's sake.

"No. It's in the company's name." He opens a desk drawer and pulls out an envelope. "And your father and I had an agreement."

"What kind of agreement?" I ask, trying to catch my breath.

He slides it across the surface, but I make no move to pick it up.

Sitting back, he crosses his arms over his chest. "If one of us passes, the remaining partner has first dibs at their shares of the company for a pre-determined amount." He nods at Yan. "It's stated in that document. Black and white."

I pick up the envelope and hold it in my hand. The room falls silent as I gently pull the tab back and look inside with shaky hands. "It's a dollar." I look up at him.

He nods. "That's what we agreed upon."

I put it back on the desk and rub a hand down my face, releasing a long breath. "What about my mother? She is his wife. She is legally entitled to what was his." Not like my mother would want fifty percent of the company—she never showed any interest—but she could sell my father's shares and that money could take care of what little time she has left.

Mr. Yan and George exchange a look.

Slamming my hands on the desk, I stand. "Quit bullshitting me." I may not be an attorney, but I'm not an idiot. He can't possibly take the house just because it's written in a trust. It may be in the company's name, but it should go to my mother. His wife.

George opens up the desk drawer again and hands me a black folder.

"What the hell is this?" I ask, mentally tired. He doesn't respond. I fall into the chair and rip it open. Pulling the papers out, I read over them, and my heart begins to pound in my chest. "No."

"I'm sorry, Emilee." George speaks. "They wanted to tell you …"

"I don't believe it." I shake my head as tears prick my eyes. *Divorce.* They got a divorce. "Two years ago?" I read both of their signatures and dates. "But …" I want to say that I've seen them together, but I haven't. Not since I graduated college and moved to Chicago. But wouldn't they have told me? That's fucking important. "This is bullshit!"

"They didn't want to burden you with their differences," Mr. Yan adds. "But unfortunately, when they got a divorce, she was no longer covered under the company's health insurance."

I let out a rough laugh because this is a joke. It has to be.

"Mr. Wilton will continue to pay for her care."

"So, that's what this is about?" Growling, I stand and begin to pace the room, my heels sinking into the thick rug. Now he's going to take care of her? *At what cost?* Is the first thought that comes to mind. But a part of me already knows that answer, so I refuse to ask it out loud. I won't give him that satisfaction. "This can't be happening." I sigh.

The attorney reaches into his folder and hands me another piece of paper, forcing me to stop. "He had a separate policy for you."

I try to scan it over, but I don't really know half the shit it's saying until I get to three million dollars. Then my eyes read the next part. "Thirty-five?" I ask, looking at him.

He nods. "At thirty-five, you will receive access to your inheritance."

That's eleven more years. "Are you the executor?" I snap at George.

He gives me that snake-like smile and shakes his head. "No."

I throw the papers to the floor.

My father is dead.

My parents are divorced.

And George controls fucking everything.

This is a nightmare I just need to wake up from.

Yan stands. "Until then, Mr. Wilton has controlling interest over the company and estate. You two can talk amongst yourself and figure the rest out." He gathers up his things, and George stands, walking him to the door and seeing him out.

Figure the rest out? What kind of attorney says that? The moment I leave this office, I'm going to hire my own.

George comes back and sits down at the desk. I look at him, and he sighs heavily. "This is not the situation I wanted, Emilee."

"Then hand it over to me," I challenge him.

He smiles softly. "That is not what your father wanted."

I look away. "The house? Give me the house." It's paid for. I know this because my father built the house for my mother. He was so proud of it, and she cherished it. He could hand it over to me, and I could borrow against it. That will be enough for me to cover my mother's medical expenses on my own. I don't want to owe this man a single dollar.

"It's in the company's name," he repeats. "I am the company."

I feel tears sting my eyes. *Is that even possible?* "So are you gonna kick us out?" I ask, and my throat tightens at the words. Make me pay rent? My mom spends a lot of time at the hospital. She's seeking treatment even though we all know it won't do her any good. She's going to die. The clock has started ticking. And as much as I hate losing her, I need to accept it and spend what little time she has left with her.

I look back at him, and my brows pull together. Why does he have this shit-eating grin on his face?

I've been away from Las Vegas two years now. I haven't come home enough. I know that now. So much was happening that I didn't even know of. I wish I could go back and spend more time with them, but it's too late. He's gone. She's fading. And I'm going to be left here with this sorry piece of shit.

He leans forward, placing his forearms on the desk. "Do you want to stay?" My heart beats faster at his words before his eyes drop to my chest. "In the house, that is?"

I look down at my hands fisted in my lap as the tears blur my vision. *I knew it.*

He's always been a fucking perv. My father chose him as a business partner because they were best friends, but that doesn't make him a good human being. There's a reason snakes hide in the grass.

"What do you want?" I ask even though I already know. I can't move my mom to Chicago when all of her doctors are here. I won't do that to her. She would want to stay here in her house to live out what remaining time she has left. Plus, my apartment is on the third floor. She would never be able to get up and down the floors easily. Even if she did take the elevator.

"It's simple really." He gets up, and I stiffen, keeping my head down.

My body begins to shake. I hear him behind me, but I don't turn around. Seconds later, he comes back to sit at the desk in my father's seat and pours a glass of scotch. He slides it to me and pours another one for himself. But I'm surprised when he slides that one to me as well. "You want your mother taken care of. And I want you."

He watches the tear run down my cheek and smiles. I stand. "No," I say and turn to walk toward the door. I'll find a way …

"She needs healthcare." My hand pauses on the doorknob. "You can't cover her under yours because you no longer have one after quitting your job. You could try to get her, her own policy now, but I doubt anyone would touch her. They don't like to dish out money for terminally ill patients. Do you make millions of dollars a year, Emilee? Do you make enough to pay for her treatment out of pocket?"

I close my eyes, and my shoulders fall. We both know I can't.

"She's got maybe four months left." He adds. "Even if the treatment doesn't work, don't you want her to be comfortable?"

I spin around, and my eyes glare at him. "You're a sorry bastard."

He gives me a smirk. "Your father put you in this position. Not me, honey."

"You're taking advantage of it," I snap. But I don't believe him. My father would not do this to me. To my mother. He loved us. He would have taken care of us. No matter what.

He shrugs. "Take it or leave it, Emilee." Then he dismisses me, turning to the computer.

Storming over to my father's desk, I smack my hands down on it. He looks up at me. "I won't …"

"Careful, Emilee. Think long and hard before you answer. I'm the man of the house now."

I scoff. "You may have a dick and balls, but you're not a fucking man."

He slaps me across the face so hard it has my entire body whipping around, and I fall flat on my face. Pain explodes in my cheek, and my breath is taken away from the impact to the hard floor. My eyes sting, and my cheek throbs. I close my eyes, biting my lip to keep from making a sound when I want to scream from the pain.

He sighs heavily from above me.

I sit up and look down to my legs and notice my dress has ridden up. I grab the hem and shove it down quickly, trying to cover myself up.

His dark chuckle fills the large office.

The door opens, and my head whips up to see a woman about my age walk in with several pieces of paper in her hand. She doesn't acknowledge me in any way. "Here are the papers for Miss Lee, sir."

That's my mom's maiden name.

He takes them from her, saying nothing, and she leaves just as quickly as she entered.

He tosses one to the floor in front of me, and I pick it up. I read over it, and it's a medical bill. Twenty-five thousand dollars and thirty cents. I swallow the lump that starts to suffocate me.

I look up to meet his eyes and they are on my legs. I try to push my dress down farther, but it's pulled too tight. I stand. What if he forces me …?

"I'm not gonna rape you, Emilee," he says as if reading my mind, and my breathing picks up.

Then his eyes run up my body, hovering on my chest before finally meeting mine. "No, you're going to open those pretty legs of yours and allow me to fuck that pussy all on your own."

My entire body goes rigid, and a coldness sets in my bones. His words sound so final as though my future is already decided. He knows he has me at a disadvantage. I don't have the kind of money for my mom's care, and I don't have any way to make that much, that fast. And I won't allow her to go without the best care money can buy.

It's extortion. But what can I do? How do I prove that?

He picks up the scotch he poured and hands it to me, saying nothing.

I hold it in my hand and look at the amber liquid. It's like he's offering me a present. Something that can dull the pain, but it won't be enough. I'm a cheap drunk, but I'm not a whore. I don't sleep around. I don't spread my legs for any guy who looks my way.

He reaches out, and I stiffen when I feel his hand on my thigh. I swallow the bile and spin around quickly to face him and throw the drink in his face. "I will not let you do this to me or my mother."

"You little bitch." He reaches for me, but I run for the door and yank it open, hitting him in the face. He falls onto his ass at the impact.

I run like hell down the hall.

"Emilee?" my father's assistant calls out my name, but I ignore her as I take the emergency exit, not even bothering to wait for the elevator.

ONE

TITAN

I SIT BACK in my seat at our custom black stone conference table. A skull is carved out of the middle. Kingdom is written in gold letters at both ends of the table. I sit at one, Bones the other. The thick, black curtains pulled closed to keep the sun out of the room.

Bones looks down at his watch and lets out a growl. "Where the fuck is he?"

"Grave is always late." I state the obvious.

Bones called an emergency meeting after we got the call about Nick York. All kinds of red flags have now gone up, and we need to discuss our next step.

Cross sits to my right, holding his Zippo in his hand. The sound of him flipping it open and then closing it is grating on my already short nerves. My headache still lingers like a one-night stand refusing to leave after I'm done with them.

"We'll start without Grave." Bones slaps the table.

"I say we kill George," Cross announces, straight to business.

I shake my head. "Dead men can't pay debts."

"No, but with Nick and George both dead, we can take the company," he counters.

I snort. "And exactly what are you going to do with it? You don't have enough spare time as it is."

"The company is not up for grabs," Bones states. "Titan is correct about already being spread too thin. Plus, I don't want the hassle."

"I'm sure Nick has left it to Emilee. She would be more than willing to sell it to us." Cross shrugs.

"How would you know what she would do?" I ask.

"Common sense. She doesn't even live here. You think she'll move back here to take it over?" He shakes his head.

Okay, let's try another way. "What do you know about construction?"

He rolls his eyes. "It can't be that hard."

Just then the door opens, and Grave enters the conference room. His blue eyes are red. His dark hair stands up in every direction and his clothes are wrinkled. He looks like he just woke up on the side of the street, which could be a very likely possibility.

Bones stands from his chair and crosses his arms over his chest as his little brother falls into a black leather chair. Lifting his chin, he glares down at him. "Where in the fuck have you been?" Bones demands.

"Don't start." He throws back his can of Red Bull like it's a shot. "You should be glad I even made an appearance."

Bones slaps his hands down on the table. "This is serious!" he shouts. "We were recently notified that George wasn't going to pay us, and now his partner is dead. Looks pretty fucking suspicious to me."

"Hey, I told you that we shouldn't have loaned George that money," Grave argues.

Cross lets out a whistle, and I shake my head.

Bones drops his head and runs his hand through his spiked hair. I'm just waiting for him to drag his brother across this conference table. It wouldn't be the first time. The only difference between Bones and Grave is that Bones is sober enough to actually do some damage at the moment. "He came to us and needed the money. We loaned it. That's it. Now that it's time for him to pay up, he wants to back out on his word, and we don't fucking tolerate that." Bones is saying all of this through gritted teeth.

I gotta say he's got more restraint than usual.

"Are we sure the money was for George?" I ask.

Three sets of eyes land on mine.

"Who would it have been for?" Cross asks with a rise of his brow.

"Nick," Bones answers, knowing what I'm thinking. He falls into his seat.

I sit up straighter. "He's come to us before, and we helped him out."

"He also paid us back," Cross says. "Sooner than we had agreed on."

Four years ago

"What can we do for you, Nick?" I ask as he enters the conference room. He had called up Bones an hour ago and said he needed to speak to us immediately.

I don't have a problem with the man, but his daughter, on the other hand ...

"I need a favor," he announces, straightening his tie nervously.

"What is it?" Bones asks, standing over by the floor-to-ceiling windows. The black curtains pulled tight to block out the sun. Bones prefers darkness in every aspect of his life.

"I need a million dollars," he announces.

The room falls silent. My eyes go to Bones, and he's running his hand down his freshly shaven face. Grave pops a bubble with his gum, and Cross is flipping his Zippo.

"Done." Bones nods. "I'll have it for you in three hours."

Mr. York's green eyes widen for a brief second, and then he makes sure to look at each of us when he speaks. "Don't you want to know why?" he asks, sounding surprised.

"No," I answer.

"The why doesn't matter to us. What is important is that you pay it back," Bones explains.

Nick nods. "Of course. I ..." He clears his throat. "Just tell me when." He decides against what he was about to say.

"Three months," I say.

He stands from the chair and buttons up his twenty-thousand-dollar suit jacket. "I won't even need that long."

We never did find out why he wanted it or what he did in order to pay us back.

"It seems fishy," I agree. "But at least something good is going to come from Nick's death."

"Which is?" Cross asks.

I smile, looking over at him. "I made a phone call and was informed that George is back in town for his business partner's funeral."

"Meaning?" Grave asks, throwing back more of his energy drink.

"Meaning, we're going to collect our money," I answer as Bones glares at him.

EMILEE

I HAVEN'T SLEPT in days. As soon as George called me, I threw some of my tubs that were packed with my clothes into my car and headed straight for Las Vegas. A twenty-four-hour drive took me thirty-five. I drove as fast as I could. I never stayed at a hotel, but I did pull over for a few hours of sleep here and there. I survived on energy drinks and fast food. They were cremating my father per his wishes, and it gave me some time to get back home. I wanted to fly to get here faster, but I needed my car here. I knew once I arrived, I wouldn't be going back for a while. If ever.

Slamming my car into park, I enter my father's house and run up the winding staircase, two at a time. Once I reach the second floor, I run down the hall to the master suite, then I shove the door open without even knocking. My mother lies in the king-size bed with her head resting on the upholstered white headboard and the red silk sheets pulled up to her neck. Her nurse stands to her right, helping her sip from a Styrofoam cup.

"When the hell were you going to tell me that you got a divorce?" I snap, trying to catch my breath.

She doesn't even seem surprised that I know. I think she's too tired at this point. Or she just doesn't care. I'm not sure which one I'd rather it be.

"Emilee ..." She softly says my name.

"Don't do that." I shake my head. "Don't talk to me like I'm five, Mother. You got a divorce." I growl. "A divorce? Why …? What?" I reach up and start yanking on the bobby pins and ponytail holder that kept the bun in place. "Fuck!" I hiss, scratching my head roughly.

"Will you give us a second?" she asks her nurse in a soft voice.

I begin to pace the large room. My eyes scan over the white carpet. My mother has always been a clean freak, but to be honest, she always paid someone to do it for her. My father gave her the ability to hire help, to allow her to be a stay-at-home mother who never had to worry how the mortgage was going to be paid or where her next meal would come from. I think she took that for granted.

Once she exits, my mother begins. "It's complicated—"

"No. It's not," I interrupt her. "You. Got. A. Divorce. Who wanted it? You or Daddy?" My chest is heaving with every wild breath I take. The news of their divorce is hitting me hard. I understand that not every marriage works out. I'm not stupid. I know how love works. People change over the years and grow apart. It's the fact that she never told me. I talked to her all the time. She had thousands of chances to come clean, and she chose not to.

She lets out a long sigh and pats the large space next to her. I cross my arms over my chest, refusing to move. I love my mother, but I'm not going to give her a pass because of her condition. She's been lying to me. Daddy had been lying to me. What else don't I know?

"Who?" I demand.

"It was mutual."

"Bullshit!" I snap.

"Emilee …"

I throw my hands up. "Fuck this." And turn to leave. As my hand turns the doorknob, she speaks.

"I wanted it."

I keep my back to her, and my chest tightens. *I knew it.* I didn't want to believe it. My mother once told me "someone always loves the other more," and my father loved her more.

"I wasn't happy. And neither was he. Even though he wouldn't admit it." A silence fills the room. "It had been a long time coming."

"Why didn't you tell me?" I ask roughly. "Why didn't Daddy tell me?"

"He wanted to." She coughs. "But I talked him into waiting."

I turn to face her, and tears fill my eyes. "So even after you left him and broke his heart, you still managed to control him?" I shake my head with disgust.

She closes her heavy eyes and runs her hands down over the sheets. "I was ashamed—"

"You should be!" I interrupt her, hearing the bedroom door open behind me. I turn to leave her but come to a stop when I see who has entered. "What in the fuck are you doing here?" I demand.

"Emilee." My mother sighs. "Please quit using such harsh language."

I watch with confusion and horror as George undoes his tie and walks past me. He goes over to the side of the bed and bends down to kiss my mother's forehead.

"Stay the fuck away from her!" I shout.

"You didn't tell her?" he asks my mother.

She waves off his concern. "She's been through enough for one day."

My eyes dart down to where he's grabbed her hand. His dark eyes lock on mine as he bends down and kisses her fingers. My blood begins to boil just as I close my fists.

"What happened to you?" my mother asks him. "You smell like alcohol."

He smirks at me. I want to go over there and knock the bitch out, but I can't move. My legs are cemented to the floor. Is this what shock feels like?

"Just an accident." He winks at me. "It won't happen again."

"You can't be serious?" I manage to choke out. "Mom?" I look at her. The blood rushes in my ears, and I'm trying to catch my breath. "Is this …?"

"I'm tired, dear," she says, closing her eyes.

"Mom …"

"She said she's tired," he growls at me. "Come back tomorrow. She needs her rest." He pulls the covers up and tucks her in. "What can I get you, darling?" he asks her.

Come back tomorrow? I live here. This is my home too. "Mom." I lick my lips. "You can't be serious. He …"

"She's had enough for one day," he snaps. "Get out or I will …"

"What?" I shout. "Have me thrown out of my own house?"

"Please don't fight," my mother whispers. "Not now. It's been a long day."

"Long day?" I gasp at her words. "You didn't even come to Dad's memorial." Since he was cremated, we just had a service at the funeral home. It was small and quick. It was all wrong. He deserved so much more than what George's cheap ass paid for.

She closes her eyes as if pained by my statement. "I'm …"

"Don't apologize, sweetheart." He leans down and kisses her forehead. Then he rises to his feet and comes over to me. I want to turn, but my feet still won't move. He comes up to me, grabs my upper arm, and yanks me out of the room, softly closing the door behind us.

"You son of a …"

He slaps a hand over my mouth and shoves my back into the wall. I glare up at him as he hovers over me. "I told you that I control everything. It would be in your best interest to shut your mouth."

I shove him off, and he steps back. "I don't know what you plan on doing, but it's not going to happen," I promise him.

He stares at me. I glare at him. It's a standoff. But we both know that he has me at a disadvantage. I need to do something. My mother may have left my father, but he had something to do with it.

Without another word, I run down the stairs and out the front door and fall into the driver's seat of my car and pull out my cell. I call the one person I want to see right now. The one person who will understand that I don't want to discuss my feelings.

"Emilee? Hey, girl? Are you okay?" The words rush out.

It's been so long since I've reached out to talk to her. My bottom lip begins to tremble, and I run a hand through my tangled hair. "No."

"Where are you?"

I begin to rock back and forth. "I'm sitting in my car outside of my parents' house."

"You're in Vegas?" she asks surprised.

I nod to myself. "Yeah. And I need a drink." My eyes look at the clock on my dash, and it's not even noon yet. I think the day I've had warrants some day drinking.

"Okay. Where do you want me to meet you at?"

That's why I called her. Jasmine doesn't ask very many questions, if any. She's a ride or die chick. And that's exactly what I need right now.

IT'S AFTER MIDNIGHT when I stumble back into my parents' house. I've been out all day with Jasmine, and I've drunk more than my weight in alcohol. My vision is blurry, and my mind foggy, lips numb. I'll regret this tomorrow.

She never once asked me a single question. Jasmine can talk the legs off something, and I was thankful for that today. Every conversation we had was about her. Every toast we did was to our past. The future never even thought of. Jasmine is the live in the now kind of girl.

I shut the door quietly and then begin to tiptoe the best I can up the stairs. Halfway to the first floor, I have to stop and remove my heels. I don't want to lose my footing and go tumbling down. I crack the door open to my mom's room and look inside.

She's passed out on her back. Her hands folded over her chest. She looks dead, and if I wasn't so wasted, my chest would hurt. I look at the cot that lies next to her bed, and it's empty.

That's odd. Her nurse stays overnight in her room with her. That's one of the stipulations her doctor gave her by getting to come home—twenty-four-hour care.

I close her door and head toward my room.

"Emilee?"

I come to a halt when I hear my name being called out behind me. *It's him.* Is he living here? Spinning around, I trip and fall into the wall.

"Are you fucking drunk?" he demands at the end of the hall. His hands are propped on his hips as though he's my father about to ground me because I came home intoxicated and after curfew.

"That's none of your business," I slur.

"Office. Now." With that, he turns and walks down the stairs to the first floor.

Rolling my eyes, I push off the wall and grip the banister to make my way back downstairs. Who knows what the bastard wants to talk about? Entering my father's office, he stands behind the desk.

"Sit," he orders like I'm a fucking dog.

I hate doing as he asks, but my feet hurt, and my legs are tired. I fall into the chair like a brick sinks to the bottom of the ocean. "What?" I blow some loose strands from my face.

He stands there, his hands still on his hips. He's dressed in a black button-down and black slacks. He looks like he just came home from the office—my father's office.

"There's something I need you to watch."

"Make it quick." I yawn, feeling my eyes grow heavy. Shit, I drank way too much.

He picks up a remote and turns the monitor on that hangs on the wall. This room fills the screen. It had to have been from earlier because the curtains are pulled back, revealing the sunny afternoon.

My mother's nurse enters; George sits at the desk.

"You wanted to see me, Mr. Wilton?" she asks, placing her hands behind her back.

"Yes, have a seat, Liv." He gestures to the chair that I'm now sitting in.

She does so and crosses her legs over one another. Liv has to be in her early fifties. Light brown hair that match her eyes. She wears very little makeup and blue scrubs.

"I'm going to have to let you go," he tells her.

"Excuse me?" She sits up straighter.

"I am unable to afford your rates," he says simply.

"You can't do that," I whisper, but he ignores me.

"But Nancy needs around-the-clock care," she argues.

He stands from his seat. "This is not up for discussion, Olivia. This is me announcing your termination." He flips off the monitor.

My heavy eyes look up at him. He has a look of satisfaction on his smug face.

"You son of a bitch." I manage to get out without slurring.

He smirks, placing his hands in the pockets of his slacks. "I told you; I control everything."

"Hire her back," I order, managing to stand to my feet. I still hold my heels in my right hand.

He tilts his head to the side. "Now all of a sudden you care about her."

"Fuck you ..."

"Because if I remember correctly, earlier you yelled at her and then stormed out of this house."

"You can't do this!" I shout, feeling my shaking legs threaten to buckle under me.

Stepping around the desk, he comes up to me. He reaches out to cup my cheek, but I slap it away. "You're right, you know. She does need her nurses."

She has two who take turns coming to the house to care for her. She can barely get out of bed, let alone take care of herself. I can't do it. I have to make money to try to get us away from this sorry son of a bitch.

"Then hire them back," I demand, guessing he fired them both.

"That can be arranged. If ..." He trails off, and I know where this is going. He's making a point that he owns us.

"If what?" I ask, swallowing. I can still taste the vodka in my mouth. Funny, I thought I had too many shots, but now I feel like I didn't have enough.

He sighs heavily. "See, I don't care if you go out and party with your friends, but you realize that I have the control here, Emilee." He steps into me. "You will acknowledge that what I say goes."

"What do you want?" I ask, already knowing the answer. He made it very clear earlier this morning in my father's office, but I have to ask. Maybe he's changed his mind and wants something else.

"You." He reaches out and runs his knuckles down my cheek.

Vomit fills my mouth, but I swallow it down.

He leans in, whispering in my ear, "Remove that dress and your underwear, then bend over the desk, and Liv will be back here first thing in the morning."

I fist my hands as tears sting my eyes. I don't have a choice. I'm fucked. Literally. We both know it. If my mom dies because she didn't have a nurse here, it will be my fault. And I refuse to have her death on my hands. He may win this round, but I will win the war.

I pull away from him, and his hands fall to his side.

Dropping my heels to the floor, I grip the hem of my dress and pull it up and over my head.

"Beautiful." He reaches out and touches my stomach.

I jump back. "I can't …"

"Shh." He reaches out and yanks me to him. He places his free hand over my mouth, silencing me. "I told you that you were going to willingly spread those legs for me, Emilee. And I always get what I want."

My eyes are heavy and my mind foggy from all the alcohol I've consumed. But I'm still very aware of what is about to happen and how right he is.

TWO

EMILEE

I STAND AT the bar waiting for the bartender to look my way for me to order another drink. I know I'm not an eye-catching woman, but *hello, over here, douche!*

I have my tits out. What else do I need to do to get a fucking drink? Remove my shirt and throw it in his face? Stand on the bar and shake my ass?

The guy at the end of the bar has seemed to notice me. He keeps staring at me, and I've made it a point to avoid eye contact.

I've only been here for thirty minutes, and already, I'm tired of it. This week has been a week from hell, and I needed a moment to myself to clear my mind. At least that's what I told myself. But it was just a lie. That house feels so much like a prison, and I needed out. I needed to get drunk and just get fresh air.

I'm getting neither of those.

My life has been decided for me. Well, at least until I can get away from George. And I'm not sure I can live it.

Not like this.

Not under his control.

In the past week, George has come to me one other time since the night I came home drunk and found out he fired my mother's nurses. And that is two times too many. The only thing about it, is that he can't last more than two minutes. And other than the first time, the other one I had plenty of notice, so I made sure to down a few bottles of whatever I could find. Afterward, I sit in my shower crying, hoping that he will drop dead and die like my father did. So far, luck is not on my side.

I pound my fist on the bar. "Hey, asshole. I need a drink …"

He nods at me, and I almost smile. "What can I get you?" he asks.

"A shot of vodka." I'm not playing tonight. "Actually, make that three." Who knows how long it'll be until he returns?

He sets out to make my drinks, and I pull out my debit card.

Setting it in front of me, I slide my card across the bar. I down the first one as he runs my card. I'm setting the glass down when he comes back. "Your card was declined."

"What?" I frown. "Can you run it again? There must be some mistake."

He shakes his head. "I ran it three times, ma'am. Insufficient funds," he states as another guy hollers at him. "I'll be back." He walks away to help the other customer, and I slump against the bar.

Has George shut off my card? No. He can't have that kind of access. Can he? I dig my cell out and send him a text.

Me: Did you turn off my card?

I'm tapping my heel on the floor as my phone vibrates with a response.

Motherfucker: All accounts have been frozen for the time being.

Me: What the fuck does that mean?

He reads it immediately, but this time, he chooses not to respond. No. No, this can't be happening. Why would they freeze his accounts? Is the IRS investigating him? Is it some kind of protocol? Was my father in trouble with the law? A million questions run through my mind.

I run a hand through my hair and then start digging through my clutch. I find fifty dollars. *Shit!* What am I going to do for money? I thought I had time. There was fifteen thousand dollars in that account.

"All I'm saying is I would totally win," a man says as he shoves his way through the crowd and comes to stand next to me.

I look up at him, and he's every bit of six feet to my five feet six. With heels on, he still towers over me. He places his hands flat on the bar, and it causes the sleeves to his leather jacket to ride up. And I see black ink cover his skin, wrapping around his wrist like a second sleeve. His fingers drum the bar top, and I see a silver ring that has a skull on it with crossbones.

I've seen that before ...

"I wouldn't bet on you," another guy says, coming to stand on the other side of him.

That voice sounded familiar ...

The man next to me gasps. "I'm offended. You know, if we were in high school playing dodge ball, I would pick you to be on my team. Why do I feel like you wouldn't choose me?" He pushes his bottom lip out that has a silver hoop in it.

"'Cause I wouldn't." The friend snorts. "You're short and too slow." Then he lets out a whistle, and the bartender looks up at him. "Usual," he calls out.

"Unbelievable," I mutter to myself, glaring at the other guy. He's taller and broader, but the guy standing next to me doesn't allow me the best view of his face. He reaches into his back pocket and removes his wallet, pulling out a couple of hundred-dollar bills. I notice he too wears the same ring on his right hand. My heart starts to pick up.

He's not wearing a jacket, so my eyes run up his ink covered muscular arm. His tattoos peek out from underneath his shirt, and a set of black wings wraps around his throat, crawling up the sides of his head where his hair is shaved close to the scalp. My eyes meet his and widen.

Holy shit!

My heart now skips a beat.

It can't be.

His eyes slide my way. He looks away, but they slam back to me, and I see recognition dawn on his face. His blue eyes stare at mine with a look of annoyance. The same way he did in college.

Weston Mathews is standing next to me. I used to date ... well, date isn't the right word. I used to *fuck* his best friend. There was a group of four of them known as Kings. The Dark Kings—Bones, Titan, Cross, and Grave. Each one darker, more enticing. Titan, Cross, and Bones were all two years older than me. But Grave, Bones's little brother, was only one year older than me.

The bartender walks up to them and hands him two shots of dark liquid. I'm not sure what it is, and he removes his eyes from mine.

I finally take in a shaky breath and drink my second shot.

I gotta get out of here. If Titan is here, then Bones isn't far behind, and I can't be around him. Not after what happened between us. I've heard stories about what kind of men they are today, and none of them are good.

He says something else to the bartender, and he looks at me and then nods. I swallow nervously and down the third, before digging the fifty out of my clutch and dropping it on the bar. I spin around to leave but run into someone. The guy I have successfully avoided who was standing at the end of the bar is now right here. In my space. Staring down at me.

"Hey, baby." Dark blue eyes meet mine, and the stranger places his hands on my hips. I shove him back, but he doesn't budge. *Dick!*

I go to walk around him, but he grabs my upper arm and pulls me to a stop. "Hey, I'm talking to you."

I yank my arm out of his hold, surprised that he let go, and the momentum has me falling back. Right into the side of Grave. Just my luck.

"What's going on here?" Grave demands. His hands grip my hips, steadying me. Once he helps me to stand, he doesn't let go.

I close my eyes and pray that I can get out of here before he recognizes me too. *Please, God. I need luck on my side.*

"Nothing," the stranger answers. He's half Grave's size. Grave will murder him. He was a fighter in high school. He did it for sport. The douche's eyes land on mine, and he winks at me.

I pull my lips back in disgust.

"I just wanted to know why you've been ignoring me," the man asks.

I place my fingers behind my ear and lean my head forward like I didn't hear what he has to say. Being the bitch that I can be. Too bad their music isn't louder. At least then I'd have a legitimate excuse for ignoring the fucker.

His friend taps him on the shoulder. "Oh man, she's deaf." They laugh.

"Run along," Grave announces to the guy and his friends, still holding my hips. He hasn't seen my face yet. He has no idea who I am.

"You can have her, man. A deaf bitch is useless. No fun when they can't take orders." The man laughs at me.

I open my mouth to give him a piece of my mind, but Grave pushes me to the side, my side hitting the bar. Then I see Titan walk up to stand next to Grave. Neither one of them looks at me as they advance on the man and his friends.

"What did you say?" Titan asks.

A shiver of fear runs up my spine. I almost forgot what his voice sounded like. Powerful is an understatement. The Kings ruled everything they touched. If their words didn't get the job done, then their fists did.

"You know what I mean, man." Mr. Blue Eyes laughs, and his friends follow.

"Enlighten me." Titan lifts his chin.

"How is a man supposed to be in charge if a woman can't hear our commands." He spells it out.

"That's what I thought you meant." Titan speaks and looks at Grave. He starts laughing, and Grave follows suit.

Then without warning, the laughter stops, and Titan clocks Blue Eyes in the face, knocking him back into the other three guys he walked over here with. Like dominos.

Shit!

Then they're dragging him through the crowd of people and to a back door that reads *exit* above it. I turn to face the bar, and the bartender places a shot in front of me. "I didn't order that."

"Titan did. And don't worry, he paid your bill." He slides the cash I put down back toward me.

Just fucking great!

I pick it up as he walks away and inspect it. *Never drink anything given to you by a stranger.* My mom's words remind me. Titan isn't a stranger, but that also doesn't make it any safer. The guy could have poured acid in it for all I know. They were mean in high school, and college wasn't any different.

Pure. Fucking. Evil.

The older they got, the more power they wielded.

The Kings ran the school, and the staff and their parents had their backs no matter what. They threw their weight around like fucking bulls in a china shop. Titan, Bones, and Cross all played baseball for the school. The staff kissed their asses because they could hit a fucking ball. The school wanted recognition, so they let them have their way. It always went badly.

And as for my mother? What does she know?

She left my dad, and for all I know, it was for his sleazy best friend and business partner.

"What the hell." I throw back the shot and slam the glass down on the bar. "Thanks," I mumble as he takes it away.

I pull my cell out of my pocket and check my messages. I have one from George. But he totally avoided my last message.

Motherfucker: Meet me in my office when you get home.

His office? He's taken over everything. Including my life. My freedom. He's going to use me for as long as my mother is alive.

I went to an attorney a couple of days ago, and he told me I needed twenty thousand for him to even look at my case. A retainer he had said. And I think George knows that I can't afford legal help at the moment. He has me cornered in every situation. Now I've got fucking nothing since my card doesn't work.

A girl bumps into my shoulder, and I delete the messages and put my cell away. I make my way back to the bathroom. I was gonna leave when I saw Titan and Grave were here, but now that they left, I might as well stay. Knowing what's waiting for me at home, I can't return unless I'm drunk. The fifty dollars I have in my purse should do the trick. I use the restroom and dry my hands off and then pull out my cell when it vibrates in my pocket. I'm expecting it to be another text from George, but it's not.

Jasmine: Not gonna make it. Something came up. Find a stranger and let him fuck you raw.

I sigh at my friend's message, then put my phone away and exit the bathroom. The blinding lights and music are giving me a headache, so I walk past the bar and out the exit. I'll go somewhere else. A hole in the wall where no one knows me. Making my way to the back of the parking lot I come to a stop when I see my front tire is flat.

Looking up at the dark sky, I silently curse this fucking planet for my string of bad luck lately.

"You know if you get hurt, Bones is gonna kill you."

I tense at the mention of *Bones*. I whip around to see Titan and Grave walking in the parking lot.

What did they do with those guys?

"Hey, Titan. It's that girl over there." I hear Grave call out, and I'm thankful he didn't recognize me.

I never hung out at Bones's father's house. He came to mine to fuck me, and that was that. We didn't date. We were both very aware of our situation. He wanted to get his dick sucked, and I fell to my knees every chance we had. The kids feared him. High school and college. He never showed any emotion over anything. His only love was baseball. He was gonna go pro until he didn't. That day was a very bad day. For the both of us.

Titan says nothing. *Why isn't he calling me out?*

"What's she just doing standing there?" Grave asks him. "Let's go find out." He removes his hands from his pocket and lifts them up in the air, walking up to me.

"What the fuck are you doing, man?" Titan asks, sounding irritated.

"I'm showing her I have no weapons," Grave says. "Don't want her to think I'm gonna attack her or anything."

Oh, Dear Lord! He really thinks I'm deaf.

Titan stops before me and looks at me expectantly. He knows I can hear, but he's not gonna say it. He's waiting to see how long I can play this game.

I narrow my eyes on him and cross my arms over my chest.

I go to open my mouth, but Grave speaks. "Fuck, her tire is flat!"

Titan looks at me. "Have a spare?" he asks me.

Like he would fix it anyway. I shake my head.

Grave smiles. "She can read lips."

Titan snorts.

"She could ride with us," Grave offers.

I go to open my mouth to say *hell no*, but the words die on my lips when an evil smile spreads across Titan's face.

He looks the same as he did in college but also different. His blue eyes darker, his jaw even more defined. The black wing tattoo around his neck moves as he swallows. He wears a black V-neck shirt, and a pair of black Aviators hang off the collar. He runs his tongue over his perfectly white teeth as his eyes look me up and down like he wants to eat me alive.

He and I never got along in school. He treated women like they were disposable. He went through them like most girls go through underwear. And his senior year in high school, their English teacher got fired. The rumor was he fucked her in the back seat of her car on school property, and her husband caught them. Of course she was the only one that was punished for their sexual activities.

"Yeah." He finally speaks and gives me a nod as he rubs his finger over his bottom lip. "We'll give her a ride."

The way his deep voice says *ride,* I think he means the kind that involves me naked and him on top of me. My heart begins to pound in my chest, and I take a step back from them.

Grave rolls his eyes. "You're scaring her."

Titan stares down at me, his arms still crossed over his chest and that snake of a smile on his face. "Am I scaring you?"

I narrow my eyes on his.

"I'll go get the car. You stay here with her," Grave announces and then walks away.

Titan steps up to me.

"Don't …"

"Look who found her voice," he muses.

"Shut up, Titan." I snap, pulling my cell out of my pocket and dial Jasmine's number. It rings once, twice. Three times. I pull it from my ear, and he snatches it from my hand. "Hey …"

His smile just widens. "So you do remember me."

Like I could forget. "Give me my phone back." I order reaching out for it.

He places it in the front pocket of his jeans. "Drop to your knees."

"Excuse me?" I blink.

His dark blue eyes look me up and down, and the corners of his lips turn up like he knows a secret. And he does. Several of them about me. "Drop to your knees and I'll give it back to you."

My blood boils at his words. "Fuck you!"

He steps into me, pressing my back into my door, and I gasp in surprise. I thought he was big, but his hard chest presses into mine, and I have to tilt my head back to look him in the eyes. Even with my heels on, this man towers over me. I always liked that about him. He's the tallest of all the Kings.

The scent of his cologne hits my nose, and I hate how much I like it. It brings back old memories that I want to drown in, but I make myself stay here in the present. The light pole I parked under casts a shadow over his chiseled face, making it glow like a ghost from my past.

"We came close that one time." His eyes go to my chest, and I know he can feel my heart pound against his. He reaches up and runs his knuckles over my neck. His skull ring burns the skin, making me shiver. "So fucking close. It was the only time I could actually tolerate you."

"Titan." I swallow, trying to calm my nerves.

"Yeah, Em?" he asks as his eyes roam my face.

A fucking whimper comes out when he calls me by my old nickname. Then my breath quickens when he places his hands on my face, caging me in.

TITAN

Emilee York!

Who the fuck would have guessed I'd see her tonight?

It's been, what? I haven't seen her since my senior year in college, and she was only a sophomore. That was four years ago.

My best friend used to fuck her. I always wanted to ram my cock down her throat, so I didn't have to listen to her. She was a fucking bitch in every way possible.

My body presses into hers, and her wide blue eyes look up at me. I reach up and run my hands through her dark hair. I wonder what it would look like sprawled out on my bed. Or twisted in my hands while her mouth was full of my cock. I wrap the long, curly strands around my tatted fingers.

"Please don't." She's panting. Her words shaking. Little Queen Bitch isn't as tough as she used to be. But then again, she never was around me. When I got close, she was a different person.

I smile. "Afraid of me, Em?"

"Just leave me alone." She places her hands on my chest to push me away.

I don't budge. "Now why would I do that?" I lean down and place my lips by her ear. She hitches in a breath, and her hands dig into my shirt. I'm not sure if she's trying to push me back or pull me in at this point. "Remember the last time I had you like this?" I ask her. I still dream about that night.

"I told you no then." She growls. "Just like I'm telling you now."

"But that's not what you meant."

She shoves her fists into my chest and growls through her pretty teeth. "No means no, Titan."

Even though she was a total bitch, it was kinda sexy. We had a love-hate kind of friendship. If you could even call us friends. I think that's why she held my attention so much. All the other girls were annoying and clingy, but she wasn't. Then again, she wasn't mine, either. "But you were so wet for me. Are you now?"

She lets out a growl of frustration, and I chuckle.

"Does Bones know you're back in town?" I ask her. With the news of her dad's passing, he hasn't mentioned her once.

Her body goes rigid against mine. Things haven't changed much since college. The guys and I still run this fucking town. After she graduated, she left and never looked back. Only Bones knows why she split, but he never shared that information with any of us. Yet now here she is, looking better than ever.

"I'll take that as a no." I smile down at her.

Her plump lips part, and she licks them. "I don't want any trouble," she whispers.

I slide my right hand into her soft hair and tilt her head back. She doesn't try to fight me. Why would she? She knows she can't beat me. "I'm not sure I believe that." She was always trouble. My friend fucked her, and I secretly wanted a piece of her. The one where she spread her legs and let me fuck the bitch out of her.

"Titan." She breathes my name, and it sends a jolt straight to my cock.

"Yeah, baby?"

Her blue eyes narrow up at mine, and her lips thin. "Give me back my phone," she demands.

"Come get it, sweetheart." I pull away and turn, giving her my back.

"Titan?" she calls out.

"You know where I'm at," I answer, keeping my back to her.

I make my way over to the car to see Grave sitting in the driver's seat, wondering why he never came over to pick us up. I open the passenger side door and get in. He's on his phone.

"I think we've waited long enough," Bones snaps through the Bluetooth, letting out a growl.

Grave looks over at me and then in the back seat. "Where's the girl?" he asks me.

"What girl?" Bones snaps.

I smile to myself. "She'll be around."

THREE

EMILEE

I WAKE UP to the bedroom door opening, and Jasmine barging in. "The fuck, boo? It's time to get up. I told you to set the alarm on your phone."

"Lost it," I lie, still pissed off at Titan for not returning it to me last night. And even more pissed at myself that I don't have a lock on it. I can't remember what pictures are on there. I had two options after he walked away from me last night. Go inside and call George to come get me or blow up Jasmine's until she answered. Thankfully, she didn't let me down.

"Well, get up, and let's go get a new one."

I don't move.

She plops down beside me. Her brows wiggle and her green eyes shine with mischief. "I got us a job tonight."

"A job?"

She nods excitedly, pushing her short red hair behind her ear.

She always does this. Finds ways to make money. Her father is a millionaire, but that's not enough. She's a greedy little bitch. That's why we are such great friends. I should be thankful since I have no money, no phone and a car that has a flat tire.

"As long as I get to keep my clothes on." There's no telling what she plans on having me do.

Her smile widens. "Well …"

"I'm not getting naked, Jasmine."

In college, she got us a job jumping out of a birthday cake wearing nothing but whip cream as a bra for a bachelor party. Technically, we were over eighteen and considered adults, but I still wasn't gonna do it. I shut that shit down really quick.

"You just gotta show some tits and ass." She shrugs.

"That's everything." I don't have much to offer in the first place. I've always been on the smaller side. In everything. My B cups are nothing compared to her DD's. Jasmine has the figure that every guy dreams of. Narrow hips, bubble ass, and large chest. She's got these perfectly shaped full lips and big green eyes. I would totally fuck her if I was a guy. Hell, there was that one night in college …

"Come on." She slaps my ass over the blanket. "We got to start getting ready."

I lean up to look at the clock on my nightstand. "It's a little after one." I had planned on sleeping in all day. "What time does this job start?"

"We have to be there at five. So, we need to start getting ready now."

"Where are we going exactly?" I ask, sitting up and pushing my wild hair from my face.

She gives me a big smile and then jumps up and down once. "Kingdom."

I fall onto my back, throw my arm over my face, and sigh in defeat. This week is trying to fucking kill me! And tonight, it might succeed.

I ALLOW HER to pull me around town for most of the day. She takes me to a salon for a spray tan, then I had my hair washed and fixed to perfection. Got my nails and toes done. It was the works. I've been nervous most of the day. Even the two margaritas I had before we left the salon haven't helped me much. I kept wondering how I was going to pay for everything, but when I reached for my purse, she refused to let me help. She said it was on her since she signed us up for this. I hated that I couldn't pay for it but was thankful for her kindness. I plan on paying her back for my half as soon as I get paid for whatever the fuck we're doing tonight.

My knees start to bounce when I see Kingdom ahead of us.

Please don't let me see him.

"You are literally sweating," she observes in the driver's seat with a laugh.

"This is not funny," I snap and lean forward to move the vents, so the cool air hits my face in her Aston Martin DB11. Placing my hands on the dash, I allow it to also hit my underarms. Fuck, can you actually sweat to death?

She smiles. "You're gonna run into Bones sooner or later."

"I just don't want it to be today." She doesn't know that I saw Titan last night. I'm pretty sure she slept with him back in college. Hell, maybe she still does. I've been gone for a long time. And I don't plan on staying in Las Vegas long. There's only one thing for me here, and it won't be here much longer. I would have already jumped on a plane and gone back to Chicago if not for my mother, since my apartment hasn't sold yet. But I can't abandon her now.

She pulls off the Strip and up to Kingdom. I look up at the buildings in awe. "Wow," I say, taking in the scene before me.

"Yeah." She chuckles.

Kingdom has been here for years. Their fathers started it back in the late eighties; they were known as the Three Wisemen. But it's had some major upgrades since I saw it last, which was before the Kings took it over.

Four black, glass-tinted buildings tower before us—side by side. It reads Kingdom across the top in the middle with gold letters.

She pulls under the carport-like structure, changing my view from the towers to bright lights that light up the four lanes. Cars are lined up, and a few limos. Tourists stand on the steps and by the curb with their luggage in tow. Others are getting out of their cars, just arriving for the weekend. She brings her car to a stop at the valet stand.

Two men open our doors, and I thank them as I get out. She all but runs up the stairs, but I take them slowly, gripping the handrail, just taking it all in. Cars honk in the distance on the Strip and in line waiting for their turn to enter the hotel and casino.

"Come on, slowpoke," she calls out, holding open one of the glass doors for me.

I enter the hotel and look down at the white marble floor. A golden K sits inside a black circle. People walk around, talking to one another. Black columns are placed throughout the lobby, with lights wrapped around them. A massive rectangular rug runs along the entrance over to the front desk, lined in white stitching. We entered on the hotel side. To the left of the front door, the marble flooring changes to carpet, and you can see slot machines lined up one after another. You can hear the ringing from the machines. People cheering at the poker tables and waitresses walking around with full trays in their hands.

She grips my hand and pulls me over to the far right where there is an inclinator. She steps onto the moving sidewalk. Mirrors on both sides are lit up with round bulbs, and I stare at my reflection. My dark hair is down and in big curls. My makeup is caked on—more than how I usually wear it—and my eyes are lined with black eyeliner. My lashes have three extra coats, making them heavy, and my lips are covered in a nude gloss. I feel like we're in college all over again, and I've allowed her to talk me into sneaking out to go barhopping.

The walkway comes to an end a couple of times where you have to walk the small distance to get on another. When the last one ends, she takes my hand and leads me down a long hallway. "What exactly are we doing?" I ask.

"You'll see." She practically bounces up and down before pressing a door open. We enter a room that resembles a locker room. It has a couple of showers, lockers, and sinks. She goes to a locker labeled twenty-five and opens it. Reaching in, she grabs a set of clothes and hands them to me.

I unfold them and hold the small scrap of material up. My eyes go to hers. "You have got to be kidding me."

She just smiles.

TITAN

I SIT IN my office at Kingdom when I feel my phone vibrate in the pocket of my jeans. Pulling it out, I realize it's Emilee's.

Motherfucker: Where are you?

It has to be a guy with that saved as a name. Probably an ex of some sort. No woman saves a guy under motherfucker that she wants to see or talk to. I scroll up to see their previous messages, but there are none.

I type back a reply.

Me: Where are you?

He reads it and replies immediately.

Motherfucker: At home. Where you're supposed to be.

I don't know much about her, but I don't think she's married. I didn't see a ring on her finger last night. I looked. And I didn't see a man there with her.

Me: And where is that?

I ask.

Motherfucker: Quit fucking around, Emilee. We have a deal, and you're not keeping your end of it!

I run a hand down my face. I look up when the door to the office flies open, and Bones enters like he always does.

"So how did the talk go?" he asks, getting down to it.

I turn her phone off and place it in my pocket. "Well, about as good as it could have gone."

He runs a hand through his hair.

"Hey, let's go out. Get some drinks." I offer, walking into Grave's office.

He's lying back in his seat with his hands behind his head and his black boots on his desk. Some Netflix shit is playing on his flat screen that hangs on the wall. His blue eye slide to mine slowly. "You wanna go out?"

"Yeah. Why do you sound so surprised?"

"Because you don't go out."

45

I shrug. "I feel like having some drinks." He's right. I used to get fucked up. But that was back before I helped run a multi-billion-dollar company. My only responsibility was to wake up, drag myself to class, and hit some balls out on the field. Things are different now.

"Sure." He sighs and sits up. "Just let me turn my computer off and I'm ready."

The car ride is awkward. Grave and I don't spend much time alone. He pretty much spends all of his time partying with Cross while Bones and I pick up their slack at Kingdom. "So ... how are things going?" I ask.

He sighs. "I knew it."

"What?" I feign innocence.

"Bones set this up." He scoffs, looking out my passenger window. "What does he want you to talk to me about?"

I sigh. "He's just worried about you."

"No, he's worried about the image I'm giving Kingdom." He looks over at me. "Anyone ever tell you you're a shitty liar?"

I chuckle at that. "Can you blame him?"

He doesn't answer.

"It's not all about Kingdom," I start. "He's worried about you."

"Well, you can tell him that I'm fine. And you didn't need to pretend to go have drinks with me for that information. You could have done that in my office." He adds.

"How are things with you and Lucy?" I change the subject. He's been seeing her for a while now.

"The same."

"Which is?" I ask digging deeper. I don't know what the fuck him and her are. So the same doesn't mean shit to me.

"We fuck." He looks over at me. "That's all we do." He pulls his cell out of his pocket. "That's all I ever plan on doing with her. She's not the kind of girl you settle down with."

"And you're that kind of guy?" I ask.

"No," he answers. "That's why what we're doing works so well."

And that was that. I got nothing out of him. We had pulled into the bar, and then we ran into Emilee. We weren't even there for ten minutes before we beat some guys' asses and then left. I dropped him back off at Kingdom where he got in his car and went to meet up with Lucy, and I went home to bed.

"Like I said, Bones, Grave is an adult. I can't force him to do something and neither can you," I tell him.

He sighs. "Maybe prison would be the best place for him."

Grave is going to either end up dead or get a life sentence. There's no doubt about it. But that's just who he is. That's who we all are.

"Aren't you being a hypocrite?" I ask.

He lets out a growl. "No. I'm very careful with what I do and how I do it. Plus, drugs don't run my life."

True. That's never been our thing. But that doesn't mean we don't live a life of sin. You can't play God and expect to be forgiven when you are questioned about what you had to do in order to achieve that title.

"So what do you want to do?" I ask, leaning back in my seat.

"There's no controlling him." He sighs.

"But?"

"But nothing." He stands and exits my office as fast as he entered, ending our conversation.

I lean back in my chair and stare at Emilee's phone. Picking it up, I turn it back on and look over the home screen photo. It's of her and Jasmine, and it looks recent. Jasmine recently dyed her hair red. I remember it being that color at Luca's wedding. Back in college, it was bleach blond. Emilee's wearing a smile, and her hair is flipped over to the side, a few strands covering her face. A shot of tequila in one hand, a mixed drink in another. She actually looks happy. Like she doesn't have a care in the world. But I know differently. Her father is dead. She always was good at covering up her true feelings.

Going back to her recent text, I pull up the number and type it into my computer just to see if I can get an idea of who this guy is. Maybe a social media page or something.

And I'm quite surprised when I see it belongs to none other than the sorry bastard George Wilton.

What kind of deal could you possibly have with him, Em?

FOUR

EMILEE

Standing in front of thousands of people, I'm in a black sleeveless shirt that's cropped, ending right below my boobs, and has an extremely low V cut in the front with a pair of black spandex booty shorts with a thick black belt that has a golden K on the front. I've worn bathing suits that cover more. My top keeps riding up and so does the fabric on my ass. Jasmine even sprayed hair spray on it and said it would help. Whatever the fuck that meant. Just made my skin sticky and itch.

She signed us up to be ring girls. Tonight, Kingdom is hosting a fight, and we've been walking around for the past two hours half-dressed and holding up cards to announce each round. Kingdom's event center is over a hundred thousand square feet and holds around seventeen thousand guests. And the event has it at full capacity.

"How did you get this job again?" I ask her, sitting down next to her ringside. Some people would kill for these seats because we are so close, we can see the blood fly and smell the sweat.

"I know a guy who helps the Kings with the promotional side of things."

"Know a guy? Or seeing a guy?"

She shrugs. "It's nothing serious." She dodges the question.

TV crews are all over the place, which she didn't mention beforehand. It's hot, and my tits and forehead are covered in sweat. The lights that shine down on the ring are unbearable. I should have worn less makeup because I can literally feel it melting off my face. And my clothes are sticking to my body. I'm praying my ass doesn't have a wet spot.

The lights shut off, and the crowd screams so loud I cover my ears to try to block it out, but it does no good. When they come back on, they're flashing, making it hard to see anything. Music begins to pound through the speakers.

"There he is," Jasmine yells, nodding her head to the aisle while yanking on my arm to pull me to my feet.

A man bounces from foot to foot as he makes his way down the aisle to the center of the arena. Women reach for him. Men slap him on the shoulders. He wears a black silk robe tied loosely around his waist.

He walks up the stairs, then bends down to crawl into the ring between the ropes. He comes to a stop in the center and drops the robe. *It's Grave.* I'm not surprised the guy fights.

He came by his name honestly. The guy always had a death wish. When he was fifteen, he ended up totaling Bones's car while drag racing it. He was high and drunk, and Bones was so pissed. I will never forget the way he fucked me. Ruthlessly. I had bruises for days. And even after he was done with me, he was still raging. He wanted to beat the fuck out of his brother, but he didn't touch him. I still don't know what stopped him.

They call his opponent out from the other end of the event center, and the crowd boos him. Grave's obviously a legend here at Kingdom. I have a feeling he'd have that kind of welcoming crowd even if he didn't own a part of the casino.

"Does he fight often?" I ask her to wonder how he got around that legal battle. It has to be illegal for an owner to participate in such activities.

She nods, her starry eyes on Grave as he smiles at his opponent. "Every weekend."

"I saw him last night."

"What?" That gets her attention, and her green eyes slam to mine. "When? Where?"

"At Brentley's. He was there with Titan."

Her eyes widen. "Whoa." She places her hands up. "You're just now telling me this, why?"

I shrug. "Didn't find it important."

She places her hands on my shoulders and shakes me. "But—"

"He didn't recognize me," I interrupt her.

"Titan?"

"Oh, he recognized me." I give a rough laugh. "The fucker took my phone."

"What the fuck, Em?" she snaps and places her hands on her hips. "Why haven't you told me all this?"

I look down at the white Nikes she made me wear, unable to meet her eyes. "I've been gone a long time. And I know you and him—"

"There's nothing going on there," she interrupts me. And then sighs. "I wish you would have told me. After this is over, we're getting your phone back."

The fight lasted two point five seconds. The guy swung at Grave and missed. Then Grave hit him—once—and he dropped to the ground like a dead body.

We pose for photos for the media crew members running around and with the men who had VIP tickets. They even asked us to sign shirts they purchased. One guy asked to take a selfie with me, said his business partner would hate himself for not coming to the fights. Whatever.

People start to exit the event center.

"Let's go." Jasmine grabs my arm and drags me up an aisle, pushing people out of our way.

"Where are we going?" I ask.

"To get your shit back," she growls.

I dig my heels into the floor. "Oh, no … it's fine. I can get it later. Or buy another one …" *Yeah, with what money, Emilee?*

She walks into a tunnel and takes a right. People crowd around with their phones out still taking pictures. A few guys are dressed in three-piece suits and others casual in jeans and T-shirts. They all wear lanyards around their necks, giving them access back here.

One guy spots us and smiles. "Hey, ladies. What are you doing later?"

"Not you," Jasmine replies with her nose up in the air.

Another guy steps in front of us, forcing us to a stop. "Hey, we're headed to a party. The penthouse here at Kingdom. You two wanna join us?"

"No thanks," I answer.

Jasmine snorts. "If we want to fuck you, we'd approach you. Move over, dipshit." She shoves him out of the way and begins to drag me along again.

We pass door after door. A few men who wear security badges look at us oddly. I don't think we're supposed to be back here, but since they can tell we're dressed as ring girls, they let us go.

We come to a door that has *Grave* written on the outside in white letters. I would say it's because he fights so often, not because he owns the casino. But either one could be why he has a designated room, and the other fighter doesn't.

"Jasmine, I don't think …"

She shoves the door open and pulls me into it. Grave sits on a black table with his legs dangling over the side. He's still dressed in his black shorts, his sponsor's name down the side. Titan stands to his left with his back toward us. Cross leans up against the far wall with his eyes down on his phone in his hands, and Bones stands to the right.

All look up at us as I hear the door shut. And my stomach drops when my eyes land on a set of blue ones staring at me. One of our many hookups come to mind.

I lie on my stomach on my bed. My math book open, and I'm writing in my notebook, solving the problems when I hear my window open.

Looking over, I see Bones climbing in. He's got a black and white baseball shirt on, a black hat backward, and faded jeans. We're in college, and he still sneaks through my bedroom window. It's kinda become tradition. My parents would flip if they knew I was sleeping with a man that I'm not in a relationship with. They've always been strict. I'm pretty sure they think I'm still a virgin.

"Hey?" I ask, sitting up. "I didn't know you were coming over tonight?" He told me earlier that he had practice.

He walks over to my bedroom door and locks it. My body instantly heats. He removes his hat, tossing it to my floor. His dark hair falls to his eyes, and he shoves it back, making it stand straight up. Then he reaches up and pulls his shirt up and over his head, revealing a hard chest and a six-pack. He and the Kings work out regularly. They have to stay fit for the baseball team. My eyes scan over his skull tattoo on his smooth chest. It has a crown tilted on the corner, and crossbones underneath it. All the Kings have them. As if it's some kind of branding. "Bones ... my parents are home ..."

"So?" he asks, already kicking off his tennis shoes. Then his hands go to work on his jeans.

"So?" My eyes widen. "They'll hear us." I look over at the window. My parents think I'm the good girl. I'm not, but that doesn't mean I want them to find out. "Let's go to your car ..."

He grabs my upper arm and tosses me onto the bed. "Bones—"

He cuts me off, placing his hand over my mouth. I look up at him straddling me, breathing heavily through my nose. His blue eyes bore down on mine. He's angry. About what, I don't know. We don't share our feelings or personal information. We are as detached as two people who are just fucking can be.

His free hand goes between my legs, and he's shoving the thin layer of my underwear to the side. I'm always wet for him. "Then I better gag you," he says, running a finger over my pussy.

I arch my back, taking in a breath through my nose. His fingers dig into my cheeks as he presses his hand over my mouth. I scream out into his hand when he enters me in one hard push. Bones likes to make it hurt. He took my virginity. It hurt. I cried. Then he made it feel better.

A knock comes on my door, and my eyes widen. He stops moving, but his eyes stay on mine.

"Emilee, you okay?" my mother asks.

He removes his hand from my mouth, and I suck in a long breath. "Yes," I say and flinch at how high my voice is. "Just stubbed my toe,"

I add.

"Okay. Dinner is in an hour."

"Okay ..."

He slaps his hand back over my mouth and leans down, placing his lips by my ear. His body weight is pinning me down, making it hard to breathe, and his cock is still inside me, but he hasn't started moving yet. "I'm gonna fuck this tight cunt of yours, and then I'm gonna eat my cum out of you. You're gonna be my dinner, Em."

I blink, pulling myself out of that memory.

Grave smiles at me. "Hey, it's the deaf girl."

Titan widens his stance and crosses his arms over his chest as he glares down at me. Cross's eyes go big the moment he recognizes me.

Bones looks me up and down slowly before he turns to fully face us. "What are you doing here?" he asks with a tilt of his head. He doesn't look surprised or mad. Just indifferent. Like I never meant a thing to him. And thankfully, Jasmine speaks before I can process that.

"She came to get her phone," she snaps. "Titan?"

A slow smile spreads across his face. "Ready to get on your knees, Em?"

"Keep it," I growl and spin around to leave, but Jasmine grabs my arm, stopping me. Why I would expect more out of him is beyond me. I thought just once, I'd get a fucking pass from this shitty string of bad luck I have. I thought that maybe putting him on the spot would work in my favor. That's what I get for thinking anything regarding the Kings.

"Hey?" Grave scratches the back of his head, jumping down off the table. "You're not deaf?"

Bones takes a step toward me. "What are you doing here, Emilee?" His voice more of a growl this time.

"Emilee ..." Grave's voice trails off, and his eyes widen. Then he whispers, "Shit."

Shit is right!

I place my hands on my hips, well aware I'm barely dressed, sweating like a whore in church, and wearing more makeup than a drag queen. This man isn't above me. I sure as hell am not gonna let him think that. "I was working."

He looks me up and down one last time, and then his cold eyes meet mine. I forgot how beautiful they are. "Well, you're fired, so pack your shit and get the fuck out." Then he turns his back on me.

I should be surprised, but I'm not. He never was nice unless his dick was hard. What Bones and I had was never complicated. I knew where we stood. I've never been that girl who made up shit in her head or thought a man should love me just because I gave him my body. He made it very clear when he declared he wanted me.

I'm putting my books away at my locker when I feel someone come up beside me. I shut the door and look up into a set of blue eyes that I know well. Dillan Reed AKA Bones. "May I help you?" I ask, looking around the silent hallway. It's just us. Everyone has left for the day. Maybe he wants me to do his homework. But I don't think that's it. He doesn't need anyone to do his work for him. The Kings get good grades because of who they are. Their fathers are the Three Wisemen.

"I hope so."

Three words. That was all it took for me to give him my virginity five days later. He wanted my body. And I offered it up to him like a sacrifice. As if lying down for a king would guarantee me salvation. But standing before them now makes me realize I never needed to be saved.

"I'm not leaving until I get my phone." First George and now him? I refuse to let them treat me this way.

Bones pauses and turns back to look at me. Then at Titan. "You have her phone?"

He nods.

Bones looks at my bare legs, exposed stomach, and then my eyes. "Well, you heard him. You want it, you get on your knees."

"You guys are fucking pricks," Jasmine growls.

I snort, shaking my head. "I see nothing has changed. You know what …?" I look at Titan, pulling my lip back to show him how disgusted I am. "Keep it." Then I turn around and storm out.

TITAN

WE ALL STAND in the room, watching the door slam shut as Jasmine chases Emilee out. Bones looks at me, and I arch a brow, silently daring him to ask me what the fuck that was about and why his old fuck was here tonight working. And why her phone is in my pocket.

He says nothing. Instead, he looks at his brother. "Get ready. We have business to take care of." Then he exits as well.

Cross looks at me. "What the hell was that about, man?"

"Long story," I answer.

Grave runs a hand through his sweaty hair. "I really thought she was deaf." He frowns, clearly disappointed that she wasn't. "And I can't believe I didn't recognize her." Maybe if he'd lay off the drugs, he'd have a clearer head.

"It took me a second to figure out who she was." Cross nods to himself. "It's been a long time."

"Let's go," I say, clapping my hands. "You heard Bones. We got work to do."

I don't have time for Emilee York to consume my thoughts tonight. Even if I wanted to rip off what little clothes she wore and throw her on this table. The Kings be damned. I'm not shy. If they want to watch, I'd let them.

FIVE

EMILEE

Jasmine drops me off, and I enter my parents' house and storm up to my room, slamming my door. "How fucking dare them …?"

"Miss York?" I hear a knock on my door.

It's Liv, my mother's night nurse. I open the door. "Is my mother okay?" I ask. It's after midnight. Why else would she be knocking on my door?

Her eyes widen as they scan my mostly exposed body and caked-on makeup. "Uh, … yes, ma'am." Her eyes meet mine, and she clears her throat. "Mr. Wilton is expecting you."

My jaw tightens. "Tell him to go fuck himself," I snap.

She sucks in a breath at my foul language.

I run a hand through my hair. It has more hairspray than a toddler in a tiara contestant. Taking in a deep breath, I weigh my options. He still has control. He's probably been blowing up my phone that I don't have. "Is he in my *father's* office?"

"No. He went home to his house for the evening. He said you know where it is." She bites her bottom lip and drops her eyes to her feet.

I roll mine. "And?"

"And he said that he's been trying to contact you all day."

I fist my hands. What in the fuck has he been texting me? Titan could be reading them. If I'm lucky, he shut the thing off or it died.

"He said that you need to keep up your end of the deal."

I slam the door in her face and hear her shriek on the other side. "Sorry son of a bitch," I hiss. We didn't make a deal. He blackmailed me. But he's right. If I want what's best for my mother, I need to give him what he wants. Fuck, I hate my life.

Looking at myself in the mirror, I decide to change my clothes, but I'm leaving my makeup on and my hair the way it is. I'm not going to take the time to fix myself for him. I need a drink, but I can't if I have to drive ... "Shit!" I throw my head back and close my eyes. I need to get my tire fixed. I had it towed to Jasmine's house. Thankfully, I made enough tonight for that, but that doesn't help me right now. "Fuck it," I say, pulling on a T-shirt. I'll go downstairs and call a taxi. I'll never make it through George touching me if I'm sober.

TITAN

AN HOUR LATER, I pull up to a driveway and turn off my candy apple red Maserati. Bones sits in the passenger seat. Silent. He hasn't said a single word to me since we saw Emilee at Kingdom. A flat black Zenvo ST1 stops behind me. I exit and watch Grave get out of his car.

"What's the plan?" he asks me.

"Collect what we're owed," I answer.

"And if he doesn't have it?" Cross asks, exiting the passenger side of the Zenvo.

"Then you get to burn something," Bones answers, slamming my passenger door shut. He's in a mood, and it's not a good one.

All four of us make our way up the concrete steps and knock on the big wooden doors.

They don't keep us waiting long. A little Mexican woman answers the door. Her black hair is up in a tight bun, and she wears a traditional black and white uniform that allows her to scrub his piss off the floor when he's too hammered to make it to the toilet.

"May I help you?" Her eyes widen as they run over the black ink that curls around my neck.

I lean forward, and she stiffens but doesn't back away. "Run," I whisper.

She sucks in a breath, and I grab her shirt by the collar and yank her through the door. She gasps as I shove her away from us. We enter the house and slam the door shut. Bones locks the door, keeping her out.

"Margarita, who was at the door …?" The man who comes to look over the railing trails off when he sees the four of us standing in his house. "Shit," he whispers under his breath.

"George, nice place," Grave says, smiling as he looks around at the expensive wall art hanging and the glass sculptures on the shelves. He walks over to the round glass table that sits in the middle of the foyer and picks up the glass vase that has a red rose painted on it. He removes the flowers, lies them on the table, and then drops the vase to his feet. It shatters to a million fucking pieces.

"Kings," the man says, swallowing hard. His big eyes go to Bones. "I was gonna call you—"

"Good thing we decided to come see you then," Grave interrupts him. That stupid grin still plastered on his face.

His hands grip the banister, knuckles turning white. "Have Margarita show you to my office."

"She won't be joining us," I state.

He takes a deep breath. His eyes shoot to the right, and I quickly look at Bones. He gives me a curt nod, silently informing me he caught that too.

"Give me ten …"

"You have three," I say.

Glass shatters to my right, and I hear Grave giggle like a fucking schoolgirl at destroying shit.

George pushes away from the banister and disappears.

"He could be getting a gun," Cross states, looking at us.

"He'll only have time to shoot one of us," Bones says.

Another sound of glass breaking and Bones sighs but makes no move to stop his brother. Grave is the little kid who destroys every-fuck-ing-thing he touches. The kid who lies down in the middle of a grocery store and throws a fit 'cause his mother won't buy him ice cream. And Bones is that parent who walks away from him, pretending he's someone else's problem.

"Two," Cross calls out.

We hear a door open, and George comes back into view. He walks briskly down the stairs but keeps looking over his shoulder.

"Let's go," I order, gesturing for him to show us the way.

"Grave," Bones calls out as we begin to walk. He doesn't follow.

We enter a door, and the man goes to sit behind the desk, but Bones grabs the back of his collar and yanks him back before sitting behind his desk himself. I shove George into a chair across from the desk.

"I have checks … my checkbook is in the drawer."

Bones places his inked forearms on the brown surface. "We don't accept checks as a form of payment."

George swallows, nodding quickly. "I have cash."

"Where?" I ask.

"It's not here."

"Where is it?" Cross growls.

"I can have it tomorrow."

"Not good enough," Bones states, leaning back in the seat. He looks up at Cross. "Go ahead …"

"No. No. No," George says, jumping to his feet. "I can get it. I just need time …"

"You're out of it." I grab his arm and pull him down onto the rect-angular coffee table that sits in the center of the room. He screams as he fights me, but I manage to get the rope out of my pocket and wrap it around his wrists. Then I yank them back and tie them to the legs of the table. He kicks his legs out, but there's nowhere for him to go as he lies on his back with his wrists tied above his head to underneath the table.

"Please … please …" he begs. "I have it …"

"You're three months behind," Bones says, slowly standing and coming around to lean back against the desk.

George flinches. "Something fell into my lap. It cost more—"

"Not our problem," he interrupts him.

We all turn to look at the office door fly open, and Grave enters. He has his right hand wrapped around the back of a neck. He shoves the girl into the room. "Look at who I found."

She stands up straight, shoving her dark hair from her face, and her eyes land on mine. They widen in recognition. "Titan," she breathes my name.

Grave laughs, shutting the door and leaning up against it so she can't exit. "Twice in one night. Must be our lucky day."

I look at Bones, and he has the same question in his eyes. *What in the fuck is Emilee doing here?*

"No," George snaps. "She's not a part of this!" He yanks on the rope that ties him to the table.

She looks down and notices him. "What the hell …?"

"He owes us money," Bones states.

Her entire body stiffens when her eyes meet his. Her feet falter, and she stumbles into Bones, swallowing nervously. He stares at her like he did earlier, with no emotion, but I notice the tic in his jaw.

"She has nothing to do with this. Get her out of here," George barks.

Bones looks away from her and at him. "She stays." Then his eyes meet mine, and he nods.

I reach out, grab her upper arm, and yank her back to my front.

"What the fuck are you doing? Titan!" she snaps, fighting in my arms.

Leaning down, I whisper, "Just watch."

She struggles some more in my vise grip, and her ass rubs against my cock in the sweetest way. She's changed clothes since earlier, but she still has her makeup on and hair fixed. She smells like fucking candy. Sweet and edible. "You're turning me on, Em."

She stiffens, her breath picking up.

Cross reaches into his shirt, pulling the silver cross that hangs on a thin chain, and removes it from his neck.

"What are you doing?" George snaps.

Cross reaches down and yanks on the man's button-down. The buttons go flying as his hairy chest is exposed.

"Are you going to kill him?" she growls.

I frown at her tone. It sounded more like a request than a question. Why is she here at three in the morning? Was she here to talk business with him? Her father just passed. Maybe he left her his half. With George dead, she'd get a hundred percent of it. Killing him would be doing her a favor.

We had a deal, and you're not keeping up your end. Is what her text from him had read. I still haven't told the Kings about what I found on her phone.

What kind of deal do they have?

"Let her go!" he shouts.

"We will," Bones promises.

"Unharmed," George adds.

Bones looks up at her. His blue eyes run from her bare feet up her toned legs and over her white cotton shorts and pink T-shirt. She shrinks back into me, and I smile. Why is she afraid of him now, but she wasn't just hours ago at Kingdom? What's changed?

"That's not up to you to decide," he finally says, looking back down at him.

Cross straddles George's stomach, and Emilee's breathing picks up even more. Her fingers dig into my forearm, her nails cutting the skin.

Cross removes the black Zippo from his front pocket and flips it open. He holds up the cross that hangs on his necklace and runs the lighter over the metal, heating it up.

"What is that?" George asks, voice frantic.

"A reminder," he answers. Running the lighter along the hard surface, he repeats the process over and over. When satisfied, he presses the cross to George's chest and holds it there. He bares his clenched teeth and arches his back, refusing to scream as he is branded.

Then Cross pulls it away and slaps his hand over the burned cross on George's chest. Emilee shakes in my arms.

"When are you going to pay?" Bones asks, sounding bored.

"Tomorrow," he grinds out.

"And what happens if you don't?"

George stays silent, probably not wanting to give us any ideas. We don't require help when it comes to creativity for those who try to fuck us.

Bones makes a tsking sound with his tongue. He walks over to us and looks down at Emilee. He grabs her chin and shoves her head back into my chest.

"No!" George says, fighting the restraints, but Cross still sits on top of him, restricting his movement even more. "Don't touch her!" he shouts.

My frown deepens at his concern for Emilee. Are they together? Surely, she's not with him.

The corners of Bones's lips curl up. His eyes run over her face before they meet hers. "You can't take what's freely given. Can you, Em?"

She swallows as a tear runs down her cheek.

"What?" George snaps. "Emilee, what is he talking about?"

"He doesn't know about us?" Bones tilts his head to the side. He's going to push George to see just how jealous he will get. He's thinking the same thing I am—that they are together.

"Stop," she chokes out.

"That's not what you used to say."

"Bones …" She whimpers.

His smirk grows to a full smile. "That's more how I remember it."

"You know them?" George snaps.

"Oh, we know each other really well," Bones adds, letting go of her jaw and taking a step back from us. "Tell him how I used to fuck you—"

"Enough!" she snaps, interrupting him. She fights me, and I let her go.

"How you used to suck my cock …"

She slaps him across the face. Silence follows, and we all watch, waiting to see what he does. Smiling down at her with amusement in his eyes, he wraps his hand around her throat and shoves her back into the wall. She gasps before he takes her air away. Her lips part, and her hands try to pry his away, but it's to no avail. "Watch it, baby." He leans down, his face inches from hers, and I watch his hand tighten around her throat. Her lips turn purple, and her legs try to kick out, but he's pressed into her. He lowers his lips and whispers something so softly, none of us can hear what it is. Then he steps back, letting go of her, and she crumples to the floor. She coughs while her body shakes.

"That's more how I remember it," he says, staring down at her. "You on your knees. Tears running down your face while you gasp for breath."

She looks up at him through watery eyes. "Fuck you, Bones." Her voice is hoarse, softening the hatred she meant to deliver.

"We're done here," Bones announces and looks at George. "You have until tomorrow." With that, he storms out.

Cross gets up off the man and walks out as well, followed by Grave. I reach into my pocket and grab my knife. Flipping open the blade, I cut the rope that binds George's wrists. He jumps to his feet and yanks her up off the floor by her hair. She cries out. Before she can get her balance, he slaps her across the face. She doesn't make a sound. Just holds the side of her face and stares down at the floor.

My hands itch to help her up, but I don't. She's not my problem and this is not why I came here.

He looks at me, gasping for air, and orders, "Get the fuck out of my house!"

I close the blade. "Don't make us chase you," I warn and exit.

We make our way back to the vehicles in the driveway. I start mine up and pull out. Bones stares out the passenger window.

"He's not gonna pay up," I tell him.

"I know."

"He's gonna offer us Em." I've seen it enough to know how this works. He knows she has a past with Bones. The man will save his own life by throwing hers away. She means something to him, but I just don't know what. But her past with Bones makes her even more valuable to him.

"I know."

My hands tighten on the steering wheel. "We don't accept any other form of payment," I growl.

He finally looks over at me, and his eyes drop to my crotch. "Then why is your cock hard?"

SIX

EMILEE

"SUCH A FUCKING slut," he hisses, dropping down into the seat behind his desk.

I'm still trying to catch my breath from Bones's hands around my neck. And the side of my face stings from George's hand. *I hate feeling so trapped.* But I feel like I have to defend myself. For my mother. "It was a long time ago—"

"You think I give a shit?" he shouts, interrupting me.

"Why do you owe them money?" I ask. What could he have possibly done? Was my father involved too? Did they do business with them? A thousand thoughts run through my mind.

The only good thing about the Kings showing up here at George's house is that they came before he could fuck me.

"That's none of your damn business!" he snaps.

"Yes, it is!" I shout, fisting my hands down by my sides. "Why the fuck do you owe them money? What have you done?" They were ruthless in college, so I can only imagine what they are like now that they are grown with more money than God and an endless amount of power.

Who knows who they have in their back pocket?

The red-hot burn mark in the shape of a cross on George's bare chest tells me they still don't fuck around.

He ignores my question once again. "Come here," he orders, and I stiffen. "I said come here!"

My heavy feet take slow and small steps over to him. When I get close enough, he yanks on my arm, pulling me in front of him. His hands run up my thighs, and I shudder, swallowing the vomit that begins to rise. I only had two drinks. I'm going to need a few more before I can do this.

He stands and whispers in my ear. "You're supposed to be my little slut."

I turn my face away from him, and he grips my hair and yanks my head back. A cry is ripped from my lips. "Please …"

"Did he fuck this mouth?" He runs his fingers over my trembling lips. "Tell me," he orders.

"Yes," I whimper as tears run down my face.

"And what about this pussy?" He drops his hand to cup me between my legs, and I close my eyes as he rubs me over the fabric.

"Yes." My voice is barely audible.

"And your ass?" he continues. "Did he fuck that tight ass?"

"George …"

He slaps me across the face again. Thankfully, he's weak at the moment and can't hit very hard. "What did I tell you to call me?" he growls.

I swallow the bile that threatens to come up, and answer softly, "Daddy."

"Good girl," he coos. "Now … did he fuck that ass?"

I nod as a sob breaks through. There was nowhere on my body that Bones did not touch. He had a way of making me want things from him. Sinful things.

He shoves me to the floor. "Pathetic," he sneers.

He plops down in his seat and stares down at me on the floor. Then a smile spreads across his face as he leans forward. "Go home and get some rest. I'll be there first thing in the morning to pick you up. We're going out."

"Where are we going?" If I wasn't so pissed off at the Kings, I would thank them for saving me from a night with George.

"You need a new dress, darling." He reaches out, and I flinch when he runs his hand through my hair. "You need to look your best."

"For what?"

He cups my cheek he just slapped. My salty tears burn the tender flesh. "You, my dear, are gonna pay my debt."

TITAN

I sit at the kitchen table in our suite at Kingdom. There are times we don't get the chance to go home, so we all share the entire fiftieth floor, The Royal floor. Our fathers may have once owned Kingdom, but we have done a lot of remodeling over the years. It has over eight thousand square feet for all of us. We have the roof to ourselves along with a pool, hot tub, and private bar. Not to mention our gym, bowling alley, and theater. It also has a locker room and a massage parlor. We have our own staff twenty-four seven. Most of us live here more than at our houses. When your business never sleeps, neither do you.

I look up when I see Bones enter the suite. He had an early meeting this morning with Luca. Walking over, he plops down across from me at a table that can fit ten guests. "May I help you?" I ask, picking up the cup of coffee in front of me.

"Busy?" He quirks a brow.

I take a drink and sit back. "What do you want, Bones?" I'm not in the mood to play games with him today. He needs to get to the point and quick.

"I got a call from George."

"And?"

"You were right. He wants to trade Emilee."

I snort. "No woman is worth five hundred grand."

He crosses his arms over his chest.

"You can't be serious." I sigh. "You want her?" *Didn't he get enough of her in high school and college?*

"No." He nods to me. "But you can have her."

"What the hell am I gonna do with her?" She was a bitch and a total prude. Well, for anyone but Bones. He kept her legs spread twenty-four seven. If she wasn't sucking his dick, he was fucking her cunt or ass. After he quit using her, it was like she never even existed. He was a fucking idiot.

His eyes slide to the double French doors that are open to my personal suite. A redhead and a blonde are tangled in the white crisp sheets. Both passed out. Their clothes from this morning scattered across the floor. They were waiting on me in the lobby when we arrived back at Kingdom. "You can think of a few things." His eyes come back on mine.

I shake my head. "She's not into what I like."

He runs his tatted fingers over his chin. "She had a pretty open mind back then."

I roll my eyes. "He abuses her."

He frowns. "How do you know?"

"I watched him slap her." I take another drink. "After you all walked out. He knocked her around. Because she had slept with you." I still can't figure out why the one was so concerned about the other.

He runs a hand through his slicked back hair, thinking over my words. Would he have stopped George if he had seen it? Doubtful. He almost made her pass out with his hand around her throat. And I couldn't show weakness toward her and intervene. George would have used that to his advantage, but it seems he's going to try anyway.

"I don't have time to help a broken woman." I shake my head. "And we can't take something that someone doesn't have." George is a problem. But not one that we can solve on our own.

He opens his mouth, but his phone rings in his pocket. "Hello?" Pause. "What is it, Nigel? Yeah." His eyes meet mine. "We'll be right there." He hangs up. "Let's go."

"Where are we going?"

"Seems Emilee has come to us."

Fuck!

We enter Bones's office to find her sitting in a chair. Nigel had let her in. Her back ramrod straight and staring straight ahead. Bones sits down at the desk, and I lean up against the far wall, not in the mood to sit. No one says anything.

Her watery eyes go from mine to Bones's. Then she drops her head and looks down at her nails. "He's not gonna pay you."

We say nothing.

She lifts her head to look me in the eye. "He wants to give me to you. Like I'm some fucking object that can be traded." She fists her hands in her lap. "I tried to explain it wouldn't work. George—"

"Are you sleeping with him?" I interrupt her, unable to wait any longer. I need to know what she is to him and why.

She sniffs and adjusts herself in the seat, looking even more uncomfortable. I look at Bones, then back at her. "Does he rape you?" Maybe what I thought I saw and what they have aren't the same. He physically abused her, so forcing himself on her isn't a far stretch. And that thought makes me want to kill him. I may have told her to get on her knees for her phone, but I'd never force myself on her.

She flinches. "You can't take what is freely given." She recalls Bones's words.

"So what? He's your sugar daddy?" I ask, not liking that idea either.

She shakes her head. "My mother is sick. Dying. I came back after my dad passed to be here with her and help take care of her. But after meeting with my father's attorney, I was informed that George has access to all of my family's money. That house is in the company's name; my father left him the company." Bones and I exchange another look because that doesn't seem likely. "He told me if I gave him what he wanted, he would cover my mother's medical bills. Although she doesn't have much longer to live, I want her to be comfortable. He said that he would pay for it as long as I …"

"Spread your legs for him," Bones finishes.

She reaches up and wipes a single tear from her face.

I run a hand down mine. "What's wrong with your mother?"

"Cancer," she whispers. "Stage four. Lymphoma. She's got four months left. Maybe."

Bones sits back and crosses his arms over his chest. This is news to us. And it makes things even more complicated.

She straightens her back. "I have a proposition of my own for you."

My brows rise.

"No offense, Emilee, but your pussy isn't worth five hundred thousand," he tells her even though he just tried to sell the idea of me taking her.

"The house." She ignores him.

"What about it?" I ask.

Her watery eyes meet mine. "There's insurance on it. It's paid up to date." I frown. "Burn it to the ground. You can have the insurance money as long as you give me enough for my mom to be taken care of."

I open my mouth, but she continues. "I have no job back in Chicago anymore. I quit. And I put my apartment up for sale the moment I found out she was sick so I could move back here to be with her. But my father died before I was able to get rid of it. My account has been frozen. Right now, I'm at his mercy," she growls. "You guys showing up gave me an idea. You take care of my mother, and you can have the rest."

"Emilee—"

"It's insured for over two point two million," she interrupts Bones.

He looks up at me. I shake my head. "Too risky."

"I'll set it," she growls. "No one will ever know about your involvement. I'll wait. Three weeks. Give it some time, then I'll do it late at night."

"What's in it for you?" Bones asks. "Two point two million is a lot of money, and all you want is for us to take care of your mother. What about you?"

"I can go back to Chicago. Find a new job. Get back to my life." She takes in a deep breath. "I want him to be there. I want his body to burn."

So that's it. She doesn't care if she gets a dime; she just wants the fucker dead. Can't say I blame her after what she just told us.

SEVEN

EMILEE

They both stare at me.

Titan frowns. "You said it's in the company's name and he owns the company right now. What if he were to die? Then who is next?"

"I am," I lie. How the fuck should I know? Like George is going to share any of that information with me.

"You sure? He doesn't have kids? A wife?"

I nod. "Positive. I've seen the paperwork." Another lie. I'll deal with this after that motherfucker is dead! I just need them on my side. The Kings can destroy him. "And no, he's never been married and no children."

Bones eyes me. "Everything would have to burn. You're willing to lose everything?"

"Yes."

"Everything, Emilee," he reiterates. "You can't rent a U-Haul to pack up all your sentimental shit and then set it on fire. All your memories. All your clothes. Shoes. Books. Pictures of you and your mom. You and your family. In order for it not to look suspicious, whatever is in that house will have to be gone. We're not willing to take that risk for you."

I let out a long breath and look down at my hands in my lap. "I've already lost everything," I say softly, making my chest tighten. "After my dad …" I pause. "George moved in and took everything that ever meant something to me."

I swallow the lump in my throat and look at Bones. His blue eyes stare into mine. Then at Titan. "If I have to run out of that house naked while it's up in flames, I will."

"Well, then you gotta think about the size of the house," Titan adds, running his fingers over his chin in thought. "It will take hours to completely burn one at that size. The fire department will be there long before it's all destroyed."

"Give me a diversion," I offer, not thinking of that until now.

Bones snorts.

I fist my hands. "There's only one road in and out to the private neighborhood. Block it off …"

"You want us to what? Cause a wreck?" Titan asks, already shaking his head. "We're not gonna give you a diversion. That makes us involved."

"It's an option," I say through clenched teeth.

"No, it's not," Titan states.

Bones speaks. "How you gonna make sure he's there? He's going to run when he finds out we're not gonna take you as payment." He looks me up and down, and my face flushes.

"Tell him you will," I argue. "If he runs, that defeats the plan and it'll all be for nothing. I need him dead."

"How will we make it believable?" Bones asks.

Glancing at him, I see he's relaxed back in his chair. He's got his right elbow on the armrest and his tatted fingers run along his bottom lip. His other hand rests on his thigh. He looks like a demon ready to swallow my soul. Asking what I'm offering in payment.

Titan pushes off the wall and I watch him walk over to me. My heart picks up when he comes to stand behind my chair, out of my line of sight. He pulls my hair off my shoulder ever so gently, but it feels like a threat.

"He'll want proof," he says just as softly.

I close my eyes and whisper, "I've done far worse."

Titan chuckles. "I bet you have, baby."

I open my eyes, and Bones's blue ones stare at me. Titan's hand lands on my shoulder, and I jump. "Five hundred thousand is a lot of money, Em."

I swallow.

"You can have it all." My voice shakes. "I just want ..."

"Your mother taken care of," Titan announces.

I look back at Bones, and Titan's fingers crawl along my neck, and my body shudders. "Please." I hate begging. Especially to him of all people. After all this time.

"I don't do charity cases," Bones states, and my stomach drops.

I shove Titan's hands off me and stand, leaning over his desk. "I'm not a fucking charity case. I'm offering you more than you are owed."

He waves it off and stands to his full height. I have to look up and instantly feel like someone he wants to squash. "We'll get it one way or the other," he says simply and then walks around his desk.

"Dillan!" I growl his real name, turning to watch him walk to the door. He's gonna dismiss me. "He's gonna run. I know he has the money to pay you, but he's just refusing to. With the kind of resources he has, you'll never find him. I'm your only option."

He smiles at me. A cruel and lethal smile that makes me remember just how cold this sorry bastard can be. "No one can hide from the Kings," he states.

I turn to face Titan. He always was a fucking dick too. "Weston ..."

"It's Titan," he corrects me.

"Seriously?" I snap

He crosses his arms over his hard chest.

"Fuck, you guys are still the same ole Kings! Self-absorbed and a pain in my ass."

Titan's eyes drop to my legs. "I'm more than willing to fuck your ass, baby."

I growl, turn, and storm out the door with my chin held high, but tears burn my eyes.

I'm so fucked!

TITAN

BONES SHUTS THE door and looks at me. "Get a tail. I want eyes on his house and the York's residence twenty-four seven. If he sits to piss, I wanna know."

"And Emilee?"

He goes back behind his desk. "I don't give a shit what she does."

I've never asked what happened between them because I didn't want to look like I cared. Maybe I should. "What if she starts the fire anyway?"

He opens his mouth and then shuts it. "Well … then I'd care. I don't want the bastard dead. I want our money."

"She seems desperate. Coming here had to take some balls. Rejection hurts." He says nothing. "We could call up Luca," I offer. "Cross helped him take out the Cathedral. We could pay the fire marshal off to do the same with the York's residence."

He sighs, running a hand down his face. "It wasn't a bad idea, but I wasn't going to tell her that. I don't want her putting herself in danger."

I arch a brow.

"What?" he asks, noticing.

"You know what."

His jaw sharpens, and he looks away from me. "It's not like that. We fucked. We moved on. Doesn't mean I want her to kill herself in a house fire over fucking George."

I say nothing.

"We have a meeting with him tonight." He changes the subject.

"Since when?"

"That's what he called about earlier. Wanted to plant a bug in my ear about Emilee and set up the meeting."

"Since when did we start making house calls? Especially two?"

His jaw clenches again, and I can tell he's irritated with this situation. And I know it's because of Emilee. Any other time, he wouldn't be so lenient with George. We'd be burying a body, not negotiating with it.

"Only you and I are going." He ignores my question.

"What about Grave and Cross?"

"Grave won't be able to sit down long enough to listen. And Cross has something to take care of." He waves me off. "Go finish playing with the girls in your bed and then get ready."

EIGHT

EMILEE

I PULL UP to the white stucco mansion and run up the stairs, passing the pillars and ring the doorbell. I get no answer and begin banging on the door. "Jasmine!" I shout. "I know you're home. I see your car …"

The door swings open. "E." She smiles at me. "What are you …?"

"I need a drink." I shove past her.

"Well, you've come to the right place." She closes the door. "Come on."

I follow her through the foyer and down a hall. Then through another door that leads down to her father's basement. Turning on the light, I walk over to the full bar and sit down on the barstool. I place my face in my hands. We used to come down here and drink all the time in high school. He never checked his inventory.

"Talk to me," she urges.

"I need money," I admit. "Lots of it."

"How much?"

"A million would be a good start." I give a rough laugh, trying not to cry at the situation I have found myself in.

"Okay." I look up at her, and she places a full drink in front of me. "A million it is."

I snort and pick up the glass. "I'm serious, Jasmine."

"Me too. I'll take it from my father and give it to you. I'll tell him I went on a shopping spree."

I shake my head. "Yeah, because that is believable."

"E, I once spent over a million on a sculpture in a Gucci store in Milan. You should have seen his face when he read the credit card statement. Trust me. He'll believe it."

I take a sip of the drink still in my hand and hiss in a breath before sitting it down.

"What kind of trouble are you in?" she asks.

"It's not me. It's my mother," I admit. "My father left George in charge of everything after he passed. He's blackmailing me to have sex with him." She gasps. "In order to pay my mother's medical bills."

"That motherfucker," she hisses. "I never liked that bastard."

"But come to find out, my mother is in love with him."

Her eyes grow big.

"The worst part is that George owes the Kings half a million, and they want their money. He wants to offer me to the Kings as payment." I take another gulp.

"The fuck?" she snaps.

"I just came from Kingdom. I met with Titan and Bones. I asked them to take the deal. Begged them actually. To buy me some time to kill George. But they denied me." I look up at her, and she doesn't look the least bit concerned about my confession. "I can sell my car. It's paid for." A present my parents gave me after graduating college before I moved to Chicago. But with the accounts frozen, I'm not even sure I'd be able to do that. The car's in my father's name. The process could take longer than I have. "After my apartment sells, I'll have that as well. But I don't have access to much right now." I didn't want to sell it now. That's my escape plan. To run away back to Chicago after my mom passes, but I can't afford not to get rid of them both.

She pulls a barstool up across from me and sits down. "Look, Titan can help you."

I shake my head. "No, he won't."

"He can. Ever heard of Glass?"

"No." I've been gone for a little over two years. Things come and go a lot in this town.

She picks up her phone. "I have a friend who can help you."

I reach out, slapping her hand and phone to the bar top. "I don't want a lot of people knowing my situation. And I'm sure the Kings don't want anyone knowing theirs."

Her green eyes soften, and she places her free hand on top of ours. "Trust me, E. I'm going to help you. And no one will know."

TWENTY MINUTES LATER, she's driving me down the Strip. "Please tell me we're not going to Kingdom." I can't deal with any more Kings today.

"Nope."

She turns on her blinker and pulls into a parking lot. I lean my head back to look out the window to see the sign that sits above a two-story brick building. *Glass* written in white letters.

The front and side parking areas are full, so she pulls around the back. Finding a spot, she backs into it, facing the building.

"What are we doing here?" I ask. "And what is this place?"

"A strip club."

"What?" I shriek. "I can't strip …"

"We're not here for work. We're here to get help."

Her phone dings in the cupholder, and she picks it up. "She has ten minutes to spare for us."

"Who?" I ask.

"A friend." She continues to stay vague.

She goes to open her door but throws an arm out and slams her hand into my chest. "Get down." she whispers harshly, yanking on my shirt.

"Jasmine, what the—?"

"It's Bones," she interrupts me.

I look over at where she's gawking and see Bones step out of a black door on the second floor. He makes his way down the metal stairs and to a blacked-out Lamborghini Reventon that's hidden back here with hers. I hadn't seen it before. He didn't have that car back when we … fucked.

"What's he doing here?" she wonders.

I snort. "Really? You have to ask that question?" His headlights come on, and the car's engine roars to life. He drives out of his spot before pulling out onto the Strip.

I look at the dash. "He wasn't here very long. I was just at Kingdom an hour ago in his office."

"Come on." She gets out, and we walk inside. There's a hallway that curves to the left and the right. Both end up at a desk where a guy sits on a barstool. "ID's?" he asks, and we both pull ours out. He looks them over. "Work or play?"

"Play." Jasmine bats her eyelashes at him.

I roll mine. *How can this help me?* I'm not going to crawl onto this stage. No matter how many drinks I buy.

"Enjoy, ladies."

She grabs my hand and pulls me through another set of double doors. The blinding lights and pounding music instantly give me a headache.

Jasmine seems to know what we're doing because she walks us up three stairs and past the bar toward the back of the room.

There's a round black leather booth that's empty. She falls into it and scoots over to allow me to sit beside her. I'm about to ask her what in the hell this is when a girl climbs off the stage next to us and slides into our booth. She has bleach-blond hair that cascades down her back. Her plump lips are painted blood red, and she has purple contacts in. She also wears nothing but a G-string. I can't help but look at her perfect tits. Honestly, I can't tell if they're real or fake.

"Jasmine." She smiles and pulls her in for a hug.

"Shana." Jasmine kisses her cheek before pulling away. "Thank you for meeting with us."

"Anything for you. What do you need?"

"I'm in a bind. And I need cash. Fast." Jasmine makes it sound like we're here for her. And I'm thankful for that.

The woman's eyes slide to mine, then back to Jasmine. "You know

I can't ..."

"Please?" Jasmine begs. "I know you can help me. I swear I won't tell anyone. Totally confidential."

I want to ask so many questions but keep my mouth shut for the moment.

Shana looks from her to me a couple of times. "I'm guessing this is for the both of you?"

Jasmine looks at me too, and I swallow nervously. I have to make a decision here. Jasmine can't speak for me. But I do trust her. So far, she's the only one willing to help me. "Yes, please."

She nods and slides out of the booth and walks toward the other side of the club. She disappears into a door by the main stage.

I look at Jasmine. "What did I just sign up for?"

"I'll explain it the moment we leave. We'll go back to my house and fill it out."

"Fill what out?"

Just then the woman returns to our booth and sets two forms down. "Here you go." She also has her cell with her, and she begins to type away on it. "I'm letting him know you're coming. If I refer you, you have a better chance."

"Message who?" I ask.

"Okay." She looks down at her phone, ignoring my question. "He'll be expecting you Friday morning. Just write my name at the bottom of your application so he knows who you are."

She turns her phone around and holds it up so we can read it. My heart skips a beat when I see who she messaged.

Her: I'm sending two girls Friday. They have their forms.
Titan: Sounds good.

WE MAKE OUR way back to her car. I'm practically running behind her to keep up with her pace. I think Jasmine knows I'm pissed. If not, she's about to find out.

"A prostitute? That's how you expect me to fix my problem?"

"A queen is not a prostitute," she argues. I get in the passenger seat and slam her car door shut.

"Let's recap, shall we? I tell you George is forcing me to sleep with him, and your idea is for me to fuck random strangers?"

"Queens don't *fuck* random strangers. You get offered a job, and you decide if you accept or decline."

I run a hand through my hair. "And why the fuck did she message Titan about this?"

She sighs. "He runs the Queens. The escort service through Kingdom. He hires the girls and gets their jobs. I told you he could help you."

"Of course, he fucking does." *Unbelievable.*

We come to a stop at the stoplight, and she looks at me. "Listen. I'm trying to help you. Queens make bank. Cash. It's exclusive and on the hush hush. You sign an NDA, and the clients sign an NDA. You make as much as you want, as often as you want. You fill out the form with what you're willing to do and not do."

"Jesus …"

"And I'm going to do it with you."

I look over at her.

"Shana spent last weekend in the Hamptons at a beach house with a man pretending to be his girlfriend at his family reunion. Easy ten grand."

"This is how women die," I tell her. You see women on the news all the time who have gone missing. Never to be seen again. "Or they get sold."

She chuckles. "I don't remember you being so cautious, E." The light turns green, and she drives through the intersection.

I look out the passenger window to see the empire known as Kingdom pass by and let out a long sigh. The only money I have access to right now is what I made from being a ring girl. Other than that, I'm fucked. "How long?" I ask.

"I'm not sure. Shana has been doing it for two years now. She only works at Glass one night a week. All her income comes from being a Queen."

I look over at her. "If I die, I'm coming back to haunt you."

"Dying is the least of your worries. You have to convince Titan to hire you."

"Convince him?" I ask.

She nods. "Oh yeah. Not every woman who wants to be a queen actually gets hired. He's going to tell you no."

I'm not sure why he would deny me, but somehow, I know she's right. "That bastard still has my cell phone."

She chuckles. "You're going to have to get it back."

"That's what I'm afraid of." Get on my knees for my phone, or fuck George again? That's an easy decision. I don't know why I didn't choose him sooner.

"It will be okay," she promises.

But I'm not so optimistic.

NINE

TITAN

We walk into George's house, and Margarita looks at me with fear as she allows us in. "Mr. Wilton is waiting for you in his office." She starts to walk us down the hall, but like last time, I grab her collar and yank her back.

"We know the way," I tell her, and she scurries off.

Bones doesn't even bother knocking on the door. He shoves it open to find George sitting at the desk. The moment he sees us, he jumps to his feet. Clearing his throat, he straightens his already straight tie. "Kings?" He looks at the door, waiting for the other two to join us. I slam it shut. "Please." He gestures to the seats behind us. "Take a seat."

"I don't do house calls, George," Bones announces, crossing his arms over his chest. "Where the fuck is our money?" Straight to business.

His face falls, but he recovers it quickly. "Well, uh … I don't have it …"

Lie. Emilee says he has it but just refuses to pay. And I believe her over this piece of shit.

"But I will. Soon," he adds.

"You've said that before." Bones nods.

"My business partner has passed. And I'm waiting for the life insurance to pay out."

"That could take months," I add. If that's even true. Who knows how much he already has access to since Nick York has passed?

He shakes his head fast. "No. My attorney has assured me just a few weeks."

"Well, we came to collect today." Bones states taking a step toward the desk.

He holds up his hands. "I have an offer for you. The girl ..."

"I don't want the fucking girl." Bones shakes his head. "I want what you owe us."

"Please, we can settle this ..."

Bones removes the gun from the waistband of his jeans, and George goes silent. "The thing is ..." Bones sets the gun on the desk but maintains hold of it. "We have killed for less, George. I don't want pussy. And I don't want excuses. I want the fucking money." He lifts the gun and cocks it. Walking behind the desk, he places it to his temple. "Now the question is, are you willing to die for it?"

"There's money in the briefcase," he rushes out, nodding to the one sitting on his desk.

"What are the numbers?" I ask, looking at it.

He rattles them off, and it pops open.

"How much?" Bones asks.

"Not enough," I answer as I pull out wads of cash.

"There's a hundred grand there. If you just give me a month, I'll get you the rest," George rushes out. "I'll ... I'll bring it to you. Meet you at Kingdom as soon as I have it."

Bones removes the gun and clicks the safety on. George lets out a shaky breath.

TEN

TITAN

I WOKE UP with another pounding headache, so I have the curtains closed to block out the light. And five new girls stand in the center of my office. All stripped down to their underwear. I'm still going through their paperwork when I hear Nigel's voice come through the speaker on my office phone. "Two ladies have arrived, sir. They say that Shana referred them, and that you are expecting them today."

I press the intercom button and order, "Send them up."

I never set a limit on how many Queens we have. At one point, we had over three hundred. But not all of them live in Nevada. One, for instance, resides in Columbus, Ohio, and comes to Vegas three times a year to work for me. The women get to choose how often and how much they work. You'd be surprised by how many I've lost due to them getting in a serous relationship with one of my clients. I wouldn't say it's allowed, but I can't tell two people not to share feelings. It is what it is. And there are always five new girls ready and willing to take her place.

Hearing my door open, I hold out my hand without looking up and snap my fingers. "Paperwork."

TITAN

Two applications are placed in it, and I slap them down on the desk. I press my intercom button for the adjoining office. "GiGi, five of them are ready for you."

Seconds later, the door to my right opens, and she steps in.

"Go with GiGi to get your measurements. Once done, come back in here, and the doctor will be ready for you," I inform them.

I place the first five applications to the side and look at the two new ones. When I read their names, my head snaps up. Jasmine and Emilee stand before me.

"Is this a joke?" I ask.

Neither one of them says anything. I run a hand through my hair. "Goddammit." I stand. Not in the mood for this today. Or any other day. "What the fuck is this shit?" I demand, picking up their papers.

"We're here to audition to be a Queen," Jasmine smiles at me. She has her short red hair half up and is dressed like she's going out on the town in a black mini dress with her tits hanging out and heels. I wouldn't expect anything less from her.

"I don't have time for this," I growl.

Jasmine reaches for the hem of the dress and lifts it over her head. Then undoes her bra and tosses it behind her.

My eyes meet her green ones. "What are you doing?" Still not believing them for a second.

"Isn't this what we must do?" she asks, tilting her head as if she's confused. "The application was very clear that we must strip down and show you what we're working with."

It does not say those exact words, but I'm not going to stop them. I'm so ready for this day to be over, and it's not even ten a.m. yet. "You're right." I cross my arms over my chest, and my eyes go to Emilee. She looks almost terrified. "Show me," I challenge her. I had no doubt Jasmine would do it, but Em won't.

EMILEE

I RUN MY hand through my hair and close my eyes. At one time, I liked him. I actually wanted him to touch me. Fuck me.

85

Twenty years old.

"Bones, this is the boy's locker room," I hiss as he drags me inside off the gym floor.

"I don't give a fuck."

"Bones ..." He slams my back into a red locker, the sound bouncing off the now silent room. I watch the door slowly shut behind us and wonder if it locks. It's the middle of the day. We just finished lunch. Who knows who may try to come in here?

He lowers his head to my neck. His warm breath hitting my skin. "No one is in here at this time, Em. It's just you and me." His hands go to my shorts. "And I can't wait ..." His lips find mine. "Need to ..." Kiss. "Be inside of you right now."

His tongue enters my mouth, tangling with mine, and I groan as that usual feeling builds in my stomach. My thighs tightening and my pussy growing wet at how much he needs me. Bones never needs anything. I'm the only one he ever shows who he really is. How broken he truly is. And I can't help but want to save him. From his demons. From his nightmares. I never turn him down.

He shoves my shorts down my legs when he realizes I'm not gonna protest anymore. His fingers go between my thighs, and he runs them over the soaked fabric of my underwear.

I open my eyes and gasp when I see a set of blue eyes staring at me in the large mirror. I look to the left of us, but no one is there. It's another set of lockers. He shoves a finger into me, and I begin to pant. Looking back at the mirror, I see those same eyes again. And I realize he's on the other side of the lockers. Only this time, he's moved forward, more into the line of sight, and it's Titan.

"Bones ..." I go to shove him away.

He rips my panties off my hips, and I cry as the fabric tears into my skin before giving in to his strength. He shoves them into my mouth, then clamps his hand over my lips, knocking the back of my head into the locker with force. I look up at him, and wetness pools between my legs. His face is in front of mine, staring down at me. "I'm gonna fuck that tight cunt, Em." He lowers his lips to my neck, gently kissing my skin. "You're gonna keep these soaked panties in your mouth until I replace *them with my cock and come all over those pretty lips."*

I whimper. My eyes still on Titan. He stands there like a statue, listening to every word. And my heart pounds. Does Bones know he's in here? Would he stop if I told him?

Bones pulls back and glares down at me waiting for me to agree.

I nod my head. My breathing ragged and heart pounding. I know they've shared girls before; I wonder if it's ever crossed his mind to share me ...

That thought gets interrupted as Bones slides into me, stretching me. I cry out around the gag, and he doesn't take his time. He lifts my right leg to hug his hip, and his fingers grip my skin, holding it in place. He's rough as he slams into me. My body hits the lockers, and the sound echoes in the room.

My eyes are on Titan. His on mine. His white T-shirt strains from his heavy breathing. He lowers his hands and unzips his jeans, and my breath gets caught when I watch him pull his hard dick through the open zipper. Lifting his hand, he spits on it before stroking his long, thick cock. Once. Twice. Girls in this school talk and their whispered memories of his dick don't do him any justice. I watch hungrily as his hand picks up pace and saliva pools in my mouth.

"Fuck, you're so wet, baby," Bones growls. "I should gag you more often." He grips my hair with his free hand and yanks my head back, making me look up at the white ceiling tiles. I can't see Titan anymore, but I can feel his eyes on us. Watching. Wanting. A part of me wishes he would touch me. Suck on my hard nipples. I still have on my bra and shirt. When Bones is in a mood like this, nothing else matters but a quickie. Hard and fast to get both of us off. No foreplay. No extra attention.

And right now, I sure do want to play. With both of them. A bigger part wishes Titan's cock was in my mouth instead of my thong.

That sensation building takes over me, and I scream into the gag as heat rushes up my back. Bones lets go of me. My shaky knees give way, and I fall to them on the tile floor. Then he's shoving his fingers in my mouth and removes the gag. I take in a deep breath, but that's all he allows me before it's replaced with his cock. I can taste myself on him. His hands grip my hair, and he doesn't slow his pace. He fucks my mouth just as he did my pussy. His grunts and the sounds of me sucking fill the room like music booming through speakers. Then I feel him. His body tensing, he pushes farther down my throat and tears run down my face. I accept him, knowing he needs it. I need it. And I want to show Titan how good I am. If he's even still here. All I can see is a blurry vison of Bones looking down at me as he holds my head by my hair. He pushes into me one last time, and cum fills the back of my throat. When he finally steps away, I fall forward on my hands, gasping for air. Cum drips from the corners of my lips, and I lick it off.

I hear Bones zip up his pants, and then he kneels before me, "I've got practice tonight, but I'll be over afterward. Leave your window unlocked and be naked." He kisses me, stands, and leaves.

My head is bowed while on my hands and knees in the boys locker room, and I look up when I hear the sink turn on. I thought Bones had left ... My eyes lock on Titan's in the mirror. He's washing his hands. I want to be embarrassed, but I can't. The rush of knowing he was watching turned me on. I even wanted him to join.

Without breaking eye contact, I get to my shaky legs. He throws the paper towel in the trash and turns to face me.

I'm breathing heavy, and my face is wet from tears running down my cheeks. He takes a step toward me and just stands there. When he sees that I don't stop him, he takes three more, closing the distance between us. I pant, but he's no longer breathing heavy like he was when I watched him earlier. He reaches out, grabs a lock of my tangled hair, and twists it around his fingers. He licks his lips.

"Titan ..." I whisper, thinking he's gonna kiss me. I'm standing in front of him naked from the waist down. Not one bit ashamed or embarrassed.

Instead, he leans forward, placing his lips to my ear. His large body pressing into my shaking one. "You looked good on your knees, Em. It suited you." He pulls away, standing up to his full height. He reaches up running a finger over my wet lips. "Anytime you need a reminder where you belong, let me know. I'll be more than happy to help you out." Then he turns and walks out.

Opening my eyes, I see the side door in his office softly shut. One look over where Jasmine was standing shows me that she has left me and Titan. And she just became a Queen. It's all up to me now. I have to swallow my pride and do what must be done. And I already hate how much I'm going to enjoy it.

ELEVEN

TITAN

"Why are you here, Em?" I ask, walking over to the minibar to pour her a drink. Vodka straight up. I hold it out to her, but she doesn't take it.

Good girl.

That was a test, and she passed.

"I want to be a Queen."

I laugh, and her eyes narrow on me. I should ask her how she found out, but that would be pointless. I can connect the dots. Shana and Jasmine are friends.

"Okay," I'll indulge her. "Then why are you still dressed?" She just stares at me. "That's what I thought." I walk back over to my desk. "I assume you can see yourself out?" I sit down in my chair, but she still stands there. "I don't have time …"

"I want to be a Queen," she repeats, lifting her chin.

"No, you don't." I gesture to the door with my chin. "Get out, I have shit to do."

She reaches down and grabs the hem of her shirt and pulls it up and over her head. Her blue eyes stay on mine as she unzips her jeans and shimmies them down her legs before stepping out of them.

I shift in my seat. "Em …?"

"Isn't this what you want?" she asks, interrupting me.

I swallow but don't disagree with her. She knows what I want, or I wouldn't have taken her phone and demanded she fall to her knees to get it back.

She slowly walks around my desk and places her hands on my knees. She pushes my chair back to allow her access to stand between my desk and me. Reaching behind her, she undoes her bra, and it falls to my feet.

"This is what you want, right? Me? On my knees?" She drops before me, and I sit up straighter. Her hands reach for my belt, and I don't stop her as she undoes it.

My heart picks up, and my cock hardens, but I keep my eyes on hers.

"I can use people too, Titan," she states, licking her pretty pink lips. "I know what must be done to get what I want? Do you?"

Reaching out, I grip her dark hair in my hands. "What does that mean?"

Her lips part, and she sucks in a breath.

I lean forward, placing my face right in front of hers. "What in the fuck did you mean by that, Em?"

"It means we both want something." Her hands run down my thighs. "Or do you no longer want me?" she asks. "I remember a time when you did. You could have had me, you know? I was just playing hard to get. And you chickened out."

"New Kings" by Sleeping Wolf plays while I sit on the couch at the frat house. I decided to go out tonight. Grave and Cross wanted to hit up a strip club, and Bones had other plans. He didn't fill me in, and I didn't ask. I figured he had plans to fuck Emilee. But that obviously wasn't it when I see her walk through the front door.

I'm not surprised when I spot Jasmine by her side. She immediately pulls Em through the living room and into the kitchen.

I tip my beer back and realize I'm empty. Getting up, I make my way into the kitchen as well. I watch Jasmine make two shots. She hands one to Emilee, but she shakes her head, refusing it.

Jasmine rolls her eyes and tosses them back one after the other. Before she can even set the second empty shot glass down, Trenton walks through the kitchen, and she follows him out of the room to what I can only guess is a bedroom upstairs.

I throw my beer bottle away and walk over to the kitchen island. "What are you doing here?" I ask her.

She jumps back and pushes her dark hair behind her ear. "Jasmine talked me into coming out."

I nod and pop the top off my new beer. "I see." I look her up and down. She wears a pair of black jeans and an ocean blue sweater. Her hair is down, and she doesn't have much makeup on. It's like she tried to downplay her look, knowing she was coming to a frat party. Emilee isn't one of those girls who likes to be seen. She prefers to stay in the shadows, but I've always noticed her.

I grab a bottle of maple Crown and pour two shots. "Have a drink. You look like you need it." I slide it across the island.

She takes it but doesn't look me in the eye. She's been avoiding me ever since I saw her and Bones in the boys' locker room a few weeks ago. She can try to avoid me all she wants, but we both know she liked me watching. That it turned her on.

She throws back the shot and hisses in a breath. "Thanks."

I walk around the island and approach her, testing the waters. She bows her head and shuffles her feet. Reaching up, I push her hair behind her ear. Her head shoots up, and her blue eyes meet mine. "Titan ..." she whispers.

I push my body into hers, pinning her back into the countertop. My hands go to her hips, and I lower my face to her neck. I inhale her scent. She smells like strawberries and cream.

"I can't get you on your knees out of my head," I admit shamelessly. "Do you think about it too, Em?"

Her chest rises and falls quickly while her fingers dig into my jeans.

"Tell me that you wanted me, too."

"Bones ..."

"Bones knew I was in there," I admit. "He knows how much I hate you. And that I want to fuck you. Why should he get all the fun?"

She slams her fists into my chest, pushing me back a step. Her eyes narrow up at me. "Go to hell, Titan."

"You were wet. Because of me," I add, keeping her in place. "You put on a show for me." Her body begins to tremble against mine. "Tell me, Em. You wanted me to join the two of you."

Those hard, blue eyes soften, and her hands wrap around my waist, pulling me closer into her. "You didn't make a move," she whispers before licking her lips.

"I enjoyed watching you," I admit. "I jacked off to you and him." She saw me. She knows what I did. But I want her to know that I know she wanted me as much as I wanted her. I'm not ashamed of what I did. "I want a turn."

And just like that, she's changed her mind. She shoves me away from her, and I step back, allowing her to take in the scene. To let everything I just told her sink in. She turns and runs out of the kitchen.

I follow her, grab her upper arm, and pull her through a door that just happens to be a bedroom.

"Titan, I can't," she whispers as I close the door behind me. I spin her around, pinning her back to it.

"Can't or won't?" I ask, cupping her cheek.

The lights are off, so it's pitch black in here, but I can hear her heavy breathing. I can feel her heart pounding against my chest. Mine does the same, and I'm hard as a rock. It presses painfully against the inside of my jeans. I know she can feel it.

"I hate you," I say, lowering my lips to hers. She sucks in a breath. "But that doesn't mean I don't want to fuck you, Em."

"Why do you hate me?" she asks, the question breathless, and I can smell the maple on her breath.

I lower my lips to her neck and feel her pulse race as I gently kiss her soft skin. "Because you won't give me what I want."

She goes silent, but I don't pull away. It's her move. I'll gladly get on my knees for her. All she has to do is give the order because as much as I hate her, I want her even more.

Her hands slide up my chest and wrap around my neck, and then she's pulling me forward. My lips touch hers, and my hand slides from her face into her hair. I grip it between my fingers, and she gasps into my mouth. Her kiss grows frantic and so do her hands.

This is it. I'm finally going to get what I want. And I don't even care that she'll go to Bones later. I just want a taste.

EMILEE

I CAME HERE to be a Queen, and I'm not going to leave until that happens. I need the money. My mother needs this money.

Titan stares down at me as if he's in a daze. He's not here with me. Not right now. He's somewhere in the past. Probably that night at the frat house. That one time I was going to go for it, but then changed my mind at the last second. I had wanted to be with both of them, but I was afraid that if Bones found out I was with Titan, he would hate me. And that thought terrified me. I may have not loved him, but I couldn't afford to lose him. But this time it's different. I don't belong to anyone. Not Bones and sure as shit not George. I'm going to choose who I fuck and when I fuck.

Right here, right now, I choose Titan.

My hands run up his jeans-clad thighs, and I wrap them around his hard cock. He jumps, his eyes focusing on me, and his hand tightens in my hair.

I lick my lips. And before he can push me away, I wrap my lips around him.

"Emilee …"

I don't allow him to refuse me. I open my mouth and push him to the back of my throat, tasting his precum.

"Oh, fuck," he groans, shifting in his chair.

I readjust myself on my knees and look up at him. His head is back, and his lips are parted. He's panting. His hips move in the chair.

My head bounces up and down as I swallow his fucking cock like he's a client. But isn't he? I may have wanted to all these years, but this is more of an audition than an actual job.

My cheeks scream, and my throat burns. My mouth is open as wide as it will go to accommodate his size. I want to pull away, but I don't. I can't. Not until he gets what he wants.

You gotta give to get.

His hands dig into my hair, pulling it from the ponytail, and he takes over. Fucking my mouth how he wants to. It's rough, but I expected it to be. Nothing about the Kings was ever soft.

After a few minutes, I feel his body tense, and without warning, he comes in my mouth. His hands fall from my hair.

I pull back and suck in breath after breath. I wipe the drool off my chin and make it to my shaky feet.

He stands as well, towering over me. His hand comes up and runs his knuckles down the side of my cheek. "You sure you want to sell yourself to me, rather than him?" he asks.

I knew there would be consequences, and he just laid them out on the table. No fucking around when it comes to Titan. It is what it is. "Yes," I answer. I don't need to be drunk to be with Titan. I won't vomit afterward. And I won't sit in a shower crying either. I can handle him. I can tolerate him.

He pulls away from me and reaches down into his desk drawer. He pulls out my cell and starts typing away on it. I walk back around to the front of his desk and get dressed. Once I'm done, I look at him.

"Here you go." He hands it over. "I just happened to have charged it last night. I've downloaded the Queens app. If you have any problems, it calls me directly."

I nod, not sure what he means about *problems*, but I can figure it out. I refuse to thank him. So instead, I give him my back and walk toward the side door where Jasmine had entered.

"Oh, Em?"

Letting out a long breath, I turn to face him. "Yes?"

"If he fucking tries to touch you again, you call me. Understood?"

I almost smile. This is why I chose him. Fucking a King is like having your own personal bodyguard. They protect their queens. "I will."

Before I can exit the office, his main door opens, and Bones enters. *Shit!*

His blue eyes drop to my cell in my hand, and the corners of his lips turn up.

Without saying a word to him, I push open the door and get the hell out of there. The moment it closes, I lean my back up against it. Shutting my eyes, I let out a long breath, hoping I made the right decision.

TWELVE

TITAN

I LOOK OVER at Bones once Emilee has left the room. He arches a brow. "I see you gave Emilee her phone back."

I nod.

"What did she want?" he asks, plopping down across from me.

"A job."

"A job?" he asks.

"I made her a queen." Not the best decision I've ever made, but I don't know why I didn't think of it before. It's a great solution to her current situation. Plus, I can keep an eye on her. "I'll control who she sees and what she does. It's the best form of a leash."

He leans forward. "Good idea."

"I'm guessing she was not the reason you came into my office."

He shakes his head. "Nope. I got a phone call, and it seems George has skipped town."

"Not surprised." I sit back, trying to ignore my hard cock that is in my jeans. I wanted more but couldn't tell her that. As far as she knows, I'm using her and not the other way around. "What is the plan?"

"We'll let him go for now. He'll come back." His eyes slide to the door Emilee just exited through.

"You think he'll come back for her?" I ask, the thought not sitting well with me. She's mine now. I've waited long enough for her; he's not getting his hands on her again.

He shakes his head. "There's no reason for him to do that. She won't get him anywhere, especially now that he knows we weren't going to trade her for the money."

I nod in agreement. "Did the detail not see where he went?"

"Nope. They lost him while on the highway. He knew we had eyes on him."

"You think someone leaked that info, or he just got nervous and figured we had him covered?"

"I don't know." He runs a hand over his hair, frustrated. "But when he returns, he's going to pay us back, in pounds of flesh." With that, he gets up and exits my office, slamming the door shut behind him.

EMILEE

A WOMAN BY the name of GiGi measured every inch of me and Jasmine. Then a doctor came and hooked us up with the Depo shot. He also took our weight and height and wrote it down. I'm guessing the clients like to know what size of woman they are paying for. We were then tested for every STD known to man and informed we would get our results within the hour. I wasn't concerned in any way. I was tested last year and was clean. The only person I've slept with since then was George, and he used a condom both times.

Then we were sent to the Kingdom spa where we had facials, got a mani and pedi, followed by our entire bodies waxed. And after that, we visited the Kingdom salon where they did our hair and makeup. The works.

Five hours after entering Kingdom, we walk out to her car parked out back.

"Have a great day, ladies." Nigel nods to us.

"You too," Jasmine calls out. "Man, I feel like a new woman," she says, falling into the car.

"Right?"

She looks over at me and winks. "So, I see you got your phone back."

"Yeah."

"And?"

"And I worked hard for that damn thing," I admit.

She laughs at me. "The Kings don't go easy on anyone."

Ain't that the truth. "Where are we headed?" I change the subject. I'd prefer not to discuss Titan. I can still taste him. Still remember the look on his face as I pleased him. The sad part is I didn't feel any shame. And I should have. How is what he did any different from George? Is it because I wanted him before? I've always been attracted to Titan, but that doesn't change the fact that he's a prick.

"Here." She hands me her cell and the business card that GiGi had given us. "Put that into GPS. Might as well figure out what the hell it is."

I look down at it. It's a flat black card with nothing written on it besides an address. I type it in. "It says it's ten miles from here."

"Okay." She reaches over and turns up the volume. "Like Lovers Do," by Hey Violet fills the small car.

"You sure this is it?" she asks as we pull up to an abandoned warehouse.

"Yeah," I say, double-checking what I put in her phone matches what the card says.

She parks in the front row, and we get out. Going up to the double doors, I push one open, and we step inside.

"No fucking way," she says in awe, looking over the massive space.

"Hello, ladies." A woman comes up to us dressed in a black business suit with a white button-down. Her dark hair is up in a tight bun, and she has a smile on her face. Her dark brown eyes do a quick sweep over us as if assessing us. "Do you have your card?" she asks.

Jasmine and I exchange a *what-the-fuck-card* looks. I dig into my back pocket and pull out the only one I have. The one GiGi handed us with this address on it. I hold it up. "Is this what you want?"

"Yes, ma'am." She hands it back to me. "Now let me show you around." She turns and walks off as we follow close behind. "We dress all the Queens. The client will notify Titan what the occasion is, and he will inform me and yourself on the app."

"No way." Jasmine smiles. "We get to keep what we wear?"

"Well, yes and no." She goes on. "You'll have an account; the item you wear will be scanned. It will withdraw that amount from your account. When you return said item, you'll scan it again and it deposits the amount. If you don't return it … well, you get the idea."

"This is amazing," Jasmine squeals.

"We have everything from bathing suits, to lingerie, to assless chaps," she continues. "To high heels, sandals, and skis. If you have something in mind that we don't keep in stock, we can have it made as long as we have a couple of weeks' notice. You'd be surprised by how many of the clients plan vacations as far as a year in advance with a Queen."

We walk past a couple of women going through what looks to be like an evening gown section.

"Do we have to wear something from here if we get a job?" I ask. Not like I have anything I could wear. Most of my things are still in Chicago.

"No," she answers, continuing to walk toward the back of the warehouse. "You may wear whatever you like. As long as it goes with what the client desires."

"Why wouldn't you want to wear something from here?" Jasmine whispers.

The lady comes to a stop and turns to face us. "I'll let you two look around." She nods over to the back right-hand corner of the store. "There are the fitting rooms. Try a few things on and let me know when you're ready."

"Ready for what?" I ask.

"Your photos."

"What photos?" Jasmine asks what I'm thinking.

"We have a studio here where we take professional photos for Titan to use when clients request a specific look, blond, brunette. Blue eyes or brown eyes, etc. Once you decide on what you want to wear, we will do the shoot and then upload the pictures to the Queens app for the clients."

TITAN

Ah, now the three pounds of makeup the lady put on me at the salon makes sense. I nod. "Can we wear anything?" I ask.

"I suggest business attire, an evening dress, and a bathing suit. We will upload one picture of each to the app and to Titan as well." With that, she leaves us.

I turn to face Jasmine. She has a smile on her face, and her green eyes are huge. "This is so awesome." She grabs my hands and starts to jump up and down. "I feel like Pretty Woman. But the best part is that I don't have to fuck one guy for the rest of my life."

I laugh. "Come on, Julia Roberts. Let's go find you something to wear."

We pick out a bathing suit and then make our way over to the evening gowns. The two women are still digging through the racks.

"Hi." Of course, Jasmine must talk to them. She's never met a stranger. That is why being a Queen is going to be perfect for her.

"Hello," the brunette says to us.

"So how long have you been a Queen?" Jasmine asks, being nosy.

"Three months," the blonde answers.

"A little over a year," the other one chimes in.

Jasmine takes a step toward them and lowers her voice. "Have you guys ever been in The Palace?"

They exchange a look. "It's a myth," the blonde finally responds after a long moment of silence.

"Urban legend," the brunette adds.

"What's The Palace?" I ask.

Jasmine is the one who answers me. "It's a sex dungeon that clients use."

I shake my head. "Count me out." Is that why the application asked questions regarding safe words and hard limits? That's one thing I hate about the situation I have found myself in—Titan knows what I prefer when it comes to doing this job. I didn't say I'd fuck any guy, but I filled in the box that I'd be open-minded.

"Really? I think it sounds like fun." Jasmine smiles.

"You would." I chuckle.

"When you've been fed vanilla all your life, rocky road sounds pretty damn delicious." She wiggles her dark eyebrows.

I roll my eyes. I know damn well that that woman prefers the kinkier kind of sex rather than vanilla.

THIRTEEN

TITAN

I'M SITTING IN my office when my cell goes off with an email. I open it up to see three attachments. They're of Emilee.

The first one has her in a red one-piece bathing suit. She stands in front of an all-white backdrop with her hands on her hips, her head tilted to the side and a smile on her face. She looks happy, almost excited.

My cock has been hard ever since she left my office earlier. I have wanted her for too long. I've been telling myself I was over it, but obviously, I wasn't.

I've been sitting here imagining her walking back in and stripping naked for me again, lying on my desk, her legs spread wide with my head between her thighs. And now here she is in a bathing suit. But it's not for me. No, it's for other men. Ones who will pay for a touch. A kiss. A fuck. How far will she let them go? I guess that depends on how much money they offer her.

And it's not like I care. She's not mine. Never has been and sure as hell isn't now.

My door swings open, and Bones enters. I never see him this much in a week, let alone in the same day. He must be restless. He walks over to my desk, picks up the remote, and presses the button to close my curtains.

I exit out of my emails and sit back in my seat. "If I haven't seen you out in the daylight, I would swear you are allergic to the sun."

He drops the remote and falls into the seat across from me and runs a hand down his face. "I was just informed that George boarded a private jet for Paris."

"Wonder why Paris?"

He shrugs. "He'll come back. He has unfinished business."

"Emilee."

"Her mother." He places his elbows on his knees, leaning forward. "I did a little research. Divorce papers were filed two years ago between Nick and his wife. But that's not all I found."

I hold my hands out wide, gesturing for him to tell me. I'm not one for guessing games.

"Marriage license."

I frown. "They married a second time?"

He shakes his head. "George and Nancy married. Three months ago."

I run a hand down my face. "That doesn't add up. Emilee told us he was blackmailing her for sex in order to pay for her mother's health care. If he's her wife, then he's got her under his policy."

"He lied to her." He agrees.

"But why?"

He shrugs. "As bad as this sounds, he could have forced his way onto her, but he wanted her to give it up willingly. Why?"

"Lawsuit?" I offer. "Consensual sex with his stepdaughter is a much better headline than girl cries rape."

"True." He sits back. "Maybe we're thinking of this the wrong way."

"What do you mean?"

"What if he did this knowing that it was going to get out? He wants Nancy to find out what they did."

"But is there any proof of their sexual relations?" I ask. "Did he record it?" The thought makes my stomach roil. If something like that is leaked to the press or online, it would make him look like a god and Em look like a slut.

"Not that I know of. But we weren't there." He sighs. "I think the only thing that's for certain is that he didn't expect us to show up. We've spooked him. Put whatever plan he had with Emilee on hold."

"What about Nancy?"

"What about her?"

"I can't see him leaving her behind. Emilee said she didn't have much longer."

He shrugs. "After everything I've found, I know he didn't marry her for love. I doubt he cares if she dies while he's gone. Plus, once she's dead, he's entitled to what Nick left her."

"But it didn't sound like he left her much. Em, said it all went to George. That's what we need to get our hands on. His wills."

He stands from the chair. "I'm already on it. I'll let you know the moment I do."

The office phone rings, and I hold my finger up to my lips as I place whoever it is on speakerphone. "Hello?"

"Titan!" The man sings my name. "How are you?"

"Good. It's been a while, Jacob."

"Yes. Yes," he agrees. "I'm flying in tomorrow, and I need a girl."

"What type of event?" I ask, logging into my computer.

"Dinner."

"I have just the one for you." I pull up Jasmine's file. Jacob loves the outspoken kind. The ones that stand out. Her current red hair and over-the-top attitude are just that.

"I want something different for this dinner. She needs to be quiet. Sit there and just look pretty. It's a business meeting, not a social event."

I exit out of Jasmine's file, and I pull up a girl by the name of Macey. "I have …"

"I want Emilee."

My fingers pause over the keys. "Sir?"

"I just saw her picture. She's new, right? I want her."

I look up at Bones, and he arches a brow at me.

"Is that a problem, Titan?" Jacob asks at my pause.

"No." I clear my throat. "Not a problem at all. I will notify her and send you the pickup instructions."

Click.

Bones smirks but says nothing as he exits my office.

Prick.

EMILEE

"Thank you," I tell my cab driver who drops me off outside of Kingdom. I walk up the fifteen stairs to the back entrance.

"Hello, Miss York. It's good to see you again," Nigel says, holding one of the double doors open for me.

I let out a long breath. I'm nervous. My boobs are sweaty, and my knees shake. It's the unknown. What's expected of me.

I got a notification on the app last night from Titan with instructions of a job. Then I received an alert from the shop that a dress had been picked out for me. Along with an appointment to get my hair and make-up done. "It's good to see you again too."

He gives me a kind smile. "The pleasure is all mine."

"Do you know much about the Queens?" I ask him, wanting to know as much info as I can.

"What would you like to know?"

That's a loaded question. I have so many. But the only one that I can seem to speak is. "Do they all get picked up here at the casino?" When I was notified of the pickup location, I was more than surprised. I mean, I was relieved that it wasn't my place. Or his. At least Kingdom is mutual ground. And I can see why they didn't want us to meet at the restaurant. He wants to arrive with me. Show me off. I understand how this works.

"No. But this is your first time with this client, correct?"

"First time period." I run my sweaty hands down my gown.

"Oh." He smiles. "How exciting."

I laugh nervously. "That's not what I'd call it."

He reaches out and takes my hand, clutching it in his. "My dear, I assure you that you are in good hands. Titan would not allow someone to be with a Queen that he would not trust."

I nod and let out a long breath. "I'm just nervous about what is expected of me." I drop my head and stare at the white marble floor and the gold K that is in the middle of a black circle.

He places his free hand under my chin and lifts it, so I meet his kind eyes. "You do what you feel comfortable doing. This is your show."

A single elevator to my right dings before the door slides open when Nigel pulls away from me. Titan and Grave step out. They both stop when they see me. Grave looks at me as if I'm an annoyance. He's mad at me, I'm sure. He thinks I tricked him by acting deaf. That was never my intention. Titan clears his throat. "I'll meet you down there," he informs Grave. "Can you give us a moment, Nigel?"

"Of course, sir." He bows and then follows Grave back into the elevator.

Nervously, I run my hand down my dress. It's black with a deep V to show off my cleavage and a slit up my right leg, all the way up to my thigh. It's silk. Cool and soft against my skin. I topped it off with a pair of red Gucci heels and my fingernails match. My hair is up in a tight bun to show off the dress per my client's request.

He stops before me. "You look …" He licks his lips. "Stunning."

Butterflies fill my stomach, and it has nothing to do with the date that I'm getting paid to go on. "I—"

"You sure you want to do this, Em?" he interrupts me.

Something about his voice makes me lift my chin higher. Stand straighter. His doubt in me makes me want to prove him wrong more than Nigel's confidence. "It's just a date, Titan," I spit out.

He crosses his tatted arms over his broad chest and smirks down at me. "What if he wants to fuck you?"

I blink at his bluntness. My heart picking up speed at the thought of sleeping with a guy for money. For any other reason than attraction. I mean, let's face it, I sucked his dick for my phone. But it was more than that, wasn't it? I've wanted Titan for years, and I finally had an excuse to do it and not feel regret, even if he had backed me up into a corner. "If the price is right." I shrug, not wanting him to see my fear.

The smile drops off his face, and his body goes rigid. He stares down at me, and I ignore the blood rushing in my ears. He's trying to scare me. He thinks that I can't do this. That I don't have what it takes. This is when I wish I was more like Jasmine. I'll just have to pretend for now.

"Titan!"

I spin around, hearing a man behind me. He buttons his suit jacket and holds out his right hand as he approaches Titan.

"Jacob." Titan shakes his hand. "This is Emilee. Your date for the night." He gestures to me. He's replaced his scowl with a smile, but it's tight.

"Well hello, Emilee." He holds out his hand to me, and I take it. Bending down, he kisses my knuckles. "I hope you like seafood."

"Love it," I say, trying to calm my nerves. It's too late to go back, and I'm not about to look like a scared little girl in front of Titan.

The guy smiles at me, showing off a set of pearly whites. He has dark green eyes, a square chin, and a kind smile. He looks to be around forty. Much younger than I thought. All I was given was a name. I googled him, but I didn't find any pictures. He stays pretty hidden when it comes to the media. But I expected him to be older with the information I had found.

"Shall we?" He gestures to the double doors he had just entered.

"Yes, sir." I smile.

He chuckles. "Please, call me Jacob."

"Jacob." I nod, and he slaps Titan on the back.

"Tell me, how long have you lived in Vegas?" he asks, spinning us both around to head toward the doors.

"All my life," I say, looking over my shoulder to see Titan still standing in the same spot watching us leave. His eyes drop to where Jacob places his hand on the small of my back, and my heart starts to race at the way his jaw clenches.

FOURTEEN

TITAN

I ENTER THE meat locker that's underground. The room where we dish out our beatings in. Grave stands off to the far corner with his phone in his hands, typing away. Cross sits in a chair to the left, flipping his Zippo open and closed. Bones isn't here. He left earlier this morning for New York. I'm not sure if it was to see Mr. Bianchi, Luca's father, or his fuck.

"What do we have?" I snap, popping my knuckles.

Why did I let her words affect me? I don't give a fuck who she spreads her legs for. I'm not sure which is worse—the fact that he's paying her for sex, or that she would willingly give it up.

I want her.

You had her mouth, my mind screams, but that wasn't enough. I thought it would be, but it's all I've thought about.

"Robert Jenkins," Grave says, pocketing his phone and pushing off the wall. "Card counter. Cleared almost a hundred grand this month alone."

I look over at the guy sitting at the table in the middle of the room. His head is down, and his arms are restrained behind his back. He's young, maybe twenty-five. I've seen the kid on the security cameras. He's known on the Strip because he hits casino after casino, but he's not really on the radar. There are thieves out here that clear more, but I'm in a mood tonight. *Too bad for him.* "Untie him," I order.

Grave undoes the rope, and Robert rubs his sore wrists. I pull up a chair and spin it around across from him at the table. I sit on it backward, straddling the chair. "Can I get you anything? A water? A beer?"

He looks up at me, his blue eyes shooting from mine to Cross, who still sits in his chair behind me. "I ..."

"A room for the night?" I go on.

He tilts his head to the side, his confusion deepening. "I don't want to cause any trouble." He holds up his hands in surrender.

No doubt he's heard about us. "What is it you want me to do?" I cross my arms on the back of the chair. His eyes scan my tattoos before they land back on mine. "Allow you to keep the money and walk out the front door?"

"It wasn't that much," he argues.

Grave throws a handful of Kingdom chips onto the table. Some roll off to the floor. Bending down, I pick one up and run my fingers over it. It's a thousand-dollar chip. Black and gold. Kingdom is written across it along with a crown. "Is this all of it?" I ask Grave.

"Yep. Stopped him as he was trying to cash out."

"I'll leave," Robert says. "You can have it all."

I smirk, rolling the chip between my fingers. "How thoughtful."

"I didn't mean—"

"To steal from us," I interrupt him, my eyes meeting his.

He swallows nervously, and sweat beads across his forehead. I watch his hands shake when he runs them down his face. "Counting cards isn't illegal," he finally says.

I throw my head back and laugh. The sound filling the room. Grave and Cross do the same.

Robert begins to follow, but he sounds unsure of what is going on.

"What if I shove these chips up your ass? Is that illegal?" I ask, holding it out in front of his face.

His laughter immediately dies. "Is ... is that a trick question?"

I smirk and stand, shoving the chair to the side. He sits up straighter, eyes darting around the room.

"This is illegal!" He slaps the table as his fear gets the best of him. "You're keeping me against my will." He jumps to his feet.

"Sit your ass down." Grave shoves him forward and back into his chair.

"You can't do this!" he cries.

"We already are."

He runs his hands through his hair frantically while he rocks back and forth. "I …" He laughs nervously. "What are you going to do to me? Kill me?" His shaky hands point at the chips. "You have the money. Keep it."

"Oh, it's not leaving here," I inform him. "Not with you anyway."

EMILEE

I SIT AT a table in the back of a restaurant on the fiftieth floor of a casino just down the street from Kingdom. The guy to my right is Jacob French—my job for the night.

He seems nice enough even though he hasn't spoken to me much. Once I got into the limo at Kingdom, he spent most of the short drive on his phone with his wife. It was more awkward than anything. He told his children good night and that he loved them. He had a bottle of champagne on ice but didn't offer me any. I didn't take offense. The info outlining my night informed me that I was limited to two drinks while in his presence.

I feel like we've lost centuries of women's rights—a man telling a woman what she can and can't do. He should have had me cover up my face entirely and just showed my tits.

I'm on my second martini at the moment and already contemplating ordering another one. My nervousness has disappeared, and now I'm just wishing this night would end. Mr. French owns several companies. Mason Sikes, his business partner, sits across from me with a woman on his right who looks high as a kite. Her brown eyes are glazed over, and she's drunk nothing but water. She must be on ecstasy. A guy sits on the opposite side of the woman. It's his son. His green eyes keep falling to my exposed breasts. He seems to be the biggest scumbag at the table.

I down what's left of my drink, and he raises his hand, signaling our waiter. He comes over and bends down so the guy can whisper in his ear. He looks at my drink and nods.

I act like I didn't see the exchange. Instead, I pull my cell out of my purse and notice a text.

Jasmine: Call me the moment you get home, bitch. I want the deets.

I hate to tell her it's not going to be as interesting as she's expecting.

"Here you go, ma'am." The waiter places the new drink in front of me.

"Thank you," I say softly and quickly hand him the empty one. Jacob will see the drinks on the tab for sure. But what's he going to do to me?

"You looked like you needed another," the young kid says from across the table, handing the woman an alcoholic drink as well.

"It looks like she's had enough," I add, noting it's her first one.

He smiles. "No such thing. Some women need the encouragement."

So the guy is trying to fuck his father's date. "Prick," I say under my breath.

His smirk just grows. Obviously, he heard me and thought it was cute. I push my chair back. "Excuse me." All the guys start to stand for my dismissal, but I walk away before they can.

"Excuse me, where is the restroom?" I ask the woman standing in the corner. She's been watching our table like a hawk. Per her job. Anytime one of the guys gets low on anything, she sends our waiter over. I saw Jacob pass her a hundred the moment she seated us.

"Down that hall and the last door on the right." She points to the far right.

"Thank you." I make my way into the women's restroom and close the door behind me. I lean my back against the door and close my eyes. I've only had two drinks, and I'm feeling them. Hard. The bartender doesn't play around here. Maybe that's why Jacob has me on a two-drink limit.

My head is starting to spin, and my eyes are tired. That could be due to the lack of sleep I had last night. My concern for my date had gotten the best of me. Now I realize I had nothing to worry about. I'm here strictly for arm candy. I've not been spoken to directly, and that bothers me more.

Guess it could be worse. Jacob could have taken me to a sex club and expected me to perform in front of his colleagues while they recorded it. Which brings me to a thought. I don't remember seeing anything about videos being prohibited while on a date on the application. I'll have to ask Titan about that next time I see him.

That's one thing I don't like about the Queens. The men tell you what you can and can't wear, but they don't tell you what to expect on your date. Or where you're even going. Just the pickup and timeframe of it, along with your requirements and restrictions.

I use the restroom and wash my hands. I open the door to be greeted by the kid himself. "Oh." I jump back, before almost running into him. He stands in the middle of the hallway, blocking my way back to the table. "Excuse me." I go to walk around, but he steps to the side, blocking me once again. I start to get aggravated. "Can I help you?" I growl.

He smirks, his eyes looking me up and down. "I think you can." He reaches for me, but I take a step back out of his reach.

"I'm not here for you." I straighten my shoulders. "If you would please …"

He steps into me, pushing my back into the wall between the restrooms. "How much?" he asks, running his knuckles up and down my bare arm.

I pull away the best I can. "Excuse me?"

"How much do you cost for the night?"

I gasp at his audacity. "You son of a—"

"Careful," he interrupts me with a chuckle. This prick is enjoying himself. "I know you're not his wife. And I also know that Jacob pays for his women."

The hairs on the back of my neck rise. I never stopped to think of what others would think of me out with my date. Did I honestly think I would come off as a long-lost lover? A girlfriend? What if someone tells his wife I was with him? How would I explain that he paid for me? And who the hell would believe it wasn't sexual?

"See …" He lifts his right hand and cups my cheek. I slap it away, and he grips my chin, shoving the back of my head into the wall, digging his fingers into my skin painfully. He lowers his face to mine. I can smell the liquor on his breath. "You are nothing but a whore. And all whores have a price. So name yours."

My body shakes but not from fear. Anger. How dare this kid speak to me this way? "Fuck you," I say through clenched teeth.

With a snort, he places his free hand on my hip, then yanks me to him. "I will. One way or another."

I slam my fists into his chest, and he lets go of me. Taking a few steps back, he slides his eyes over me one last time before he walks into the men's bathroom to my left laughing.

After spending a second to collect myself, I make my way back to the table. I plop down in my seat and pick up my drink. This date can't end soon enough.

FIFTEEN

EMILEE

"Everything okay?" Jacob asks me once we leave the restaurant.

"Yes," I answer, staring out the back window at the lights on the Strip.

The kid never said another word to me. He just stared at me from across the table. It made me nervous, so I just kept ordering drinks. After my fifth, Jacob looked over at me, but he never stopped them from coming. As long as I wasn't making a scene, he was allowing it.

Fucking bullshit!

"I had a nice time tonight." He goes on.

I finally look over at him but say nothing.

He types away on his phone. "I know it was boring …"

I snort. "Boring would have been nice."

He stops typing. "Did something happen?"

"No," I lie. As far as I know, he knows what the kid did and didn't care. It's his business partner's son, for fuck's sake. He'll take his side over the whore he hired to sit there and look pretty.

The limo pulls around to the private back entrance of Kingdom and comes to a stop. I grab my clutch off the seat beside me.

"Emilee ..."

"Thanks for the dinner," I say, exiting. I've already been paid, and the date is over. No need to make this longer than it has to be.

The limo drives off, and I turn to walk to catch a cab. I had too much to drink tonight to be driving home.

"Miss York?"

I spin around to see Nigel standing at the top of the stairs, holding one of the doors open with one hand and a cell to his ear in the other. He nods a couple of times and whispers something before placing it in his pocket. "Please come in."

I grab my dress and pull it up to be able to walk up the stairs and into the building.

"Is something wrong?" I ask confused. Did Jacob call and complain about how many cocktails I had?

"No, not at all. Titan would like to speak to you."

I nod. He pulls out a black key card and scans it for the elevator access. We step inside, and he scans it again, and the door slides closed.

I scan the buttons to see he pressed the one with an R. We stand silently while it makes its way up. I avoid looking at myself in the mirrored walls. It opens, and he gestures me to exit. I do so and see a set of black double doors ahead of me at the end of the single hall. *The Royal Suite* is written across the top of them. "What is this?" I ask.

He doesn't answer me. Instead, he presses in a code on the keypad located on the door and opens it.

It's a suite. A fucking mansion overlooking the Las Vegas Strip. The floor-to-ceiling windows allow the city lights to illuminate the open living room. White marble floor with dark gray furniture and a glass coffee table. On my right is a large kitchen with black cabinets that have gold hardware. The countertops match the white marble flooring with stainless steel appliances. "This is beautiful," I say in awe.

"It will only be a moment."

I look over to see he has walked toward a set of French doors. He holds them open for me. I make my way over. Walking through them, I turn to face him, but he's shutting them, leaving me alone in a bedroom.

I turn around to look at the room I'm in. It's large. A bed sitting on a platform dressed in white. More floor-to-ceiling windows open to Sin City. I walk over to a wet bar and pour myself a drink. *What's one more?*

Once done, I walk over to the sliding glass door and step outside onto a balcony. The fresh air feels good on my face. A soft breeze has my dress rubbing against my legs.

I take a drink.

"It's beautiful, isn't it?"

I spin around to see Titan has joined me. He leans back against the now closed glass door with his hands in the front pockets of his slacks. The sleeves to his black button-down are rolled up to his elbows, exposing his tatted, muscular arms.

"Bring all the Queens back to your room?" I ask, taking a sip of my drink.

"Are you drunk?" His eyes drop to the glass, ignoring my question.

I give him a drunken smile and throw it back. As I gulp it down, I'm wondering why in the hell I'm here. And why I can't get what happened yesterday in his office out of my mind. I should have told Nigel that I couldn't come up here. This was a mistake. "As much fun as this is, I'm leaving. My job for the night is done." I place the now empty glass on a side table and walk toward the glass door. As I go to reach for it, he places his hand on my stomach, bringing me to a stop.

"Did he touch you?"

I arch a brow. "Excuse me?"

"You heard me."

Another man who feels entitled to what I do with my body. "That's none of your …"

"Did you fuck him?"

My eyes narrow, and I shove his hand off me. *Does he ask all the queens this after their jobs?* "I'll fuck whoever I want, whenever I want."

He wraps his hand around my throat, spins me around, and slams my back into the cold window. I gasp. "Titan …"

"Yes or no, Em?" His hard chest vibrates against mine with his words. His eyes bore down into mine, almost glowing with his rage. His jaw clenches, and he's breathing heavily.

I'm so turned on. And my body is starting to warm up from the drinks I've had. "What if I did?" I lift my chin, pushing him. I allowed the kid to talk down to me tonight, but I won't let Titan do it. He's not above me.

He tilts his head to the side and releases my neck. I take a deep breath as he runs his knuckles down over my collarbone. They make their way lower over my chest bone and gently caress my nipple over my dress. It instantly hardens.

"Jealous?" I challenge at his silence. It's the alcohol. It's making me more confident than I would normally be around Titan. The Dark Kings are far from jealous of anything, let alone another man over a woman.

"What if I am?" he asks.

I open my mouth to laugh, but his thumb running over my pebbled nipple replaces it with a moan.

"Hmm?" He reaches up and undoes my bun, allowing my hair to fall over my chest. He brushes it back and over my shoulders. "What if I said I have thought of nothing but you all night?"

I just stare up at him. Half dazed, half in shock.

"What if I told you that the thought of you out with him made me angry?"

He places both of his hands on the glass on either side of my head, caging me in. I find myself reaching out to him. My hands grip his narrow hips, pulling him closer. Silently begging for him. I lick my numb lips. "I'd say you're lying." My voice comes out rough. Needy. I'm failing so badly at playing hard to get. And I'm too drunk to tell if he's fucking with me or not. Or maybe I just want it to be real. For him to want me like I wanted him all those years ago.

He smirks. "I'll prove it to you." He reaches down, grabs the silk fabric, and rips my dress, making me gasp.

"I loved that dress."

"I'll buy you ten more." His lips meet mine as his hands grip my thighs, and he lifts me off the ground. I wrap my legs around him.

TITAN

I wish what I had said to her was a lie, but it wasn't. I've thought about nothing other than her since he requested her on a date.

What would she do for money?

I know how desperate she was. How she begged Bones and me to help her. What would she do with a stranger who would pay her anything?

Carrying her back into my bedroom, I push her off me and her back lands on my bed. Her ripped black dress barely hangs on her thin body. Her hard nipples press against the black silk. She stares up at me and licks her lips as her eyes drop to my slacks. My dick is as hard as stone, and you can clearly see the outline of it. I reach down and undo my belt. She sits up, propping herself on her elbows.

"You never answered my question."

"Hmm?" She bites her bottom lip, eyes still on my slacks, watching me carefully as I lower my zipper.

"Did he touch you?"

Her eyes trail up over my button-down and meet mine. "No." She makes her way to her knees. "He didn't touch me." Her hands go to my shirt, and she starts to unbutton it. "You look disappointed."

I grip her wrists, stopping her actions. "I …"

"You think I'd whore myself out?" She tilts her head to the side.

"I think you're desperate."

She throws her head back and lets out a laugh that makes her boobs bounce. My hands itch to rip what's left of that dress off her. "Aren't we all desperate for something?" she asks.

My brows pull together. "What does that mean?"

"What have you always wanted, Titan?" Before I answer, she goes on. "What have you always wanted that you would do anything for?"

I don't even have to think about it. "You." The answer is that simple, and as long as I've tried to ignore it, she knows I wanted her, but she had chosen Bones. And now? It doesn't matter. I'll make her mine tonight and face the consequences for that tomorrow.

She pulls her wrists free of my hands and holds her arms out wide. "Well, here I am. The question is, what are you going to do with me?"

This is it. I should tell her no. That it just won't work. If she hadn't fucked my friend for all those years, then I would take her up on this offer. But she did, so I can't. Instead, I hear myself say, "Whatever I want."

She gives me a big smile. Lifting her hands, she rips my shirt open instead of taking her time with the buttons.

I grab the hem of her dress and pull the ripped fabric off her legs and toss the remains to the floor. She kicks off her heels, and I yank her underwear down her legs. My lips find hers frantically. I can taste the alcohol in her kiss, and I swallow her in hopes to get drunk. "Lie on your stomach," I mumble against them.

She does as I say, and my cock jerks when my eyes land on her ass. I yank all the pillows off the bed and throw them to the floor as well. Then I slap her ass. "Put it up in the air."

She moans, arching her back, and pulls her knees up underneath her, giving me a great view of her shaved, soaking wet pussy.

I shove the shirt off my shoulders and kick off my shoes and slacks. Then I crawl onto the bed behind her and use my knees to spread hers farther apart. My hands run up her smooth thighs, over her round ass and up her back before tangling into her hair.

She hisses in a breath when I yank it back off the bed. Leaning over, I whisper in her ear, "Do you know how long I've fantasized about you like this?"

"Titan …" She whimpers.

"So fucking long," I answer, telling her the truth.

Letting go of her hair, I watch as her head falls to the bed. I grab my hard cock and stroke it a few times while running my free hand over her pussy, smearing her wetness.

She reaches between her legs to finger herself, but I slap her pussy with my hand.

She cries out, her body jerking.

"That's all mine, baby." Then I push into her without warning.

"Oh, God …"

Leaning over her back, I slide my arms under her shoulders and up over her head, locking my fingers together behind her neck. The position buries her head into the mattress while restraining her arms above her head at the same time.

And I fuck her. Hard. My hips slam into her ass, making her cry out. I fuck her relentlessly. As hard and fast as I can. Her body trembles, her pussy tightens, and she screams my name louder than any woman has before. But that's to be expected. I've never fucked anyone like this. I've loathed this woman since grade school, but a part of me has always wanted her. She was like an itch you can't scratch. A high you could never reach. She was unobtainable. Until now.

"Titan … oh God, Titan …" Her pussy tightens around my cock, and her entire body stiffens against mine as she comes.

I don't let up as her orgasm rocks her body. I go for a few more minutes, then unlock my fingers from behind her head and sit up. Both of our bodies are slick with sweat, and her thighs shake. She's gasping for breath, her hands now fisting the sheet.

I pull out and flip her over onto her back. My cock stands to attention, covered in her cum. It runs down her inner thighs and onto my sheets. I should have used a condom, but honestly, I didn't want to. I want to feel her. All of her. I know she's clean, I saw her results. It's part of the process to be a queen. And I know I'm clean.

Reaching up, I push her wild hair from her slick face. Her makeup is smeared, and her lips parted. This is what she should always look like for me. A beautiful, fucking mess. "Open up for me, Em."

She looks up at me with her heavy eyes. She's on a high, and I feel pride that I put her there. That I did this to her.

I'm not done.

Shoving her arms down to her sides, I straddle her chest, pinning them in place. And without question, she licks her lips and opens up for me, knowing exactly what I want.

"Good girl." I take my cock and slide it into her parted lips. She's like a pro. Licking, sucking, not giving two shits that my cock tastes like her. I always knew she was a freak. Bones never told me about their sex life. He didn't have to. My best friend knew I wanted her, so he would let me watch.

I wrap my hand in her hair and push her head back, opening up her throat for me. Her pale blue eyes look up at me through watery lashes as I fuck her mouth just as hard as I fucked her pussy. "You're gonna swallow, Em."

SIXTEEN

EMILEE

I OPEN MY eyes to a dark room. Sitting up, I wince. Shit. My entire body hurts.

Why am I …?

Titan! I slept with him.

"Fuck." I cover my face and fall back down onto the bed. Removing my hands slowly, I look next to me, afraid he's there, but he's not. Throwing my arms to my sides, I release a heavy sigh. My hand hits something hard, and I pick it up, then drop the damn thing on my face. "Fuuucckk," I moan and try again.

It's my phone. And it's almost dead because I didn't charge it last night.

Sitting up, I look around to see I'm the only person in the room. I quickly go to my recent calls and call the one person I need to talk to.

"Hello?" Jasmine answers sleepily.

"Wake up."

"Emilee?"

"Yep."

"Wait ... Do you know what time it is?" She yawns. Obviously, I woke her up.

"Doesn't matter."

"You okay? Do I need to come get you?" she asks in a rush, sounding more awake. She knew I had a job last night. "Your date ..."

"No. I'm at Kingdom, and I'm fine."

"At Kingdom? Why would you ..." She trails off, and I hope she's figured it out because I'm not sure I can say it out loud. "Did you stay with Titan last night?"

I fall to my side and bury my head into the sheets. They smell like sex. "Yeah," I mumble.

She laughs. "How was it?"

Rolling onto my back, I stare up at the ceiling. "Amazing."

"You've gotta tell me all about it. How about I meet you at the buffet there in thirty?" She yawns. "I need some breakfast."

"Okay," I say but pause. "Call Haven and see if she wants to join us." It's been so long since I've seen her. And Jasmine hasn't mentioned her once.

She's silent for a moment. "When was the last time you spoke to her?"

"I don't know." I try to add the months in my head. "Maybe four months ago. Why?"

"Well ... she's married."

TITAN

I sit at my desk, my cell in one hand and a pen in the other. My door opens and when my eyes meet a set of dark green ones, I inwardly sigh.

"Let me call you back," I say to Luca on the other end.

"I'll see you in a few. I'm about to head that way."

Click.

I set my cell on my desk, then cross my arms over my chest. "Mr. Bates. What can I do for you today?"

He's dressed in one of his Armani suits ready to mow over anyone who gets in his way of ruling the world. Starting his day with me. "Fire her," he demands, coming up to my desk.

I lean back in my seat, getting comfortable. "I don't know what you're talking about."

"The fuck you do!" he seethes, pointing his finger at me. "You hired my daughter as a fucking Queen."

"I can't disclose that information."

"Cut the shit, Titan." He slaps my desk. "I saw her pictures. And in one of them, she was wearing fucking lingerie!"

My door opens, and Bones enters, shutting it behind him. "I was walking by and thought I'd check to see if you needed some assistance."

I stand from my chair. "I'm good."

Bones looks from me to Mr. Bates. They have history. Not a good one. He wants to stay but reluctantly exits.

"I will not allow her …"

"To what?" I arch a brow.

His jaw sharpens. "To be a fucking whore."

I snort. *Pot meet kettle.* "You spent over two hundred grand last year on Queens," I remind him.

He pulls his shoulders back and bows his chest.

I walk around my desk and come face to face with him. "I will not fire her. And the only reason you know she's a Queen is because you're a client." I reach up and grab his suit jacket, yanking him to me. "If you want to continue to pay for your sex, then I suggest you keep your mouth shut and not tell me how to do my job." I shove him back.

He trips over his own feet and falls into the chair. I make my way back around to my desk and sit down across from him.

He bows his head and runs his hand through his hair. His concern is getting the best of him. "Do you know what this will do to me if it gets out that my daughter sells her body?"

"It won't."

"You can't guarantee that," he growls.

"My airtight NDAs do."

He stands. "And if someone talks?"

I stand as well. "Then I will take care of them just as I would if any of my clients leak any info about my Queens." I run a no tolerance kind of business. "I protect my assets."

He seems to be satisfied with my answer because he turns to the door but stops and faces me once again. "Jasmine is not to know that I was here."

SEVENTEEN

EMILEE

"Y OU GOT MARRIED?" I demand as my best friend sits down beside me in the booth.

She nods and gives me a big smile as her amber eyes light up. "Yeah."

"What the fuck, Haven?" I ask, my jaw still dropped at the news.

She sighs. "It was …complicated."

I frown. "Are you okay? Is Luca treating you right?" The guy is in the mafia. We've all known it since high school, but that never stopped her from loving him.

"Yeah, it started out a little rough, but everything is perfect now." She pushes a piece of brown hair behind her ear. Her amber eyes soft and full of love as she speaks about her husband.

I look over to see a man by the name of Oliver Nite standing at the entrance of the restaurant. "Is he here with you?" He grew up a Bianchi. Luca's father took him off the streets when he was just a kid and raised him as one of their own. He wears the gold ring on his right hand to prove it. The Bianchis adopted him and made him one of their own even if it was for their own selfish reasons.

"Yeah. He's my bodyguard."

"Why do you need a bodyguard?" I ask worried. "Are you in danger?" The Bianchis have a lot of enemies. I never thought my best friend could be in danger due to who she loves.

She waves me off. "Everything is fine. Luca is just paranoid."

"Well ... that's good to know." I'm glad he's making sure she's safe, even if she feels it's overkill.

"I tried calling you. Several times," Haven says. Narrowing her eyes on mine, she changes the subject.

My chest tightens. "I'm sorry." I've been a shitty friend. And I hate that I wasn't here for her.

"I left you messages." She takes my hand. "Did you not get them?"

It's also complicated, but instead, I say, "I lost my phone and had to get a new one."

"Voicemails transfer over," Jasmine states, cramming a piece of pancake into her mouth across the booth from us.

I narrow my eyes at her.

"It's okay." Haven wraps her arms around my shoulders and pulls me into her. "I'm just glad you're here now."

"Yeah." Jasmine nods her head. "We know how you get."

"What does that mean?" I ask.

"That you pull away."

I can't argue with her or be mad about what Jasmine says because it's true. I've never allowed myself to get too close. Not even to them. Haven and Jasmine were the closest.

"And your mom is sick ..." Haven goes on. "I can't even imagine how hard that must be." She rubs my back. "How are you and your dad holding up?"

Jasmine drops her eyes to the table. She hasn't told Haven what happened to him. I imagine Haven doesn't watch the news often anyway. If she did, she'd see nothing but bad things regarding her husband.

"My father ..." I take a deep breath. "My father passed away a few weeks ago."

The table falls silent, and I drop my head to stare at my hands in my lap. "It was a heart attack. Happened at his office while in a meeting."

I swallow and leave it at that. "He left everything to George. And he is blackmailing me." I'm like a drunk girl who has reached her limit of drinks, and they're all coming back up. "But George owes the Kings five hundred thousand dollars. And he has offered me up to Titan in exchange for repaying his debt."

As the words finish rushing out, I'm met with silence. But I can't look up at them. I'm ashamed. Not sure why, since the girls and I have never kept secrets from one another. And let's face it, we've all three done some stupid shit when it came to boys. I don't know why this would be any different.

I hear the vinyl in the cushion shift as Jasmine gets up from her side of the table and comes to sit by me. I move closer to Haven to make room for her. And then I feel both of their arms around me.

Closing my eyes, I feel a tear run down my cheek. These are my sisters. We've only ever had each other, and I've missed them so much.

"I'm so sorry," Jasmine whispers, either pretending like she didn't know, or she truly is sincere.

"Me too." Haven sniffs. "We should have been there for you …"

I pull away from both of them. "No. I should have been there for you," I tell Haven.

"Hey." She smiles. "I'm fine. Promise. Don't worry about me. But Jasmine …" She looks over at her. "She needs help."

I laugh, wiping the tear from my cheek.

"I'm just fine. Thank you," Jasmine says, lifting her chin. "Hey, that offer still stands, Nite," Jasmine calls out.

"Offer?" I ask, confused.

"Yeah, I told him I'd fuck him with a strap-on."

"What? Why would you say that?" I ask.

"Because he's gay." She rolls her eyes.

"No, he's not," I argue.

"He is. But that's okay. I don't discriminate. And I'll have you screaming my name all night."

"He's a mute," I remind her. He took some kind of vow of silence back in college. That's where he got his nickname *Silent Nite* from.

"He won't be when I'm done with him." She winks.

He ignores her.

Haven rolls her eyes. "You fucked him at my wedding."

"What?" I gasp, looking at Jasmine.

She lifts her drink to take a sip. "For the hundredth time, we didn't have sex. He ate me out."

"At her wedding?" I ask wide-eyed. "Where did that happen at? In a closet?"

"A woman never tells."

"Well, good thing you're not a woman," Haven jokes. "You're that cocky frat guy who brags to all his friends."

"She's fucking Titan." Jasmine obviously has no problem telling important information about my life.

Haven gasps. "No way."

I nod, and Jasmine adds, "Yep. She's a dirty little whore."

I flinch at the way she says whore. I know she's joking, but the thought of the guy from last night still has me on edge. God, he was such an ass.

Haven laughs. "Well, you're screwing Trenton."

"What?" I ask wide-eyed. "Jasmine, he's married." I follow his wife on Instagram. She went to college with us but was two years younger.

She shrugs. "It's complicated." Then her eyes slide over to Nite.

I look over at him as well, and he's already staring at her. *What the hell have I missed?*

"Anyway, back to you and Titan." Haven whistles. "I always knew it would happen. You two had this crazy chemistry going on. He always wanted you."

AFTER MY LUNCH with the girls, I walk through the casino with a smile on my face. It's the first real one since my father passed. George is MIA, and I have a job. It's not exactly my dream job, but being a Queen has its perks. Like the three thousand dollars I made last night. That's what I got to keep. For sitting next to a man and not having to hold up my end of a conversation, it was pretty easy money. Plus, my clothes stayed on.

I make my way toward the back, private entrance to find Nigel at his desk. He sits on his chair with a newspaper in his hands. "I didn't know anyone still read those."

He looks up at me, folding it. "Everyone seems to get their news through social media these days."

"But not you," I add.

"It's overrated." Chuckling, he stands and walks over to the single elevator. Using his key card, the doors open, and he looks at me. "Going up?"

I bite my lip. "I'm not sure …"

"Titan informed me this morning that you are granted access whenever you want."

My cheeks flush, and I drop my eyes, but I find my feet walking me over and entering the elevator. I decide to test the waters with how much info he will give me as we ride. "What does the R stand for?"

"The Kings live on the Royal level when they are here," he answers.

I knew that. But I choose to focus on … "When they're here?"

"Yes, ma'am. Sometimes they go home. Sometimes they stay at Kingdom."

The elevator comes to a stop, and he exits with me. "You have full access to the Royal floor."

I look over the jeans and t-shirt that I wear along with a pair of Converse. "Thank you for the clothes." I tell him. After I spoke to Jasmine this morning and told her I wanted to meet for breakfast I found some clothes folded neatly in a bag on Titan's nightstand with the tags still on them. I'm not sure how, but I just knew Nigel had delivered them to the suite.

He just gives me a wink and punches in a code, and the door opens to their suite. "Thank you." I didn't get all the information I wanted, but I got more than I had ten minutes ago.

I walk inside as he leaves to go back downstairs. "Hello?" I call out, wondering if anyone is up here, but I'm met with silence.

Looking to my right, I see a hallway. I slowly begin to walk down it, running my fingers along the wall. It leads to a glass door. Pressing down on the gold handle, I open it. I step inside to see a gym. It has everything from treadmills to benches and free weights. It even has yoga mats rolled up and stuffed in cubby holes up against the far wall. The wall to my right is nothing but mirrors.

When I open another door to the left, I step into a locker room. Four lockers are to my right, then a set of showers on my left. Why would they ever leave Kingdom? Everything they could ever need is right here in the Royal Suite.

Walking over to the counter, I look at myself in the mirror that is lined with lights and frown. "I look like shit," I mumble, pulling on my cheeks. I didn't put any makeup on this morning because I don't have any here. I never planned on staying the night with Titan.

Continuing through the bathroom, I come to another door. This place is like a fucking maze. I turn the black knob and step inside.

I instantly come to a stop at what I see. It's a massage room. It's dark, soft music plays, and there's a black table in the center. It's what I see there that has me pausing. It's Grave.

He's fucking a blonde bent over the table from behind. The room is filled with his grunts and her moans. "Fuck," she cries out.

He slaps her ass, making her whimper before reaching up and grabbing her hair with both his hands and yanking her head back at an odd angle, but it gives me a clear view of her face. Her eyes are closed, and she licks her parted lips. Makeup that looks a couple of days old runs down her face. "Grave. Oh, God …"

"Lucy." He growls her name as he stares down at their bodies slapping.

I slap a hand over my mouth and step back, closing the door as quickly yet quietly as I can. "Shit," I hiss and run through the bathroom, gym, and down the hallway.

"Oh, my God. Oh, my God." I run through the double French doors into Titan's room and turn around, watching the doors. I wait for Grave to enter. To yell at me. To kick me out. But as the seconds tick by and my breathing slows, I begin to think that maybe I got lucky, and they didn't see me.

TITAN

SHE HAS DOMINATED my thoughts today. I haven't been able to do a single thing without thinking about her. My cock has been hard, and my mind's been a jumbled mess. The guys noticed. Bones even commented on it, but I ignored them all. They don't know she was the reason, and I wanna keep it that way.

Walking into the Royal Suite, I go straight to my room, knowing I'll have the place to myself tonight. Bones has plans with Luca, or so he says. He still thinks the business they have is a secret, so I'll let him have that for now. And I overheard Grave and Cross say they were going to close the strip clubs down.

I enter my room, and my eyes go straight to my bed. She's not there like I had hoped. I know she's up here. Nigel had informed me he escorted her up here hours ago. Spinning around, I see the bathroom door is cracked, and I hear the shower running.

Even better.

I open my nightstand drawer and then enter the bathroom. Steam fills the large room, and I look over at the glass shower. She stands under the sprayer, her hands running over her hair to get the suds out.

I remove my shirt, jeans, and kick off my shoes. Entering the shower, I come up behind her. "Fuck, you're sexy."

She shrieks in surprise, and I chuckle. "Titan … You scared me."

I stand before her naked and hard. Her perfect tits rise and fall quickly with her heavy breathing. Her wet hair sticks to her cheeks, neck, and chest. I reach out and push it back, seeing the bruises I left on her last night. They're not terribly bad. Just a light shade of purple from my aggressiveness. They're mainly on her hips and a couple on her chest. A few dot her thighs.

"How long have you been here?" I ask.

Her face falls, and she bites her bottom lip. "About three hours. I took a nap." Her eyes go wide, and she looks nervous all of a sudden. "Should I not have come—"

"No," I interrupt her. "I wanted you here." I had messaged her this morning to meet me in my room, but the guys kept me longer at our fucking meeting than I had intended.

She turns to face the showerhead, and I step up behind her again. Not allowing her any time. "Bend over and place your hands flat on the wall. And spread your legs for me," I order in her ear.

Her breathing picks up, and she does as she's told.

I grab what I brought in here with me, knowing what I was going to do and smear the silicone lube over my cock.

My feet hold hers apart. Her back flat. I run my hand down her spine, feeling every vertebra. She shudders. Gripping my hard cock in my hand, I put it against her ass, and she tenses. "How long has it been?" I ask.

"A while." She pants.

I smile. *Good.* Showing more restraint than I'd like, I push into her, stretching that tight ass. She cries out and goes to move, but I hold her down with my hand on her back. "Let me in, Em. Relax."

I fill her just a little, then I push in farther. "That's it, baby. That's it." I close my eyes as I push all the way into her tight ass.

She whimpers, and I'm panting. I grip her hips.

"Take your right hand and fuck that pussy, Em."

She lets go of the wall and begins to play with herself.

"Fuck your pussy, baby. I want three fingers fucking yourself. I want you coming all over those fingers. Then I'm gonna lick them clean."

"God …"

"That's right, baby." I'm going to own her. Just like Bones used to but only I'm not going to stop where he did. I'm going to demand more because I'm nowhere near done with her.

EIGHTEEN

EMILEE

For the second morning in a row, I wake up in Titan's bed. My body is just as sore as the day before. Getting out of the bed, I make it to the bathroom to brush my teeth and use the restroom. I see a T-shirt of his lying on the end of the bed, and I place it over my head, pulling my very tangled hair from the collar. I open the French doors, not thinking anything about it but come to a quick stop when I see three sets of eyes on me.

Grave sits at the kitchen table with a fork paused halfway to his mouth, which is wide open as he spots me. His eyes drop to my bare legs, and I tug at the already long T-shirt. This is payback for catching him in the act yesterday.

Titan stands in the open kitchen flipping pancakes. He looks me over once, and my body heats from the intensity of his gaze. I clear my throat and rub my neck awkwardly.

My eyes go to Cross. He looks less surprised than Grave did to see me here. He's leaned back in his chair relaxing with his legs open and his left hand flipping his Zippo open and close. Cross always had a mysterious vibe about him. I was the least close to him because he kept to himself. Even between the Kings. Or maybe I was just never close enough to pay attention. All I know about him is that he has secrets. Murderous secrets.

Nineteen years old

I'm digging around in my trunk, trying to find my bag through all of my shit when I'm slapped on the ass. I whip around about to give whoever did it a piece of my mind but laugh when I see Jasmine. "What was that for?"

She laughs. "Bones can't be the only lucky son of a bitch to hit that ass."

I roll my eyes and turn back to my car, picking up the blanket that my mother made me put in there just in case I'm ever stranded in the winter. She forgets we live in fucking Vegas. "Aha," I say, finding it hiding under there.

"Did you hear about Oak Grove?" she asks as I throw it over my shoulder.

Oak Grove is the Baptist Church that Cross's father preaches at. "No. What about it?" I slam my trunk shut, and we begin to walk toward the school.

"It burned down last night."

"What?" I gasp, coming to a stop.

She nods and looks over my shoulder. I turn to follow her line of sight.

The Kings all stand by Bones's car. He has both of his hands in the pockets of his dark jeans and a white hoodie on. Titan stands facing him with a cigarette between his lips, and Cross has his ass leaning against the front passenger door. His bag lies at his feet. He has his right ankle crossed over his left. His left hand is in his pocket while the other flips his Zippo lighter open and close.

I look back at her.

"Now Father James is missing."

"No way," I breathe before looking back over at Cross. His eyes are on mine, and I wonder if he can hear us all the way across the parking lot. He snaps the lighter shut and then opens it again.

TITAN

"What are you girls doing?" Trenton, her on-again, off-again boyfriend, gets our attention as he comes up to us with his best friend.

"Talking about what happened at Oak Grove last night."

"The police suspect arson and murder."

"How do you know that?" she asks him.

"Heard my father talking about it this morning. Guess a witness called the police and said that they saw Cross enter the church with his dad an hour before and then saw him leaving. Alone. Just before the place went up in flames."

She covers her mouth with her hand. "His dad was left inside?"

He nods. "So they say."

His friend Liam snorts. "I heard it was suicide." Then his eyes go to Cross. "I mean, wouldn't you kill yourself if Cross was your son?"

My eyes narrow on him. "That's a horrible thing to say."

He shrugs.

Trenton just shoves him. "I'd like to see you say that to his face."

Jasmine laughs, and he throws his arm over her shoulders and walks her toward the school along with Liam.

I turn back around, but the Kings are no longer standing by the car. Taking a look around the parking lot, I see a few people standing around. A couple are on their phones. Others are walking to classes. It's early on a Monday. Jasmine and I have class, but the Kings have ball practice to get to. Turning back toward the door, I go to take a step but run into a hard body. "Sorry ..."

My voice trails off when I look up to see it's Bones. "Hey," I say, trying to slow my racing heart.

He takes a quick look around. "You shouldn't be out here by yourself."

I ignore that statement as he grabs my hand in his. "What's going on with Cross? I heard about what happened with his dad ..."

He yanks me to a stop and spins to face me. The look in his eyes has me taking a step back. "What did you hear?" he demands.

I swallow. "Uh, that ... just that there was a witness who saw him at Oak Grove with his dad and then him leaving right before it burned down ..."

He steps into me, and I shut my mouth when he grabs my upper arms, digging his fingers into my skin. "Dillan ...."

"Don't say a fucking word, Em. To anyone. Do you hear me?"

"What?" My eyes search his. "I don't know anything ... It's just a rumor ..."

"Who told you?"

"Tr ...?" I stop myself before I finish that sentence. I don't wanna throw Trenton under the bus. No matter how much I dislike the guy. And I'm not sure if the Kings are involved in the death of Cross's dad. But I don't wanna be responsible for anything that happens. "Dillan ..."

"Who the fuck was it, Emilee?" he snaps, using my full name.

"I ... I don't remember," I lie and hang my head.

He steps into me and grips my chin in his hand. I try to pull away, but it just tightens. "Ow, Bones ..."

"Lying to me isn't going to save him, baby."

I dig my nails into his forearm as he holds me in place. "You're hurting me," I whisper as tears sting my eyes.

His blue eyes search mine for a little longer before he lets go, and I take a step back from him until my ass bumps into my car. Then he turns and walks into the building, leaving me standing in the parking lot all by myself and confused as to what the hell just happened.

I never brought it up again. Bones never let me into his personal life. I never discussed what he and the Kings did, and he never offered any information.

Silently, Cross stands from the table and walks out the door.

"I, uh ... can ..."

"Sit," Titan orders with a spatula.

I pull out a chair and fall into it, avoiding Grave's stare as he goes back to shoving pancakes in his mouth.

"So ..." he begins once he swallows.

"Save it," Titan orders.

Grave just shakes his head, letting out a chuckle. "It's your funeral, man."

My eyes shoot to Titan, and his are narrowed on Grave. He doesn't even look his way as he grabs the hoodie off the back of his chair before exiting the suite as well.

Titan walks over to me with a plate full of pancakes, bacon, and some strawberries on the side. He places the syrup in front of me.

"This was a mistake," I say, just staring at my food.

"Em."

"No." I stand quickly. "I don't want to cause any trouble between you and Bones." I push the hair back from my face.

"Look." He sighs, running his hand down his face. "I don't want to tell you that Bones won't care because that makes it sound like you never meant anything to him."

I didn't. But that doesn't mean he could be okay with it either.

"But I will tell you that Grave has no idea what he's talking about." He walks back over to me. "Grave lives in his own little world that does not exist to others."

He always has. Grave has had a problem with addiction since he was young. And he doesn't allow anyone to get close to it. Because that would make it real. And he can't handle that. Bones has always let his little brother do whatever the fuck he wants. And their father was never really around. He spent all his time up at Kingdom when he and the Three Wisemen owned it. I'm not sure about now because I've been gone for a couple of years, but I haven't seen or heard anyone mention him.

"But—"

"But nothing," he interrupts me. "Now sit down and eat before your food gets cold." He kisses my forehead and goes back to the kitchen.

NINETEEN

EMILEE

I TAKE A deep breath and pull back my shoulders as I make my way up the back stairs to find Nigel standing behind his desk in the corner.

"Miss York." His dark eyes meet mine. "It's nice to see you."

"I'm here to see Bones," I blurt out before I lose my nerve.

"Oh." His brows pull together. "Is he expecting you?"

"No." He opens his mouth to speak. "Can you call him for me, please?" Titan has given me access to their suite, not their office.

He nods once and picks up his desk phone. He punches in one number and holds the receiver to his ear. "Hello, Bones? Yes. You have Emilee here in the lobby wanting to speak to you." He nods once to himself. "Yes, sir." He hangs up and looks at me. I hold my breath. "He will see you."

I let it out. "Thank you."

He ushers me upstairs, and the door to the elevator slides open. There is a conference room to my right. It's a glass box that overlooks the city. "This way." He takes me down a long hall and to the door at the end. He knocks once and then pushes it open.

TITAN

I step inside to see Bones sitting behind his desk. The room is dark. Thick black curtains pulled shut hide him from the city he loves so much. The carpet a dark gray and black leather couch to the right and two black leather chairs sit across from his desk. He stands and nods to Nigel, who exits the room without a word.

I bite my bottom lip nervously, knowing the last time I was in this room Titan was also present and I begged them both to help me. Which was just an embarrassment. I have a feeling this time will be a repeat of then.

"What can I do for you, Em?" he asks, gesturing to one of the chairs.

My eyes scan over his tatted arms. He has the sleeves of his button-down rolled up to his elbows and his tie sits on his desk. He has the top two buttons undone. Bones never liked having to dress in business attire; he preferred jeans and a T-shirt.

"Em?" he asks again.

I don't move. Instead, I stay where I'm at and force my eyes to look up to meet his. "I … I wanted …" I clear my throat, and he crosses his arms over his chest. "I wanted to let you know that I'm sleeping with Titan." It rushes out in one breath.

He doesn't look the least bit surprised, and it just unnerves me more. I run my sweaty hands down my jeans.

"I'm assuming Grave told you—"

"He didn't have to," he interrupts me.

"Oh," is all my mind can gather at the moment.

He walks over to me, and my heart picks up. The smell of cologne surrounds me, and I have to force myself to stay here in the present and not fall into a memory of him.

"I just didn't want you to be mad at him," I add quickly as he nears. "We're …"

"All adults," he finishes my sentence.

I swallow nervously.

He reaches out and grabs a lock of my hair. He twists it around his finger like he used to, and my knees begin to tremble. "Bones …"

"I'm not mad." His blue eyes roam my face.

"You're not?" I ask, feeling the sweat bead between my breasts.

Fuck, it's hot in here. I don't love Bones, but I can't deny we had some amazing chemistry.

He shakes his head once. "No, I'm jealous."

I tense.

He presses his body into mine, and his finger that was twirling in my hair slides into my hair, gripping my scalp and tilting my head back. "I do miss you, Emilee."

My lips part, and my eyes grow heavy at his words. "I'm …" I stop myself.

"What?" he urges me to answer. "Miss me too?"

I was going to say I'm with Titan now, but am I? I was never really *with* Bones. We just had an understanding. He was horny—he came to me. He was angry—he came to me. We never had a label; we didn't need it. But when it comes to me and Titan, I'm lost. I don't expect him to only fuck me. I'm a queen, for fuck's sake.

"Bones …" The door opens.

He doesn't even bother looking away from me. "Get the fuck out!"

The door slams shut after that. It was Grave. I know his voice well enough.

Fuck!

"I'm sorry I came up here," I manage to get out.

"I'm not." His other arm snakes behind my back, pulling me closer to him.

"Bones." My hands grip his white button-down.

He doesn't allow me to finish that thought. He presses his lips on mine, and I stiffen against him but only for a second. My body reacts to him like it used to.

My arms go up and around his neck, and I open for him, letting Dillan Reed take what he wants like he always did.

TITAN

PULLING UP TO the York's residence, I get out of my car and walk up to the door, knocking on it. I place my hands in my pockets, rocking back and forth when the door opens.

"Titan." She stands before me in a pair of jean shorts and a black tank top. Her hair up in a messy bun and no makeup on. She's so gorgeous. But Emilee York always was. She could have had any boy she wanted.

"I got your message," I say.

Her eyes drop to the floor for the briefest moment before she forces them back up to meet mine. She squares her shoulders, stepping to the side. "Come on in."

I enter the house and she shuts the door behind me.

"Let's go up to my room." She grabs my hand and pulls me up the stairs.

Entering her room, I close the door and look around. I've never been in here, but I imagine it looks the same as it did before she left for college. White walls, pink décor. A white four-post bed that sits up against the wall with pink and silver throw pillows. She lets go of my hand and turns to face me.

She had messaged me earlier today that she was coming home tonight to spend time with her mother, and that she wanted me to come by and see her. That we needed to talk. "What was it you wanted to talk about?"

"I kissed Bones." I barely get the question out before she answers.

I just stare at her.

"I'm sorry." She runs a hand through her hair. "I didn't know where we stood. I didn't want you to think I'm one of those girls who expects you to be faithful to me. And I didn't want you to think I have any expectations," she rambles, "because I don't." She throws her hands up in the air. "But I don't want you mad at Bones. I went to see him." She swallows nervously at my silence. "I needed to tell him that we slept together because I didn't want him mad at you."

"Em ...?"

"I didn't want Grave to tell him."

"Em?"

"I'm so ..."

"Em!" I growl her name this time.

She takes a step back and bows her head, breathing heavy after her rambling.

I step into her, grip her chin, and force her to look up at me. "I know."

"What?" Her lips part and blue eyes widen.

"Bones told me."

"I didn't mean for it …"

"Will you stop?" I give her a soft smile. "Emilee, I'm not jealous of your past with Bones. I'm also not jealous about what happened today in his office."

"So you're not mad at him?" she asks cautiously.

"No." I can't help but chuckle.

She runs a hand through her hair. "Well, now I'm embarrassed," she mumbles to herself.

Bones and I have an understanding. He had her; I wanted her. I wouldn't call my friend stupid, but I would say when he wouldn't commit to her, it was a mistake. Emilee is the full package. She's the kind of woman you use in the bedroom but parade her around as a fucking queen in the streets of peasants.

"I just didn't know what we are."

I frown.

She explains further. "I didn't want you to think I was putting a label on us. But I also wanted him to know what we were doing. I'd hate to come between the two of you."

"It's not like that." I smile at her concern. "But as for us …" I run the pad of my thumb over her bottom lip. "You're mine, Em."

"Yours?" She seems shocked.

"Yes." I run my hands down over her neck and feel her pulse race. "Have a problem with that?"

She swallows and shakes her head, whispering, "No."

"Good." I lean down and press my lips to hers. "Now pack your bag and let's go."

I EXIT OUR private elevator underground to the meat locker. Nigel is already waiting for me and Bones. "Good afternoon."

Yes, it is. I find my days to be much more tolerable when I open my eyes to see Emilee next to me. Naked. I love the way she moans when I wake her up for sex before I start my day. "Good afternoon." I nod and walk down the long hallway to the heavy metal door at the end. I open it up and step inside the cold space. Bones enters behind me and locks us inside the concrete room. Grave and Cross are not present, but Luca and Nite are. Along with three other men I know all too well.

They each sit in a chair at the single table in the middle of the room. They jump to their feet the moment they see me.

"Titan, I can explain ..."

"How you failed at the only job you were supposed to do." I interrupt him.

Matt fists his hands and his jaw sharpens. "He outsmarted us."

Bones arches a brow. "Did he, though?"

"Woah." Tommy throws his hands up. "You think we did this on purpose?"

So defensive right off the bat. I cross my arms over my chest but say nothing.

"You can't be serious," the last one, Steven hisses. "We had the house surrounded."

"Exactly." I hiss. "How the fuck did you let George get away?" These were our three guys who were supposed to be our surveillance. We put them on George's detail because I thought they could be trusted. Now the fucker is gone and these three are going to tell me exactly what I want to know. "Where the fuck is he?"

"We don't know." Matt growls, taking a step back from the table. He runs into Nite who shoves him forward.

"Bullshit!" I snap.

"We heard that there was movement out back," Steven speaks up. "By the time we made it around to there, he was already in a car and on the run." He swallows. "We managed to catch up with him on the highway, but when we looked closely there were three identical cars. We followed the one that we had had eyes on since the house. We managed to run it off the road, but it was not him."

"So, you followed the wrong one?" I make sure I heard him right. "There were three of you, why didn't you each follow a car?" It's not fucking rocket science. There's more at stake here than five hundred thousand dollars. *Fuck the money*! Now our concern is him coming back for Emilee.

Tommy steps forward. "We were only down to two cars. When we went to take off my tires had been slashed."

"Unbelievable." Bones hisses beside me.

Quite so.

"This wasn't our fault. They had the drop on us." Matt snaps at him.

"Sounds like you allowed them to have that advantage on you." Bones shoves him backwards. "Now the question is was it on purpose or just a coincidence?"

"Wait a minute." Steven looks from him to me. "This was not intentional. We were set up."

I look over at Bones and he shrugs at me. It's my show. "You're right. You were." I say and pull three bullets out of the front pocket of my black slacks. Luca walks over to me and hands me his Smith and Wesson 629 classic revolver. I open it up and insert the three .44 magnum bullets into the cylinder and then spin it before snapping it close.

I raise the gun and pull the trigger, shooting Steven in the leg. The sound so loud in the concrete box that it has me momentarily deaf. He falls to his side, holding his thigh. His eyes wide as he watches the blood cover the floor. He starts screaming.

"It's a through and through. You'll live." Bones tells him.

I point the gun at Matt's head and pull the trigger. Nothing happens.

"What the fuck, man?" he ducks and steps away from me. "What the fuck are you doing?" he shouts, grabbing his chest.

"Growing up, my father always told me that we were gambling men. It was in our blood." I point the gun at him again, and he runs to the corner of the room. I almost laugh. Nite grabs him and brings him to the center. He throws him over the table and pins his arms behind his back. I grip his hair and lift his head, so he has to look up at me. His lips pulled back in a snarl. "Have you ever gambled with your life?" I ask.

"Fuck you!" He seethes. "All of you!" He fights Nite but he's too strong for him. Mr. Bianchi bred Nite for this. To be a soldier. A killer. We've all been trained for battle, so we win the war.

Letting go of his hair I grip his chin and pry his teeth apart. He cries out as I shove the barrel of the revolver into his mouth. I pull the trigger. *Again, nothing happens.*

Nite steps back and Matt falls to the floor. He's gasping for breath and tears run down his cheeks while he shakes uncontrollably. One look at his jeans and he's pissed himself. "Shit!" he gasps, looking over at Steven who is still bleeding on the concrete floor from the gunshot in his thigh. But he's removed his shirt and has it wrapped around tightly to try and stop the bleeding.

"Luca." I nod towards him and he tosses a piece of paper on the table.

"What is this?" Tommy demands.

"This is a bank statement for fifteen grand deposited into your account." I say to him. "Luca so happens to own the bank where you keep your money." I smile. All he had to do was look up his account and check transactions. It's easy to trace when it's wired from another account. Don't wanna get caught? Then always do hand-to-hand transactions with cash. No paper trail equals no evidence.

"What is he talking about?" Steven growls from his spot on the floor.

"I ... I don't know ..." Tommy stutters.

"Your friend here. Took a bribe from George Wilton to let him get away." Bones explained. Steven is losing blood, so he may have a hard time comprehending what is going on.

"You what?" Matt shouts at Tommy. "You put our lives in danger for fifteen thousand fucking dollars?" He runs at him, but Nite grabs the back of his shirt, and holds him captive again.

"He came to me!" Tommy snaps, pointing at his chest. "Me! Said you were too weak and that you'd never be able to get the job done. He needed a man."

Bones snorts from beside me.

"You're a fucking idiot." Matt shouts.

"Be that as if may." I speak. "I want answers. I've got three more shots and two more bullets. Who wants to gamble?" I ask.

"We didn't do this." Matt growls at me.

"Call it guilty by association." Bones adds.

I step up to Matt and gesture for Nite to let him go. "Where the fuck is George?"

"Why are you asking me? I didn't make a deal with him."

I tilt my head to the side. "That has yet to be determined. You guys could have split the money."

"Five grand a piece?" He shakes his head angrily. "Fuck that. Nothing is worth screwing over the Kings."

"Ahh he's smarter than he looks." Luca finally speaks. He's got a smirk on his face and his hands in the pockets of his slacks. He's in a cheerful mood today. But I'm not surprised. He likes blood as much as the rest of us.

"We were told from a source that he's in Paris, but I don't think that is true either." Bones adds. "So for the last time, where is he?"

Tommy squares his shoulders and I refrain from sighing. Matt was right, he's an idiot. "He'll come back for her. And he'll give me fifteen more." He spits out. "I won't fucking tell you a goddamn ..."

I lift the gun and pull the trigger. This time it goes off. And the bullet goes right between his eyes.

That is how you flush the system.

TWENTY

EMILEE

I EXIT THE shower and grab the white towel off the hook on the wall. Wrapping it under my arms, I tuck the corner into itself between my breasts.

I've been staying at Kingdom with Titan for a week now. I spend the day with my mother; it's been tolerable since George is still *gone* on his work trip. I'm hoping his getaway plane crashed down in the Atlantic somewhere. But I'm not sure my luck is that good.

My mother doesn't talk about him. I think she's giving up on trying to sell me on the idea of them together. And she just hasn't had the energy.

I haven't had any jobs since that one as a Queen. But it paid pretty well. It wouldn't pay my mother's bill a hundred percent, but it's enough for me to survive. But at this point, I can't get her to take any of my money. She says George has it covered.

Fuck that cunt bastard!

I step up to the white marble countertop and look at myself in the mirror. My hair is up in a messy bun because I didn't wanna get it wet and have to bother with drying it here. My face now clear of makeup after scrubbing the layers off from my night. I worked with Jasmine as a ring card girl earlier this evening again. Grave fought in the main event and of course kicked ass. After we were done, she tried to talk me into going out. I didn't want to, and I wasn't quite in the mood to go to bed either. Titan went off to Grave's private room after his fight to be with the rest of the Kings, so I came up to their Royal Suite and ran on the treadmill for thirty minutes. I needed to clear my head. Try to figure out my plans for the future. I can't be a queen forever.

"Half God Half Devil" by In This Moment plays softly through the speakers in the ceiling.

I go to remove my towel and start getting dressed but stop when I hear voices on the other side of the door. Stepping back from the mirror, I turn to face it just as it opens. Bones and Titan both enter.

"Call him again," Bones snaps, just as his already narrowed blue eyes meet mine. He comes to a sudden stop.

Titan shoves a hand through his hair, looking over at him. "The fucker …" His words trail off as he realizes Bones stopped and follows his line of sight. He too halts when his eyes meet mine. The door gently closes behind them, caging me in.

My heart begins to pound in my chest at the sight of them together. The three of us. In one room. I haven't seen Bones since he kissed me in his office last week. And last time I saw Titan was this morning when I crawled out of his bed.

I open my mouth to say something—to explain what I'm doing in here—but nothing comes out.

I wait for them to excuse me or order me to leave the bathroom. But they remain standing perfectly still and silent.

I look over Titan in his dark jeans and plain black T-shirt. He has a silver-studded belt that has a chain leading to his back pocket. He wears a bracelet on his right wrist that matches it. His muscular arms make his shirt strain, showing me every defined muscle and all his tattoos.

Bones wears black slacks and a white button-down with the sleeves rolled up to his elbows. His black ink that covers his arms and neck make him look out of place. Like he can't decide if he wants to be the sinner or the saint.

They are both so different, yet so much the same, it scares me.

"Em," Titan says my name, and I can't hide the whimper that slips out from the roughness in his tone.

Fuck, these men have this way of making my body need them. They pull me in, and I'm not strong enough to fight them.

I lick my parted lips, "Sorry," I mumble, not really knowing what I'm apologizing for exactly. I'm not doing anything wrong. I look down at the floor and force my heavy legs to take a few steps.

As I go to squeeze between them, a hand presses into my stomach, and my breath quickens as it brings me to a stop.

I look up and Titan stands there, his eyes looking into mine. I hope he doesn't see the want in them. Or notice the way my body shakes.

I'm standing in a bathroom with both of them. Alone. And the only thing that separates me from them is a towel.

His eyes drop to where his large hand is pressed into the plush material, right over my navel. My eyes shoot to Bones. His baby blue eyes watch me without any emotion—giving nothing away.

The air in the room grows hotter; steam lingers from my shower, and I feel sweat bead on my forehead. "I should go," I manage to whisper.

"Stay."

My eyes widen at the single word Titan speaks, and my thighs tighten at what's to come. When I don't make a move to run, he steps forward and slowly walks around me, his hand remaining on my stomach over the towel. He comes to stand behind me and presses his front to my back. I moan when I feel his long and hard cock pressing into my lower back.

"Titan," I pant, but my eyes go to Bones still standing before me, not saying a word. I'm not even sure he's breathing.

Titan's free hand comes up, and he wraps it around my neck, pulling my head back, and I swallow roughly against it. He lowers his lips to my ear, and whispers, "Isn't this what you've always wanted, Em?" His hot breath makes my skin break out in goose bumps. "Don't be shy now."

His hand on my stomach slowly begins to travel south. I close my eyes due to shame 'cause I make no move to stop him.

"Look at him," Titan orders, and my eyes snap open. His hand reaches the bottom of the towel—right below my pussy. He slides his hand between my legs, and my lips part as my breathing picks up. His fingers run along my pussy. "Soaking wet. Just like I expected."

A choking sound escapes my lips, and my body heats from embarrassment. I wanna close my eyes or look away, but Bones demands my attention by just standing in front of me. His eyes still don't give anything away, but the bulge in his pants does. "Titan," I pant.

"Shh." He coos as he slides a finger into me. "Let him watch you come, baby."

My breath gets caught as he adds another one. His hand tightens around my throat, and his fingers become forceful.

I bite my bottom lip to keep from crying out while his fingers move in and out of me in a way that has heat running up my back.

"Say it," Titan's voice demands.

I close my eyes. *God, please don't make me ...*

"Beg me to make you come, Em. We wanna hear it."

His fingers slow, and I whimper at the loss of that feeling that was growing. He chuckles from behind me, then I feel his breath on my ear again. "Look at Bones while you beg me to make you come, sweetheart."

I'm having trouble breathing as it is with his hands pulling my throat back at this odd angle. His fingers stop altogether, and my stomach knots at the loss of what I was so close to getting.

They're just words, I tell myself. Words that will get me what I want.

I open my heavy eyes and look up at Bones. His tatted arms are crossed over his chest, and his eyes are burning holes into mine. "Please," I choke out.

"Please what?" Titan growls.

"Please make me come." My voice shakes just as much as my legs. And Bones's jaw sharpens at my words.

"My pleasure, sweetheart." He thrusts his fingers roughly into me once again, and I can no longer fight it. My hands come up, my nails digging into his tatted forearm that holds my throat as a wave washes over me, pulling me down into the deep. My lips part, and I cry out into the bathroom while I come all over his fingers.

When I finally open my heavy eyes, I notice Bones is standing closer to us. So close that he has his hands over my towel, gripping my hips.

"Beautiful," Titan whispers removing his fingers from my pussy, and I whimper at the loss of them.

Then without a word, he lifts his hand up that is covered in my arousal and Bones parts his lips, allowing Titan to place his two fingers in his mouth.

Bones's eyes blaze down on me as he sucks them clean. "Does she taste as good as you remember?" Titan asks him, amusement in his voice.

Bones doesn't answer. Instead, he removes his hands from my hips and lifts them. He gently tugs on the towel where I have it tucked into itself on my chest to keep it in place.

I don't stop him. It's been so long since he's touched me.

It falls to the floor, and my breath gets stuck in my throat when he follows it, dropping to his knees. "Bones," I pant.

"He wants a little more," Titan says to me as he reaches up with his free hand and yanks my ponytail holder out of my messy bun. My hair falls down around my shoulders.

Bones grips my right thigh and lifts my shaky leg over his shoulder. I look down at him wide-eyed and in shock, silently begging him not to stop. Not to ask me if I really want this. Because I'm not sure I can lie and say no.

Titan lets go of my throat, and I take a deep breath, my chest rising and falling quickly. His now free hand lowers to grab my breast. I moan, closing my eyes when his other hand tangles in my hair. He yanks my head back, and I cry out when I feel Bones's tongue lick over my throbbing pussy.

"Oh, God," I pant.

Titan's fingers pinch my nipple, and I stand on my tiptoes, letting out another cry of pleasure. Bones's hand on my thigh squeezes to the point I know I'll have a reminder of this tomorrow. Then his tongue enters me, and my body jerks involuntarily as my heart pounds in my chest. I'm gonna come again. "Please ..."

Titan's hand in my hair jerks my head to the side at an odd angle, and then his mouth is on mine. His lips devouring mine, swallowing my moans as Bones fucks my pussy with his tongue.

My head swims, my eyes fall shut, and my body heats once again. Every muscle tightens, and just as Titan pulls away, I scream out in pleasure into the bathroom from Bones on his knees with his head between my legs.

My legs buckle, and I go to crash to the floor, but Titan catches me. He slides an arm under my shaking knees and my back, cradling me to his chest. "Please," I beg even though my mind says stop. I can't take anymore.

"You want more, baby?" he asks.

My eyes begin to sting with embarrassment, but this may be my only chance to get what I've always wanted.

"Please." My hands fist his shirt, and I bury my head into it. Then I feel us moving. A door is shoved open, and then I'm placed on my feet. I sway a little bit. I open my eyes to the dark room. We're in the massage room, right off the bathroom. I remember walking in on Grave when he was in here with that blonde.

The walls are painted a dark gray, to help reduce lighting and there's a large massage table in the middle, and a basket sits by the far wall with lotions and oils in it. A set of towels folded neatly next to it.

Titan gets my attention as he rips his shirt off and then he's shoving his jeans down his muscular legs. He stands before me completely naked. Black and blue ink cover every inch of his arms, chest, and neck. His stomach is a sculptured perfection that shows off his six-pack. I like how he has a tattoo on his side, but that's it as far as stomach. He's got a black skull on his right pec that has a tilted crown on top of it with crossbones underneath. It's what all the Kings have.

I turn to see Bones standing behind me. His blue eyes drop to my pussy, and he licks his wet lips. My shaking thighs are still wet from his head being between them. He's still dressed in his button-down and slacks. I walk over to him, and his eyes meet mine. They give away nothing, but I can see he wants this too when my eyes drop to his slacks. He's as hard as I am wet. I reach out and undo them. He stands completely still as I push them down, freeing his hard cock. He wasn't wearing anything underneath them. My hand wraps around the base of it, and his body lightly jerks. My mouth begins to water when I feel the cold metal underneath—I count five piercings when my fingers run up his shaft. He never had those before. I want to taste him. Feel him. It's been so long since we …

My body breaks out in goose bumps when I feel Titan come up behind me. His hand pulls my hair back and off my shoulders. He leans his lips down to my ear. "Wanna taste him like he did you?"

I bite my bottom lip nervously. I want to. God, how I want to. But what will Titan think of me?

He must sense my unease 'cause he speaks again. "Go ahead, baby. Let me watch him fuck your mouth."

TITAN

She stands before me, practically panting as she stares down at Bones's cock longingly. I look up at him, and his eyes are on her.

He's as fucking hard as I am.

Emilee York has this effect on men. To see her want us as much as we do her makes me smile.

"Get on your knees, Em," I order her when she just stands there. I know she wants it. She's just nervous. Possibly ashamed. But there's no reason to be. Any of us could have walked out of this room at any time. Yet here we still are.

She takes in a deep breath and falls to her knees. I reach down and wrap her long hair around my fist, and I gently pull her head back, so she has to look up at him. He wraps his hand around the base of his hard cock and strokes it a couple of times. She watches the motion, licking her lips. Then he guides it into her open and willing mouth.

My own dick throbs, standing to attention at the back of her head as she takes his.

He pushes his hips forward, and she goes to pull back, but my hand in her hair holds her in place, forcing her to take however he wants to give it to her. He goes slow at first—gentle—which surprises me. Nothing about Bones is ever gentle. But maybe he's feeling her out—giving her a chance to tell him no. To shove him back.

She makes a moaning sound, still looking up at him. His head falls back, his neck tattoo moving as he swallows. His hips pick up, and he starts fucking her harder. She shifts on her knees, and I know her pussy is dripping wet from what we did to her in the bathroom and for what is to come. Her hands grip his thighs. Her nails digging into his skin. She clings to him.

We're going to devour her.

Tears run down her face along with drool as he fucks her face like he once loved her, and she hurt him. Even though we know that's not what happened.

His abs tense, and his jaw sharpens. Just when I think he is about to come, he pulls out of her mouth. I don't blame him. I'd rather go inside her tight cunt or ass than in her mouth. Her head dips forward, and her breathing fills the smaller room as "Saints," By Echos begins to play.

How fitting.

Wasting no time, I lean down and pick her up. I position myself on my back on the massage table, pulling her on top of me. Bones goes over to the wicker basket that holds the oils before he gets up on his knees behind her, and she whimpers.

I wrap my hand around the back of her neck and yank her face down to mine. I kiss her desperately. My tongue sweeps her mouth, tasting a little bit of Bones on her. She pulls away, gasping for breath, and her head falls to the crook of my neck.

I look up over her shoulder to Bones. He reaches forward, grips a handful of her hair and yanks her head back, using that roughness that he prefers. She cries out, and the sound makes my cock jerk.

He leans over her back, lowering his lips to her ear. His eyes hold mine. There's no challenge in them. No jealousy. Just pure want. "You're gonna have to say it, Em."

It's the first time he's spoken to her since we entered the bathroom to find her fresh out of the shower. Wrapped in a towel and silently begging us to use her.

Her hands are on my chest, and her tits right above my face. My hands skate up her sides to her chest. I grip a handful of her luscious tits. And she gasps. We're both patiently waiting for her to give us the green light. It'll be worth the wait.

His tongue comes out and licks at her tears before pulling her earlobe between his teeth. "Say it." She's still trying to catch her breath, and her heavy eyes are closed. "Tell us that you want both of our cocks fucking you. At the same time."

She squeezes her eyes tightly and licks her wet lips. Her face is free of makeup, and she looks absolutely beautiful. This is how I always imagined her—wet, needy, and fucking begging. "Please," she whispers.

"Louder!" he demands. His hands still fisted in her hair.

I release her breasts, and what sounds like a growl escapes her parted lips. I place my hands on her hips, refusing to touch her anywhere else until she gives us the go.

She rocks her hips back and forth, and I can't help the smile that spreads across my face. *Just say it, baby.*

"Please." She clears her throat when the single word comes out rough. "Please fuck me. Both of you."

His hand goes between her parted legs that straddle my hips. He shoves two fingers into her pussy without warning, and she whimpers at his force. She's already so sore. *Just wait until tomorrow, sweetheart.*

He removes them and runs them over her ass, getting it ready for his cock.

Her eyes open, and they look down at me. My hand slides between her legs, and I rub her clit while he finger-fucks her. Her body jerks, and she cries out at the sensation. When he pulls his fingers out and goes to grab the oil to coat his dick, I slip two fingers into her myself. Her breath catches, and then I pull them out. Her body sags the best it can against mine 'cause Bones's right hand is still fisted in her hair. I lift my fingers and rub them against her lips. Her tongue flicks out to taste herself.

"Suck on them," I demand, and she opens her pretty lips for me. I slide them into her mouth, and she moans, rocking her hips against me.

Bones shifts on his knees, and I know he's ready. I take my free hand and lift my hips, sliding my hard cock slowly into her soaking wet pussy. Her walls clamp down around me, sucking me in, and my balls tighten. *Fuck, how am I gonna keep from coming too soon?*

She bites down on my finger, and Bones shifts again. Her body stiffens above me.

"Relax, it's gonna feel good, Em," I tell her, and he lets out a growl as he enters her a little more. "We're gonna make you feel so good."

She tries to pull her head back from my finger, but Bones's hand is still fisted in her hair, holding her in place. There's nowhere for her to go.

I begin to move my hips up and down slowly, and I feel her body begin to ease up. When I remove my thumb from her mouth, she's gasping for air. Eyes shut and with the way he has her head pulled back, I watch her throat work as she swallows.

I trail my fingers down over her chin and to her delicate neck. My hips pick up their pace, and the table starts rocking back and forth when Bones begins to fuck her ass.

"Gooodddd," she chokes out, and her slick body begins to move with ours. I wrap my hand around her neck and squeeze it as we take over.

Fucking her like she is just another whore we found on the streets and wanted to use for the night. But the reality is far worse—we both love her. Just in completely different ways.

TWENTY-ONE

EMILEE

This morning, I had rolled over onto my stomach and moaned at the pain my body was in.

I took inventory on my body. My hips hurt. My pussy hurts. My ass hurts. I had a pounding headache.

Fuck, it all felt so good. I can't tell you the last time I felt like this after sex. There was always something missing—leaving me unfulfilled—even after all those years with Bones. He was great in bed and made sure to take care of me every time, but afterward, it was like my body never really reached that high you hear women talking about.

I hit it last night!

"You okay?" Haven asks.

"Huh?" I nod quickly, blocking out last night. "Yeah."

I stand next to Jasmine and Haven in line at Starbucks inside Kingdom. It's almost eight in the evening, and I needed some coffee. I've been dragging ass all day. I had spent the day with my mother, like usual and then called up the girls on my way back here for the night. I order and then step aside for Jasmine to place hers.

"Just fuck me up." She has her red hair up in a high pony and sunglasses on her face. She's dressed in an off the shoulder black T-shirt and a pair of cut off shorts that are so short the pockets peek out of the bottom. Pretty sure she hasn't been to bed yet because her makeup looks like it's a day or two old.

"Ma'am, this is a Starbucks. Not a bar."

She sighs. "If I'm gonna spend ten dollars on a drink, it better make me …"

"She'll have a salted caramel mocha. Venti," I answer for her.

"Add some of those Xanax sprinkles," Jasmine adds.

"Ma'am?" He arches a brow.

"She's joking." I give a fake laugh, pushing her away from the counter.

We find a table to sit down, and I sneeze. "Bless you," Haven says.

"Thank you." I lift my hand to signal I feel another one coming on.

Jasmine plops down in a seat across from me. "I once sneezed while on my period and gave birth to a jellyfish."

The woman sitting at the table next to us gasps, obviously hearing her.

"Oh, like it hasn't happened to you?" she asks. "I swear I just need to stay home. People don't like me, and I hate most of them."

"Or maybe you should just think before you speak," Haven suggests.

She just snorts. "Where is the fun in that?"

Haven just shakes her head.

"So how's the sex life coming?" Jasmine asks out of nowhere. I wanna say I'm surprised but I'm not. Sex is always on her mind. I'm pretty sure the girl has a sex addiction.

I clear my throat. "I don't know …"

"Yes, you do. We can see it written all over your face," Jasmine interrupts me.

"Well." I push a stray piece of hair behind my ear. "I slept with Titan."

"We know that." Haven nods once.

"And Bones."

Haven drops her blueberry muffin she was about to take a bite of.

TITAN

"Does Titan know?" she asks wide-eyed.

"Yeah, it was at the same time," I whisper.

"Holy fuck!" Jasmine shrieks, shoving her glasses to the top of her head.

The old lady next to us gasps at her choice of language. I ignore her and wave them off. "I told you mine, now tell me yours." *Let's move on.*

Haven gives a laugh. "Well, I've never been with two guys at once, and there's no way in hell that Luca would allow that. Not that I want to," she adds quickly.

"I was about to have sex last night but got out of it." Jasmine shrugs.

"How do you get *out of it*?" I ask curiously.

"I was with a client. It was actually a great one. We had a great dinner, then went back to his place. He wanted to go all the way, and I was totally willing. The guy was cute. But once he removed his pants, and I got a look at his dick, I was like nope. I'm out."

"What was wrong with it?" I ask.

"It was too small. I mean I'm not saying I need an elephant trunk, but it was the size of a pinkie. And my pussy needs more than that to work with."

Haven is coughing now, possibly choking. I'm laughing, and the old woman gets up, shaking her head as she walks away from us.

"Wait! What do you mean a client?" Haven asks, just picking up on what she had said.

I bite my bottom lip, and Jasmine smiles. "We're Queens."

"You're what?" she barks. "I know you did not just say Queens?" She narrows her eyes on me. "You're doing it too?" Her eyes dart around as she lowers her voice. "You're an escort?"

"I need the money." I shrug. "Not all of us are married to billionaires," I tease.

"Yeah," Jasmine adds.

Haven points a finger at Jasmine. "Your father is a millionaire. You don't need to prostitute yourself out."

Our table falls silent. Jasmine closes her lips tightly, and I watch her clench her fists. She has never had a great relationship with her dad, and I feel he has a lot to do with why Jasmine is the way she is. She has *daddy* issues. But we've never spoken about them before. Some things are better left alone. Talking about them to her girls isn't going to make them any better. That's something she needs to speak to her dad about. Only they know the problem and can fix it together.

The barista calls out our order number, and Jasmine stands to get it, letting us know the conversation is over. Haven gives me a look that tells me we will be getting back to it later.

I see Grave enter the Starbucks. "One second," I tell Haven, and stand, walking over to him.

He looks over and sees me coming. "Hey," I say clearing my throat still unsure how to act around him. First, I saw him fucking a girl, and then he caught me and Bones together. Not everyone is going to understand what me, Bones, and Titan did. Hell, even I don't know what it was. But I know I'm with Titan and he didn't mind sharing me with Bones. I have a feeling he won't be that understanding if I asked to bring some random dude into the bed with us. Not like I need to. He and Bones are plenty.

"Hey." He nods at me, coming up behind Jasmine in line. "Jas." He recognizes her. His eyes on her ass.

"Grave." She observes, turning and looking him up and down.

He smirks at her. Grave is six two but still the shortest of all the Kings. He has that cute baby face and panty dropping smile. His eyes are blue like his brother's but they're softer. More approachable. Bones's are always hard and intimidating.

"I see you're still alive." She takes a sip of her drink and pulls her lip back after swallowing. Clearly she doesn't like what I ordered her.

"There's always tomorrow," he states.

She rolls her green eyes and heads over to our table.

"What do you want, Emilee?" he asks, looking down at me.

"Have you seen Titan?" I ask.

He chuckles. "Did he ghost you already?"

I place my hands on my hips. "No." He was already gone when I left this morning to go see my mother. And when I returned to meet the girls, Nigel said he was out for the day. He didn't mention anything about going anywhere to me.

He pulls his ringing phone out of the back pocket of his shredded jeans. I don't think Grave owns any type of business attire. "He's up in The Palace."

"Palace?" *Where have I heard that at?*

He nods. "Sixteenth floor. Code 1275."

I go to ask him what the code is for, but his cell rings once more. "I have to take this." And with that, he dismisses me.

I sit down and have my drink with the girls. But the entire time my mind is on Titan. Is that here in Kingdom? The girls and I hang out for about thirty minutes and then I tell them goodbye.

I go to the main lobby where the elevator banks are and wait with the crowd of people. I step in and frown when I don't see an option for the sixteenth floor. "Excuse me," I say and squeeze my way out before the door closes. I try five other ones, and none of them stop on a sixteenth floor. *Strange.*

Getting impatient, I turn in a circle, trying to think where the other elevators are that I could use when I see the tattoo shop. I walk over to it and enter.

"Hello. How may I help you?" a girl asks with a smile on her face from behind the counter.

"Is Cross here?" Cross is a tattoo artist among many other things. He opened this place up inside the casino when they took over. From what I've heard over the years, he does really good work. I wonder if he has given the Kings any of their ink.

Her smile drops, and she crosses her arms over her chest. *Bitch mode activated.* The spike between her eyes and hoop that hangs from her nose doesn't help to make her look any friendlier. All she's missing is the smoke coming out of her ears and she'd look like a cartoon bull about to charge me. "Do you have an appointment?"

"No. But he is here?"

"He's not available. For you," she answers slowly as if I'm hard of hearing while her hazel eyes sweep me over. Obviously judging me for what she sees—lack of ink and piercings I'm sure.

I push off the desk and walk down the narrow hallway.

"Hey, get back here," she calls out.

I ignore her.

"Hey ... I said he's unavailable ..."

Taking another turn, I walk past the open doors. The last one on the right is closed. I shove it open without knocking.

A woman lies on her back. Her legs up in what look like stirrups. All she wears is a pair of soft pink underwear from the waist down. Her jeans lie over the back of a chair in the corner of the room. And Cross is between her legs tattooing her inner thigh. "Oh my gosh ... I'm so sorry ..."

"Emilee?" He looks up at me. "What are you ...?"

"I told her you were busy," the young girl snaps, coming in behind me.

"She's fine." He waves her off, and I hear her growl.

"What can I do for you?" he asks, pushing up his black rimmed glasses to his head and removing his gloves. Cross always had that bad boy—I'll fuck you on the couch while your parents are in the other room with the door open kind of guy. All he'd need is to wrap a hand around your throat and cut off your air to keep you from screaming his name. He's always been mysterious but the guy could get any girl he wanted. And he lined them up. He had daddy issues just like Jasmine. I wonder if they got together and talked about them if that would help?

He has thick, dark hair that most women dream of. He's always kept it long. Right now, it's hidden under a backward baseball cap. And his beard—it matches his hair in thickness and color. I never cared for them because I felt like they covered up too much of his handsome face. But Cross has his own way of making everything look hot. His eyes are what make him, though. They're a deep emerald shade. I avoided him back in school. Every time he makes eye contact with you, you feel like he's undressing you. It's intimate and makes your legs weak. Like now. He wears a black T-shirt with a skull on it that looks like it's on fire. The top of the shirt reads—light up my soul. With faded blue jeans and black combat boots. He is every dad's nightmare and ever mother's wild fantasy.

I stop eye-fucking him and remember why I'm here. "How do I get to the sixteenth floor?"

His brows arch.

"The Palace?" I continue when he just stares at me.

He nods. "Right. *Palace.* Nigel can help you with that. I'll let him know you're coming."

"Got it. Thanks." It must be one of those levels that only he has access to.

He laughs and shakes his head, grabbing a new set of gloves. "No problem."

I close the door and head back to where I entered the shop. "Thanks for nothing, bitch," I say to the girl still glaring at me as I walk out.

It takes me ten minutes to get to the far side of Kingdom—tower one.

"Hello, Miss York," Nigel greets me before we step onto the elevator. He's always happy. I also notice that he's always working. I'm not sure the guy ever gets a day off. Or if he sleeps.

"I was given a code."

"Ah, yes. You will need it to enter the room." He nods.

What in the hell? What kind of room is this? Is it the vault? Is it where they stash their billions of dollars? Dead bodies?

We come to a stop, and he gestures for me to exit. "You have a great day, young lady."

"Thanks for your help."

He nods. "Anytime." Then the elevator closes, and he's gone.

I look over the flat black painted walls and dark purple carpet. Black sconces hang on the wall, shining purple lights down onto the floor. The carpet is so thick, my shoes sinking into it. I turn in a full circle to look at my surroundings. I can either go back to the elevator or toward the door at the end of the hall. Those are the only options I have.

The door it is. I make my way toward it and see a keypad. On the door is written *The Palace* in rose gold letters and then *every queen needs a palace* written below it. I press in the code I was given, and a lock clicks. I push down the gold handle and open the big black door. It's darker than the hallway. A purple light is all that shines from the top of the ceiling in the rather large entrance.

"Thank you, Titan." I hear a woman's voice. My body instantly stiffens.

"You're welcome," he says. "Everything went okay?"

"Yep."

A woman comes into view at the end of the entrance. She wears a black dress that has a deep V in the front and high up on her thighs. It looks see-through. "Hello." She gives me a warm smile, catching me before I can make up my mind whether to run away or barge in.

I blink and lick my dry lips. "I'm, uh, looking for …"

"Em?" Titan asks as he comes to stand next to her. He looks down at the blonde, and says, "You may go, Sandy."

She nods, and as she walks past me, she whispers, "Enjoy."

I watch her leave and then turn to him. We stand silently just staring at one another. I want to ask him what in the fuck he's doing in a hotel room that I didn't know existed with a woman. But I don't have that right. *Do I?* I mean, I literally let him and his best friend fuck me the other day. I can't tell him he can't do the same.

"Stop," he orders.

"What?" I blink.

"I can see what you're thinking. It's written all over your face, and you couldn't be more wrong."

My shoulders sag. I don't get jealous. I don't get feelings for men. It's just sex. "I wasn't—"

"Don't lie to me," he interrupts me.

I straighten my shoulders and lift my chin. "Then what were you doing in here with her?" I'm not going to play this game. I never used to get jealous, but I'm also not one of those girls who beats around the bush. If I have a question, I'm going to ask it.

"She's a Queen and just finished a job."

I frown. A job? In here? I open my mouth to ask him just that when he speaks.

"What are you doing here?"

"I've been calling you. Grave said you were up here."

He says nothing. Just stands there at the end of the entrance. I think he's mad at me. I cross my arms over my chest and give him my back.

"Where are you going?" he asks. I stop and slowly turn to face him once again. He holds his arms out wide. "You were looking for me. Here

I am."

My eyes narrow on him. Even though my knees shake, I'm so confused on what I saw and what I can and can't say to him. He doesn't love me. And she's a Queen. Maybe he was her job? I mean, he fucks me, and I'm a queen. He doesn't pay me for sex, though. I'm sure he has them lined up to give it for free.

"I was," I say, taking the five steps to close the distance between us. He reaches out, pulling me into him, and I gasp. "What …? What is this place?" I ask, stepping farther into the largely open room, looking at all the foreign devices.

"This is The Palace."

I catch myself in a massive floor-to-ceiling mirror. "I don't understand …" I trail off, my eyes shooting over to look at an old looking wooden bench that has a black leather seat on it

"It is reserved exclusively for our clients," he adds.

"Clients?" I ask.

"The Queens."

That's where I heard that name. It was at the warehouse when Jasmine questioned the two girls we met about The Palace. They said it didn't exist. An urban legend.

They were wrong!

I turn away from the mirror and walk over to the far wall. A tall chest that stands every bit of six feet tall. Both French doors are wide open. Chains, whips, belts and rope of various lengths and widths hang on metal hooks. I reach up and run my hands over the thick material. "What do they do?" I ask.

"Act out scenes."

"What kind of scenes?"

"Whatever they want."

I turn and look at the Alaskan king-size bed that sits in the middle of the large room. It's got black silk sheets and two pillows that match. The headboard consists of vertical bars. The footboard looks like a stockade from back in the day when people were publicly beaten for their crimes. It's raised high off the floor. I look underneath it. "Is that …?"

"A cage," he answers.

"For what?" I ask wide-eyed. It reminds me of an overly large dog cage with its iron bars. They start at the floor and stop at my knees, where the bed begins.

"For the submissive."

I take a step back and bump into him. I jump, and he chuckles.

I turn, cheeks red with embarrassment, and see a table. Walking over to it, I reach out and run my fingertips along the black leather. It has white leather straps connected to it in various places. They remind me of the type you see used in hospitals for patients to prevent them from harming themselves or others. The table is completely flat and has to be longer than seven feet. But maybe only three feet wide. "What is this used for?" I ask curious.

"Forced orgasms."

"What?" I gasp.

He smiles at me. Walking around to stand at my back, he says, "A woman or man lies down on the table and is strapped to it. The Dom then brings the sub to orgasm. Multiple times." He places his hands on my hips, and I jump.

"Don't be nervous," he whispers. "All you have to do is lie there." He kisses my neck, and my head falls to the side. "And get off. Again." His hand trails down my waist. "Again." His hand slips between my legs, and I whimper. "And again. Your body will be shaking. Your skin covered in sweat. Your mind foggy. And limbs heavy."

"Have you done this before?" I ask breathlessly. Not liking the heat that rushes up my spine in preparation of him saying yes.

"No. But I'd be lying if I said I didn't want to do it to you." He presses his hips into my ass, and I shiver when I feel how hard he is.

I feel the tension drain from my body knowing he's never done it before. "How long?" I question.

"As long as they want. The sub is the one strapped to the table. Naked. Wide open and vulnerable. But they have all the power. The sub says when they've had enough. When they want to stop, the Dom stops."

I close my eyes. "Do it to me?"

His hands come up the back of my neck, and he grips my hair. Slowly, he pulls my head back, and imagining the picture he just painted for me has me already panting. It sounds breathtaking.

"Get undressed for me, Em." Then he pulls away, not even bothering to question my words.

I undo my shoes and kick them off along with my jean shorts and T-shirt. Then my bra and underwear. I stand naked, facing the table. My heart is pounding, and my hands are sweaty. He stands silently behind me, but I can feel his eyes on me.

"Crawl on the table and lie on your back," he orders.

I comply.

He goes to the foot of the table and spreads my legs wide. He places my right ankle over the strap and buckles me in the belt-like restraint. The inside is lined with fur, so they're cool and soft. He goes to the other ankle and secures it as well.

Then he moves to my side. He secures another belt across my hips. It's tight, pinning me to the table. His eyes meet mine as he reaches around my neck. "Look up," he orders, and I do as he says, tilting my head back. Another thick belt is placed over my throat, and I swallow as he buckles it in place. I take in a shaky breath.

"You okay?"

I go to nod but can't. The thick leather strap across my neck prevents any movement. I have to keep my head tilted back. "Y-Yeah," I stutter and then cough to clear my throat.

He pulls my arms above my head and secures both of them. I'm stretched tight and strapped down.

I begin to pant. My heart races. Sweat beads across my forehead and chest, and my backside is sticking to the black leather. He places his hands on my thigh and I jump. Leaning over, he looks down at me. "You let me know when the pain outweighs the pleasure. Understood?"

Pain? I thought this was about orgasms. I feel like that would be a stupid question, so I just say. "Yes."

"Your safe word is black. Repeat it."

Safe word? "My safe word is black."

He nods. "Good girl." He walks away leaving me alone strapped to this table, and I hear him on the other side of the room. A drawer opens and closes, then I hear him walking back over to me. "After each orgasm, I'm going to ask you if you're okay. Say yes if you are, and black if you want me to stop. Understand?"

"Yes." I lick my lips and hear a vibrating noise. "What is …?"

Something presses against my pussy, and my body arches. I cry out as the sensation tickles my clit. "Oh God …" I gasp. My body fights the restraints. What felt cool seconds ago now feels like needles pricking my body. "Tita …" Before I can even finish his name, I'm coming. Harder and faster than I ever have.

The sensation stops all of a sudden, and my body sags against the table.

"Are you okay?"

I'm sweating, panting, and every inch of my skin feels extra sensitive. "Yyyeess."

This time, I feel his fingers spreading me wide before he shoves two into me while placing the vibrator back on my clit. He finger-fucks me while the amazing toy takes me to a whole new level. The room spins. My eyes close, and I'm breathing so hard I feel like I'm hyperventilating. I'm coming again.

"You okay?" I hear his voice in the distance.

"Yes," I croak out. Why does my voice sound hoarse? My throat is sore. My body tenses again. I'm riding another wave. I don't want it to stop. Ever. I'd be his sub if this meant being strapped to a table. His voice gets farther and farther away, but I always say yes. I always want more.

TITAN

Turning off the wand, I place it on the stand next to the table. I undo her wrists first, then her neck, hips, and ankles and pick her limp body up off the black leather. She shakes uncontrollably in my arms. If I hadn't just watched her come six times, I would say she's having convulsions. She's covered in sweat. Her eyes are closed, and she's gasping for each breath. She kept telling me yes. To the point she was going to lose her voice from all the shouting she was doing.

Entering the bathroom, I place her in the large Jacuzzi tub that sits in the center of the large room and turn on the water. When it's the temperature I want, I quickly undress. Climbing in behind her, I lean her back against my front. I pick up the cup next to me and fill it with water before pouring it over the front of her.

She moans, and her head falls to the side. I check her pulse. It's racing. Maybe I pushed her too hard.

"I'm okay," she whispers, reading my mind. "I could have … kept going."

I snort. "You were about to lose consciousness."

She gives me a faint smile. "So worth it."

Opening her eyes, she looks around the dim bathroom aimlessly. She lifts her hand, wrapping her fingers around the steel eye hook that is on the inside of the tub. "That's a weird spot for a towel hook," she muses.

I laugh. "That's not to hang towels on."

"What then?"

"It's for water play." Everything in The Palace is set up for dominance. Nothing is for convenience. It's for total domination.

"Oh." Her eyes light up. "I wanna—"

"Absolutely not," I interrupt her. "How do you feel?" I get serious.

"Amazing."

"Sore?"

"In the best way."

I kiss her hair. It's knotted in the back where she struggled with her neck being restrained. "Come on. Let's get you cleaned up and into bed."

I WAKE TO the sound of a vibrating noise. I yawn, wondering what time it is. This room doesn't have any windows for a reason. And after we finished in the tub, we passed out. It isn't being used until tomorrow, so we just stayed here. I knew she needed the rest.

I hear the noise again and realize it's my cell vibrating, and I get out of the bed and dig it out of my jeans on the floor. Noticing it's almost nine in the morning. I never sleep in. I'm ready and sitting at my desk by six-thirty every day. This casino doesn't run itself.

I open up my emails and scroll through them, responding to the ones that need immediate attention. I send Bones a message that I will be down in about an hour. My phone vibrates in my hand with a new email, and I read over it.

Titan

I need a date for my annual company party. It will be on my yacht off the coast of Hawaii. Next week. I would say the duration will span across three days. Given time for flights and event. I want to reserve Emilee.

I run a hand through my hair and look over at her sleeping in the bed. Her naked body tangled in the black silk sheets. She's on her side, facing me. Her eyes are closed as she breathes deeply. I don't mind her being a Queen as long as I know the situation she is in and she's not out of reach for me. A date night here at one of our many steakhouses? Sure, I'd let her do that. A date on an island, while on a yacht with a client that I know prefers to fuck his queen? Absolutely not.

I write out a quick response.

I'm more than happy to secure you a queen for the event. Unfortunately, Emilee is unavailable at that time.

She's mine, and I don't plan on sharing her with anyone. Other than occasionally with Bones because that is what she wants.

"Morning."

I place my phone back in my jeans and crawl back into the bed, pulling her into my side. "Good morning, gorgeous." I kiss her forehead.

She smiles. "I could get used to this."

"What is that exactly?" I ask.

"Endless amounts of orgasms and waking up next to you."

Me too. I hate to admit that I'm already falling for her. I knew it would happen, but if I'm being honest with myself. It was why I wanted her all those years ago, there was just something about her. When she turned me down, it just made me want her more.

I walk through the crowded hallway of the school and see her coming toward me. She has her eyes down staring at her cell, typing away. Probably talking to Bones. I haven't seen her since I kissed her at the frat party last weekend. When I was ready to go all the way and she changed her mind.

I purposely step in front of her, making her run into me. "Oh, sorry ... Titan?" She looks up at me.

"Hey, Em. Can we talk?"

She pushes her hair behind her ear. "I can't ..."

"It'll only take a second." I grab her arm and yank her into the nearest classroom that I know is vacant this time of day. I shut the door behind me and lock the door.

"Titan, I don't have time."

I grab her arm, yank her to me and press my lips to hers. She opens up for me immediately and moans into my mouth. My hands find her hair and I deepen the kiss. She tastes like a cherry lollipop.

But she pulls away too soon. "Titan, we can't," she whispers, licking her lips.

"Because you love Bones?" I question.

"No." She runs her hands through her tangled hair. "We're not like that."

"So you're just his fuck?" I know what they are, but I want to hear her say it. I want her to admit that what they have isn't what we could have.

Her eyes narrow on me. "No."

"Then what the fuck is it?" I snap, getting irritated.

"I don't have to explain it to you," she growls. "It's none of your business. And why do you care so much? He's your best friend; you shouldn't want to fuck me."

"Because I know that he doesn't give a shit about you," I say.

Her face falls, and her eyes sadden. Shit!

"Em, that's not what I meant." He doesn't love her, no, but he does care about her. She's the only woman in the world that he gives the slightest fuck about. He always talks shit on Grave and his drug problem, but Emilee is his drug. He can't quit her.

"And you do?" she asks, arching a brow.

I clamp my mouth shut because I'm not sure what to say. How to make her understand. Does she think I watch her and follow her around for nothing? She's right. I'm not supposed to want her. Not like this. Not this way.

"That's what I thought," she states, and I step out of the way, letting her out of the room and out of my life.

"What are you thinking about?" she asks me.

I let out a long breath. "Nothing."

"It's not nothing. I can feel your heart race."

I run a hand down my face. "You. Me." I pause. "Bones."

She rubs circles on my chest with the tips of her fingers but stops when I mention him. She sits up, the black silk sheet falling off her chest, and stares down at me. "Are you mad at me? For what we did?"

"No." I sit up as well. "I told you I was okay with it. I wouldn't lie to you."

"It's just ..." She bites her bottom lip.

"Can I ask you something?" She nods. "Why did you guys stop seeing each other back then?" I've always wanted to know but some things you just don't ask. And she was right. It was none of my business. No matter how badly I wanted to know.

She bows her head and sighs. I push her hair behind her ear so I can see her face. "You know that night I kissed you at the frat party?" she asks.

"Yeah," I answer slowly, wondering what that has to do with it.

"That night before, Bones had come over to the house. My parents were out of town, and we had sex." I knew he was going over there because we had plans, and he was late due to seeing her before. "After we were done, he was getting dressed, and he said that we needed to stop seeing each other." She frowns. "I was confused at first because it was just sex, but then he said that he loved me, but he couldn't love me the way that you did." Her soft blue eyes meet mine.

I tense at her words.

"I loved Bones, the most he would allow someone to love him." She sighs, averting her eyes again. "We started hooking up my sophomore year in high school when he was a senior. It was a couple of months before his mom passed, and honestly, I thought it was going to go somewhere. But after she died, he became more closed off than he was before. He was unreachable. It was like he felt nothing. Not even physical pain. I saw Grave spiral after that, worse than he already was, and I was afraid Bones was going to do the same. I clung to him, became his lifeboat because I didn't want him to drown." She takes in a deep breath. "Then he got injured in baseball while in college, destroying his chance at getting out of this town and going pro like I knew he wanted to do. There was never a good time to walk away. But you ..." She looks up at me. "You didn't have that problem. I remember saying how could Titan love me? He doesn't even know me. I was attracted to you, yes. And I wanted you, yes, but that would be as far as it would have gone."

"How do you know that?" I ask like I could have seen the future back then. I can't say for certain that we'd be sitting here right now if she had let me love her back then.

"The next night, I saw you at the frat party, and after that first kiss we shared, I just knew ..." She trails off.

"Knew what?" I ask.

"That I wouldn't be able to do with you what I did with Bones." She drops her head. "That I wouldn't have been able to separate feelings for just casual sex, so I pushed you away."

"Is that how you felt about me?" she asks. "Did you have feelings for me?"

"Yes," I answer without any hesitation. This is my chance. To be there for her in a way that Bones never wanted to be.

"But ... you were a dick to me." She narrows her eyes at me.

"I was jealous. I wanted you for myself."

She straddles my hips, and I readjust myself onto my back, staring up at her. "Why didn't you say something?"

"What was I supposed to say? Hey, I've liked you since you were in third grade. But by the time I wanted to approach you, you were already fucking my best friend?"

"Third grade?" She chuckles, thinking I'm joking.

I nod. "Yep. Duncan Wiltz walked behind you and shoved you out of the swing."

She bursts out laughing. "How did you know that?"

"I had Mrs. Hollan's class, and her window faced the playground." I can remember that day like it was yesterday. I was two grades ahead of her, and it was our last year at the elementary school. Her mother always dressed her in bright colors. She was hard to miss.

Her mouth opens wide as she stares down at me in shock.

"I watched you lie there on the ground and cry while he sat there swinging, laughing at you."

"I can't believe you remember that."

"You were wearing a pink shirt with white polka dots and jeans. You had pigtails. A pink ribbon on the right one with a yellow wrapped around the other."

"That is …" She blinks.

"Adorable."

"Kinda stalkerish." She laughs. "But I remember that day too. Well, not what I wore, but the best part was that he came back to school that next Monday with a …" She trails off as I smile. Hers drops off her face, and she tilts her head to the side. "No … did you …? Titan." She slaps my bare chest. "Tell me you didn't."

"I don't know what you're talking about."

"Liar. You broke his arm, didn't you?"

I shrug "Must have been karma." I followed that motherfucker home after school and broke his arm with my bare hands. And I told him if he said a word, I'd break the other. He never touched her again.

TWENTY-TWO

EMILEE

IT'S BEEN A week since I found *The Palace*. I've been trying to talk Titan into taking me back, but he's not having it. I haven't gotten to see him much since then actually because he's been crazy busy. He gets to the Royal Suite late and leaves early. If I was paranoid, I'd say he's ignoring me on purpose after the conversation we had that morning in the bed at The Palace. How he had feelings for me, and I knew I wouldn't be able to walk away from him if I had slept with him. *Good thing I'm not.*

This morning, I decided to go downstairs and get breakfast instead of ordering room service. And I called up the girls, so Jasmine and Haven both sit across from me at the buffet. We're waiting on our food when I see the blonde from the other day walk into the restaurant. "Sandy?" I call out.

She turns to look at me and smiles. I'm guessing she remembers me.

"Who the fuck is Sandy?" Jasmine asks, looking over her shoulder to where I am.

"A queen," I answer.

"Oh." Her eyes light up.

"Hi." Sandy comes up to our table. "Em, is it?"

"It's Emilee, but you can call me Em." I reach out and shake her hand. "This is Jasmine and Haven. My best friends."

"It's nice to meet you, Em. Jasmine and Haven." She nods to each of them.

"You too," I say, scooting over to allow her to sit down next to me. I'm curious about her, and Titan isn't going to tell me anything.

"So you're a queen?" Jasmine comes out and asks.

"Yep." She nods.

"Did you guys do a job together?" Jasmine wags her eyebrows.

I roll my eyes.

"No. I saw her in The Palace the other day," I inform her.

Her green eyes widen at that. "No way."

I nod.

"Was that your first time there?" Sandy asks me.

"Yes."

"Is it what you thought it was going to be?" she asks.

"Well …" I'm not sure how to answer that since I didn't really have any expectations, considering I didn't know that it existed.

"I've been in there three times," Sandy adds at my silence. As if she gave me info, I'd give her some.

"Three times?" Jasmine asks, all but salivating. "What's it like?"

She shrugs. "Like anything else. But some were better than others."

"What is The Palace?" Haven asks finally speaking. She's been typing away on her phone most of our breakfast. As always, Nite stands over in the corner like a statue with his eyes on the room the entire time. He's become our fourth wheel who doesn't mind being alone. A part of me feels bad for him and how uneventful his life must be.

"A sex dungeon," Jasmine answers, waving Haven off. Deeply invested in whatever Sandy has to say. "Have you used the cage under the bed?"

Jasmine and I haven't exchanged Queen stories, but she's obviously been in the room to know about the hardware.

"Cage?" Haven swallows, her eyes growing bigger. Her full attention now on us. She even puts her phone on the table.

"Yep," she answers Jasmine, ignoring Haven.

"Oh, come on. Don't leave us hanging," Jasmine begs.

Sandy gives a soft laugh before she takes a drink of my water. "This one guy ordered me under the bed. Followed me, where he tied me up spread eagle and put a ball gag in my mouth. Then he went into the bathroom, going along with his nightly routine. Once done, got naked, crawled into bed and proceeded to FaceTime his wife."

"No way." Jasmine laughs.

Haven looks like she's seen a ghost. All the color has drained from her face. I bite my lip to hide my laughter.

"Oh, yeah," Sandy goes on. "She asked how Atlanta was. He made up this elaborate meeting that kept him late at the office and then proceeded to have phone sex with her."

"Holy shit," I say.

"What did you do?" Jasmine asks, placing her elbow on the table and her chin in her hand.

"I got wet as fuck." Sandy laughs.

I sit back in my seat. "What does that do for a guy?" Why would he hire Sandy for a night and then spend ten grand on a room just to call his wife? That doesn't make any sense to me.

"I don't know. I have this one client who dresses as a dog. Like has a full-on Halloween costume. And I pull him around the room with a collar." Sandy shrugs. "Not sure what he gets from that other than hard. He does me doggie style and barks as he comes."

"Do you get off on that?" I ask curious. I know some people are into some weird kinks, but that?

"Fuck no." She bursts out laughing. "But I do go home and roll around in the cash it pays me." She gives me a big smile.

"Why would you guys do this?" Haven asks, shaking her head.

Jasmine turns to look at her. "Ever heard that saying, find what you love most and have someone pay you to do it?"

Haven shakes her head. "I don't think that's exactly how it goes."

Sandy and I laugh.

"But you've always had an addictive personality," Haven adds.

Jasmine places her hand over her heart and gasps as if she's been insulted. "Are you calling me a nympho?"

Haven nods quickly. "An addict would be more like it. Sex, gambling, alcohol ..." She pauses. "Anything you try once, you can never get enough of."

Jasmine laughs it off, but I don't miss her looking over at Nite before averting her eyes. And I wonder if he's her newest addiction. Because Haven wasn't lying.

TITAN

"What are we going to do about it?" I ask Luca as we walk through the casino.

He places his hands in the pockets of his black slacks, releasing a sigh. "At this point, there is not much we can do."

That's what I feared. But that's not where I stop. "Dig deeper."

We enter the buffet, and I see the girls sitting at their booth. Luca stops to speak to Nite at the door, but I continue my way over to them. I haven't gotten to spend much time with her. I've been swamped with work. But it has given her more time to spend with her mother.

Emilee looks up to see me. She gives me a big smile. "Titan? What are you doing down here? I thought you had a meeting."

"I did." I grab a chair and pull it over to the end of the table. Spinning it around, I straddle it backward and place my arms across the back rest.

"Joining us for a cocktail?" Jasmine asks me.

"It's too early for a drink," I counter.

"Never." She winks at me before throwing back a Bloody Mary.

The girl has always been a heavy drinker. I look over at Em to see she has a water in front of her, as do the others.

"Hey." Luca walks up behind the booth and kisses Haven on the head. "Ready to go?" he asks.

"Yeah." She picks up her phone and nudges Jasmine's shoulders for her to slide out so that Haven may leave.

Jasmine crawls out, and Luca takes Haven's hand. "I'll call you later, Titan."

"Sounds good." I wave him off, then look at Em. "You ready to go too?"

She tilts her head to the side. "Where are we going?"

"Where do you want to go?"

"Paris," Jasmine answers.

Emilee laughs. "I think he was talking to me."

"What happened to the more, the merrier?"

"I've always liked that saying." Bones speaks as he plops down next to Jasmine.

Emilee ducks her head, but I don't miss the smile that covers her face. This is the first time that the three of us have been together since we both slept with her. I don't know if she's embarrassed or just uncomfortable about the situation. But I'm not.

I hate to admit it, but I'm jealous when it comes to Emilee York. I would cut off a man's hand if he so much as touched her. But Bones? I don't mind it. Because I know that no matter what happens between Em and me, he would protect her with his life. And I wouldn't even have to tell him what she means to me. He'd do it because he loves her. Even if he won't admit it.

"Me too," Jasmine agrees with Bones, then looks at me. "So where are you taking us?"

"I'm not taking you anywhere," I answer.

Jasmine always was a flirt, but she's harmless. We had sex once back in high school. I was drunk. She was high. It was a mistake that we both agreed to never repeat.

"Thought you didn't sleep with a queen?" Sandy asks, looking at me.

The table falls silent. Sandy had overheard my conversation with Whitney in my office. When she had asked if I *sampled* the product.

"I don't," I answer, looking her in the eyes.

She frowns but drops it.

Emilee is not a queen. Not in the way Sandy sees her. Em can do as many jobs as she wants, but she's only going to do the ones that guarantee she keeps her clothes on. Bones and I will be the only men she fucks.

I open the door to my suite, and Emilee enters. I shut and lock it behind me.

"What did Sandy mean by you don't sleep with Queens?" she asks the moment we're alone. "Where would she have heard that?"

I undo the top button of my button-down. "The day she came into my office to audition for a queen, another girl asked if I *sampled* the product. And I told her no." I'm not going to lie to her. I have nothing to hide.

She turns to face me and places her hands on her hips. "Why would you say that?"

"Because I don't."

She frowns. "I'm a queen."

"And?" I shrug my shirt off my shoulders. Her eyes go to my chest and then fall to my hands as I undo my belt.

"And we've had sex."

Cute. "Having."

"Huh?" She licks her lips while I lower my zipper.

"We're having sex," I state and kick off my shoes.

"I'm a queen."

"We've established that." I shove my pants down my legs along with my boxers. My cock isn't hard, but it won't take much. Just looking at the way she stares at it is doing the job. She seems to be in a daze. I bet her pussy is already wet.

"And we have sex."

I reach out, grab her hand, and pull her body into mine. "Why are you still dressed?" I run my hands up and over her ass, gripping her jeans.

"I'm trying …"

"Shh." I place my hand over her mouth. "Quit thinking about it. It doesn't matter."

"But it does." She pulls away from me. "Are you breaking some rule by sleeping with me?"

"I'm the boss. I can do whatever I want." All the Kings break the rules at some point. That's how you succeed.

She snorts. "Spoken like a true gentleman."

I arch a brow. "Is that what you want? A gentleman? Because I promise you, what I'm about to do to you is not something a gentleman would do."

"I'm serious, Titan," she growls.

"I'm standing before you naked, and you want to argue with me?" I ask, starting to get irritated. I don't have a lot of time.

"I want to know how many queens you've actually fucked because you're their *boss* and can do whatever you want." She crosses her arms over her chest.

I open my mouth to say none, but she continues. "And how many have you and Bones shared?"

I don't know why her words piss me off, but they do. Maybe because I expected her to see me differently. Maybe I expected her to understand the connection between the three of us. Either way, stepping into her, I say the first thing that comes to my mind. "You didn't think you were special, did you?"

And just like that, I fucked everything up.

TWENTY-THREE

EMILEE

As I TOSS and turn in bed, my mind is in a hundred different places right now. Plus, my blood is still boiling from Titan and what he said to me earlier today.

It hurt.

I don't know why I thought I was special. I guess because of our conversation we had last week in The Palace. He had said that he had feelings for me once, but that doesn't mean he has them now. Too much time has passed.

The Kings have always had girls falling at their feet. But even though me and Bones weren't exclusive, I knew for a fact that he only slept with me. He didn't have time for anyone else. Believe me, he kept me busy. But we never had to say it. And as much as we used each other, he never made me feel that way.

Titan was always fucking random women in high school and college, and apparently, he hasn't changed a fucking bit. The fact that I did him and Bones at the same time should have been my first hint.

I didn't expect him to be faithful, but I did expect honesty. He made me feel worse than any client could, but maybe that's my fault due to the expectations I had. I thought things were going to be different. I allowed myself to fall for him. And why? Because I needed someone to save me? Fuck him. I never asked him for a dime. He hasn't bought me expensive things or handed me money. He gave me a job. That I auditioned for. On my knees. That wasn't even a job requirement.

Getting out of bed, I pick up the robe that hangs over the back of my leather chair in the sitting area. I tie off the sash and exit my room. Tiptoeing down the stairs, I stop on the second floor and take a peek in my mom's room. She's sound asleep like usual. The chemo takes so much out of her.

My fight with Titan allowed me to spend extra time with her today. I've been so wrapped up in him and spend too much time up at Kingdom. I'm needed here. I'm wanted here. Even if my relationship with my mother isn't perfect, at least I know she loves me. Titan was just that itch I wanted to scratch. I wish it would have been a letdown.

I go downstairs and enter the kitchen to grab a drink but hear a noise coming from down the hall. It sounded like glass breaking. "Hello?" I call out.

My mother has two nurses that change shift. One is always here and stays upstairs with her. Maybe Liv couldn't sleep tonight either. "Liv?"

No answer.

I make my way down the hall and see my father's office door ajar. "Hello?" I ask again, pushing it all the way open. "What the hell?" I say when I get a look inside.

His desk drawers are open. One lies on the floor. Papers scatter the room. A picture has been removed from the wall and shattered on the Persian rug, to reveal a safe that I didn't know was there. It's still closed.

I place my hand in the pocket of my robe. "Shit." I left my cell upstairs on the bed.

"Open it." I feel something shoved into the back of my head.

My heart begins to pound, and I throw my hands up in the air. I don't need to see it to know that it's a gun. "I … uh …"

"Open it!" a man shouts, shoving me forward with his hand on my back.

I trip over the rug and feel glass puncture my bare feet. "I don't know it." My voice shakes.

"Bullshit!" he says through gritted teeth. "Fucking open the safe or I will put a bullet in your head."

I'm trying to think of what my father would use for a combination. My mother's birthday. Maybe their wedding anniversary. But I quickly squash that idea. It turns out, they didn't like each other as much as they made me believe. "I don't know …"

He grabs a hold of my hair, and I cry out. He shoves my face into the wall beside the safe but holds me up with his tight grip.

"Please?" I beg as tears run down my face. I try to catch my breath and can taste the blood in my mouth.

"Last time," he growls in my ear. I feel his spit hit my neck, and I want to vomit. "Fucking open this safe or I will splatter your brains all over it for Daddy to find."

I blink. My heart stops, and my body goes rigid at his words. *This guy thinks he's alive.* "He's … dead," I manage to get out.

"Fucking open it!" He shakes my head, my scalp burning from how tightly he holds my hair.

I grit my teeth, place my hands on the wall, and try to get out of his hold. "He's fucking dead!" I shout, thrusting my elbow back and making contact with his ribs.

He lets out a grunt and slams my head into the safe. Once. Twice. Then he shoves me to the side. My body hits my father's desk before falling to the floor. I try to look up at the man in the room, but my busted face can't see anything. I feel his shoe to my ribs, though. I curl up into a ball for protection when he does it again. This time, it was my back.

"I'll get that money," he growls, out of breath. "I'll be back, and you better have the code."

He runs out of the room.

I grab the side of the desk and manage to get to my feet as I hear the front door open and slam close. On shaky legs, I make my way up the stairs.

"Emilee." Liv gasps as she exits my mother's room at the end of the hall on the second floor. "What the hell happened to you? Are you okay?"

I nod and wrap my arms around my stomach. "Fine," I hiss. "Check on my mother."

"She's okay. I was in there with her."

I make my way to the third floor and enter my room and grab my phone. I dial the only person who I can think of to help me right now.

TITAN

I BRING MY car to a stop. Bones and I exit and run up the stairs and into the York residence. "Where is she?" I ask the nurse who had opened the door for us.

"Office."

I take off running with Bones on my ass. We enter the room to find Luca pacing back and forth on his phone. Nite stands in the corner, and Haven sits on the couch next to a beat-up Emilee.

I make my way over to her and kneel. "Emilee?"

She looks up at me the best she can, which isn't much, considering her right eye is swollen, and her left eye has a cut across it.

She sighs. "Why are you here? Did Luca call you?"

"I did," Haven answers.

"I told you not to," she snaps, then winces.

"Will you give us a second?" I ask.

Haven nods and stands. "I'll be right outside the door." Bones and Luca follow her. Nite leaves as well and closes the door behind him.

"I'm fine," she says the moment we're alone.

"You're not." I run a hand through my hair. "Why didn't you call me?"

"Isn't it obvious? I didn't want you here," she states and gets to her feet. She starts to fall over, and I reach out to steady her. "I'm—"

"Do not say fine," I interrupt through gritted teeth.

She lets out a shaky breath, and I feel her body soften in my arms. I pull her to me, wrapping my arms around her shoulders, careful not to hurt her.

When Haven called me, she had said that Em had called Luca and woke them up in tears. All she knew was that there had been a break-in, and Emilee had been hurt. I didn't know what state I'd find her in.

She buries her head into my chest, and I feel her body shake before I hear her crying.

"You're okay now." I rub her back. "I'm here."

"He wanted money," she cries. "The safe. I didn't know it was there …" She sniffs. "I tried to tell him …"

"Shh." I rub her back. We can discuss this later. Right now, she needs a warm bed and pain pills. Crying isn't going to help the situation.

The door opens, and I look over to see Bones, Luca, and Nite enter. "I made a few phone calls and was informed that Nick York owes money," Luca announces.

"No." She pulls away from me. "That can't be true."

He places his phone in the pocket of his slacks. "I'm sorry, Emilee. He owes a million dollars."

I exchange a look with Bones. That's how much we loaned him, but he paid us back.

"No." She wraps her arms around herself. "The source has to be wrong."

"One million?" I question, and he nods. I walk over to him and lower my voice. "Are we sure this isn't George?"

"No. It's Nick," he confirms.

Bones crosses his arms over his chest and widens his stance. His eyes look over at Emilee for a brief second before coming back to us. "What if George was pretending to be Nick?" he offers.

Luca thinks about that for a second. "It's possible, but it's also easy to prove. All we need to do is get a description. But I'm just not sure how they can mix up the two. York and Wilton are very well-known in Vegas."

I nod. "Make a call and set us up a meeting for later on today." It's nearly five a.m. The sun will be rising soon. I need to move her and her mother. Then I'll worry about whose ass I'm going to kill for touching her.

"In the meantime, Nite can stay here—"

"No," I interrupt Luca. "The women aren't staying here. They're

TITAN

coming home with me."

"Do you need extra security?"

I go to say no, but Bones speaks. "We have it handled."

Luca nods. "I'll send you a text with an address and time once I have it."

"Thanks, man." I shake his hand.

"Don't mention it."

TWENTY-FOUR

EMILEE

For three days, I lived in a world of pain and fog. It came and went. I would wake up in agony, Titan would give me a pill, and then it'd fade away and so would my consciousness.

Today, I don't feel so bad. I can actually open my eyes, and my ribs don't hurt as much as before. Sitting up in the bed, I look down and see I still wear the bandage. I vaguely remember the doctor who takes care of the queens in this room, wrapping it up for me.

The door opens, and a woman enters. "GiGi." I give her a weak smile, excited to see a familiar face.

"Hello, dear." She comes to my side of the king-size bed and places a tray on the nightstand. "I'm here to give you your daily meds and some food."

"Oh, I don't think I need them anymore."

"Titan's orders."

I let out a long breath. "Where is he?" I know he brought me and my mother to his house. I didn't even try to argue. I may not believe that my father owes money, but I no longer felt safe at that house. If I'm being honest with myself, I haven't felt safe there ever since I found out that George was with my mother. It's one of the reasons I avoided going home at night and stayed at Kingdom so often.

"He's in his study with the Kings." She picks up two pills and holds them in front of my face.

I take them from her along with the glass of water. I swallow, and she places the water back on the nightstand. "Eat your toast and get some rest. I'll be back in a couple of hours to check on you."

The moment she closes the door, I spit the pills out into my hand. Getting up, I make my way to the master bathroom and use the restroom. Then I flush the evidence.

I look at myself in the large mirror. I do look much better. The bruises have turned a greenish color, but I can open my eyes. I have a few stitches here and there but nothing too major.

I enter his walk-in closet and find a white T-shirt along with a pair of sweatpants. They swallow me up, but it'll have to do.

Leaving the bedroom, I look over the balcony down into an open living room. I've never been in his house before. Crème walls, with dark brown trim that match the doors. Dark wood floors cover the hallway and staircase. It hugs the wall and takes a sharp left turn at the bottom, ending in the grand foyer. I turn left and step down into an open living room. The dining room is to the left. I see two sliding glass doors to the right that are open, showcasing the study. I can see Bones sitting in a chair from here. I make my way over to it.

"We could dig him up," Luca says as I enter.

"Why?" Bones asks. "It's too late for an autopsy."

"One should have been performed," Titan growls.

"There was no foul play," Bones argues.

"That's what she was told. And she just took George's word for it."

"I didn't know I had any reason to be suspicious," I add, making my presence known. "Plus, he was cremated. Even if we needed to, there's nothing we can do about it now."

"Em, you should be resting," Titan growls, standing from his chair.

"I think I have a right to know why I was attacked."

"Em ..."

"I'm not a child." Someone has been fed wrong information. They were after my father when he was not the intended target.

"You're right." Luca nods. "You're not. The Kings and I had a meeting two days ago. We found out that your father owes Nicholas Royce one million dollars."

There he goes again. "No ..."

"He had proof."

"I don't believe it." I swallow the knot that forms in my throat.

"It was a video. We saw your dad sitting in an underground poker tournament. He was there over twenty-four hours and ..." He pauses. "Well, you can connect the dots."

My knees give out, and I fall into a chair. "They killed him for it?" I whisper. That has to be the only explanation. Why they are concerned about an autopsy and foul play. He made a mistake, owed money, and his life was payment.

"That's the thing," Bones starts. "Nicholas didn't send anyone to collect payment. He gave your dad six weeks to come up with the money, and it had only been four."

"So ... who was the guy at the house?" I sniff, hanging my head. Ashamed that I continued to stand up for him when he had obviously done what he was being accused of.

"We don't know." Titan sighs and places his hand on my back. He begins to rub it, but I pull away. "Em ....?"

"He was looking for more than money," I say.

"He told you that?" Bones asks.

I shake my head. "He didn't have to. The picture on the wall covering the safe was already on the floor, but when I entered the room, the drawers to the desk were open as well. One on the floor."

"Maybe he thought the combination was there somewhere," Luca adds.

"Maybe," Titan agrees. "Let's go back and look around."

"I want to go." My head snaps up to look at him.

"I don't think—"

"Let her go," Bones interrupts Titan.

They exchange a look that is far from friendly. Something is up between them. And I'm that something.

TITAN

"SHE DOESN'T NEED to go back to that house." I close the glass doors to my study once she leaves to go change.

"I don't see why you want to hide what a piece of shit her father obviously was from her," Bones states.

I run a hand through my hair. "It has nothing to do with her father and more to do with the fact that the house is not safe."

He snorts. "She's the safest when she's with us. And we will all be there."

"He has a point."

"I didn't ask for your fucking opinion, Luca," I snap.

He throws his hands up in surrender. "I'm just speaking from experience. If you try to hide something from them, then they will go behind your back to get what they want." His hard eyes go soft. "And that is when things can get very bad, very fast."

TWENTY-FIVE

EMILEE

I RIDE WITH Bones and Titan back to my house, and Luca and Nite follow us. Titan had called Grave and Cross over to his house to stay with my mother and Liv while we were out. It made me think that there is more going on than they're telling me.

We pull up to the house and walk inside.

"How did he get in?" Titan asks. "There doesn't seem to be any forced entry."

"You guys didn't check the cameras?" I ask.

Bones answers. "No. The security system had been disabled."

I come to a stop. "George. He had to have done it."

"As far as we know, he's still out of the country," Titan argues.

"How far back did the footage go?" I ask.

"To that night," Bones answers.

I wrap my arms around myself. How had someone disabled the security system? How could they have known where to look? Or even what to do? I guess with the access to the internet now, it's not hard to find out anything.

"Come on." Titan takes my hand and pulls me into the office. It looks the same. Things thrown about. Glass broken. Computer monitors shattered.

"Did he have a weapon?" Bones asks me.

"Yeah, a gun," I whisper. "He held it to the back of my head ..."

I hear Luca enter the room, and I spin around to see him and Nite.

"He held it to the back of your head?" Titan snaps.

I nod. "Told me that if I didn't open the safe, he was going to blow my brains all over it for *Daddy to find*."

His eyes go from murderous to surprised. "He thinks your father is still alive?"

"I told him he was dead."

"And?" Bones demands.

"And he didn't seem to care about that. He was just indifferent. He wanted in that safe. He said he wanted the money."

Titan runs his hands through his hair.

"Well, then let's get in it and see how much is in there," Luca states.

The guys go to work looking around the office. I go over to the bookshelf that sits on the back wall and run my fingers over the spines. They're dusty. My father wasn't much of a reader, but I was. These books were for me, but I hadn't been home in two years. They had been untouched, left to rot on a shelf. It breaks my heart.

I come to the last one on the second shelf and pull it out. It was my favorite, *Pride and Prejudice* by Jane Austen. Opening it up, a piece of paper falls to the floor. I bend down and see numbers written on it, but I don't recognize them. They don't go with any birthdates or milestones that my father would consider important.

"I think I found something," I say, walking over to the safe on the wall. I punch in the code and then hear the lock click. The door kicks open just a tad.

I reach in and see stacks of papers. But no money. "What are these?" I ask, opening up the black folder.

I read over the papers before me, and my heart picks up. "No."

"What is it?" Titan asks, taking them from me.

TITAN

THE FIRST SET of papers are of Nick and Nancy's divorce. The second set is of Nancy's marriage certificate to George. Along with a will. One that leaves everything Nick owned to Nancy who then would give to George.

"Emilee?" Bones asks, walking over to her.

She falls down into a chair and places her face in her hands. "No. This can't be." She looks up at me. "They're not married. She would have told me."

I look at Bones, and he sighs. "Emilee …"

She jumps to her feet. "Did you both know this?"

Fuck! "Yes," I tell her.

"When did you find this out?"

"Weeks ago." Bones answers that one.

"What?" She gasps. "Why didn't you tell me this?"

"Because who your mom chooses to marry is none of our concern," I snap.

"How can you say that?" She sniffs, and tears fill her eyes. "This is why my father is dead!" she screams.

"You don't know that!" I argue.

"And you can't prove that it's not!" She throws the papers at Bones. He tosses them onto the desk. "George wanted his money. Then he blackmailed me for sex in order to pay for my mother's medical bills. And now there's proof that they were already married! Then a man shows up, demanding money from a safe he knew was here. A safe that I had no idea about. And you want to say that this had nothing to do with it?"

"Em …" Bones reaches out for her.

"No!" She takes a step back. "This all started because you wanted what George owes you." She crosses her arms over her chest. "Maybe you did this."

I step into her, fisting my hands down by my side. "You better be careful what you're accusing me of."

She gives a rough laugh. "What are you going to do, Titan? Hire a

TITAN

guy to break in and knock me around?"

"Emilee!" Bones snaps at her.

"Fuck you both!" She looks me up and down with her lip pulled back, but I see it quivering. "Oh, we've already done that." She tosses her arms out to her side, and her voice shakes as she announces, "I'm done." Her watery eyes go to Bones. "With both of you. Get out of this house before I call the police!" Then she storms out.

Silence fills the room after the door slams shut. I fall onto the couch and run a hand down my face.

"That was ... informative." Luca speaks first.

I place my hands behind my head and look up at them. "Let's wrap everything up."

"You really want to go?" Bones quirks a brow. "We own the cops. Her calling them to the house isn't going to slow us down."

No, it won't. I lean forward and lower my voice. "Let her think she's getting her way." I rise and walk over to Nite who stands like a statue in the corner. "I need a favor."

He nods.

TWENTY-SIX

EMILEE

AFTER I STORMED out of my father's office, I went back to Titan's and brought my mother along with her nurse back to my parents' house. I hate moving her so much, and I hate that we're back in the house, but it's better than the alternative. I can't be around Titan right now. Or Bones. They both lied to me.

It's been five days since the Kings walked out of my house, and they haven't returned. My wounds have completely healed, and I can show my face in public again without the girls questioning me. And the fact that Haven hasn't said one word about it lets me know that Luca hasn't told her about my fight with Bones and Titan. They think everything is as it was a week ago.

That's how I want it to be.

Haven and I are sitting down at the table as Jasmine comes strutting into Empire—the steakhouse on the twentieth floor of Kingdom. I want to do this as often as I can. Being around them made me realize how much I missed them and how lonely I was in Chicago. A part of me wishes we were all roommates now so I could spend the majority of my

TITAN

time with them.

She plops down in front of us and shoves her hair back off her face aggressively.

"What's wrong?" Haven asks her.

"God is testing my intelligence. And right now, I'm at the bottom of the scale."

I rub my finger over my lips to hide my smile at her obvious anger. "And how is he testing you?" I ask.

"Since when are you religious?" Haven speaks.

Jasmine grabs a fry off my plate and sticks it in her mouth. "Trenton messaged me this morning."

I roll my eyes.

"Not this again," Haven mumbles under her breath.

"It was a picture of his dick." Jasmine bites down on another fry. "And he was hard. And then I was wet."

I reach across the table and place my hand on top of hers to stop her from eating another. She stuffs her mouth when she's nervous. With anything. Food, cock, drinks. Whatever she can get her hands on. "Don't let him get to you. He's married," I remind her.

She shakes her head. "He filed for divorce."

Haven and I exchange a look.

"That was in the second pic he sent me."

"Jasmine …"

"I mean, I don't love the guy. Not anymore. But the sex was so good." She eats another fry. "How am I going to tell him no? Like I said, God is testing me." Another fry. This one drowning in ketchup. "My grades are dropping as fast as I am to my knees."

My eyes slide over to Nite who stands by the entrance. *He's still on Haven duty.* Probably will be until the day he dies. He just stands in the shadows, watching us all the time. It's kinda creepy, but I understand why Luca wants a protection detail on my best friend twenty-four seven. She's pretty important. "Why don't you get with Nite?" I offer.

She snorts.

"You guys have already had sex." Haven shrugs as if that's enough to start a relationship.

"We didn't have sex," she mumbles around a mouthful.

"But it was good," Haven goes on.

Jasmine begins laughing, and I look over at Haven. "She needs an intervention," I whisper. "She's losing it."

Her phone dings, and she picks it up. "Fuck," Jasmine growls. "He wants to come over tonight." Her fingers are running over the keys.

"You'll regret that in the morning," Haven informs her.

She looks up at us. "I'll sleep until noon. Problem solved."

"Jasmine …"

She holds her phone up to my face. "I told him no, okay?" She drops it to the table and buries her face in her hands. "Fuck, I have the worst taste in men."

"Maybe try celibacy again," Haven offers.

I burst out laughing but begin to cough to try to cover it up when her eyes narrow at mine. "Sorry." I slap my chest and whisper, "I didn't know that was a thing." *Jasmine not have sex?* That's like telling the sun it can't shine—impossible.

"This morning, I tried to make a shake after my run, but it turned into a shot of Fireball," Jasmine goes on, ignoring my comments.

"Since when do you run?" I ask, more and more confused about the girl sitting across from me. It's like I don't even know her.

"I'm making all kinds of mistakes today." She grabs my water and takes a drink.

Haven and I sit in silence as Jasmine finishes off my fries. She has her red hair pulled up in a half ponytail high on her head. She doesn't have any makeup on, and she wears a white sundress with spaghetti straps and no bra.

Her phone dings again, and she picks it up.

"Let me talk to him. I'll make him go away." Haven reaches for Jasmine's cell.

She pulls it out of reach. "It's not Trenton. It's Titan."

I sit up straighter, my heart instantly starting to pound at the sound of his name. "What does he want?" I clear my throat at my high-pitch voice, and Haven notices.

"I have a job." Her fingers type out some sort of response. "I gotta go. I'll call you bitches tomorrow." She jumps up and walks out just as fast as she entered, not even bothering to look at Nite when she storms past him.

"I'm really worried about her." Haven sighs.

I sit back in my seat, and my shoulders slump. I'm worried about her too, but Jasmine doesn't allow anyone to help her. "She'll be okay," I say even though we both know I'm lying.

TITAN

"THE PAPERS ARE legit," Luca says while we sit in Bones's office. He was finally able to get his hands on Nick's trust.

"But why would he leave everything to George when Nancy was still alive?" I wonder.

He shrugs. "He and Nancy were divorced. Maybe he hated her."

"But that is what makes this even more unbelievable. His business partner and friend married his ex-wife. That had to have pissed him off."

"Maybe he didn't know they were married," Luca offers.

"Maybe …" I rub my chin. "Any word on the guy who broke into the house?" I ask him.

He shakes his head. "No."

I look at Bones. He sits behind his desk with his arms folded over his chest. He hasn't spoken much in the last few days. "Let's put another detail back on the house." I killed one of the three from the last detail we had on George.

Bones looks at me. "You think he'll come back?"

"I think if Nick owed someone a million dollars, then it's possible he owes others."

"True." He picks up his phone and places it to his ear to call in a new detail.

Luca leans in and lowers his voice to not interrupt Bones's phone call. "How is Emilee doing? Haven said she hasn't said much about what happened."

"Haven't spoken to her."

His dark eyes widen.

"I'm not going to push her. She wants to be left alone, so I'll leave her be for now."

TWENTY-SEVEN

EMILEE

Entering my mom's room, I just stare at her. I haven't spoken to her either. I never told her I found the papers of her divorce and marriage.

I'm too pissed at her. Too hurt. A part of me blames her for this. If she hadn't left Dad, then maybe he wouldn't have gone and gambled everything away and put us in this position. Who knows what all she hasn't told me? At this point, I'm just waiting for the bank to show up and take the house from us. Closing her door, I head to my room and shower. Afterward I crawl into my bed. Snuggling into my pillow, I close my heavy eyes and pass out.

I wake to the sound of voices in the house. Sitting up, I look at my phone to see it's a little past six in the morning. My door flies open, and I pull the covers up to shield my chest from a guy I've never seen before. "Excuse me …"

"I'll talk to her." My mother's nurse, Liv, enters behind him.

"What the hell is going on?" I demand.

"I said I'll do it. Now get out." She points at the door, glaring at him, but tears cover her face and her dark eyes are bloodshot.

He spins on his heels and exits my room.

"What the hell is going on?" I ask her, reaching for my phone again.

"Emilee ..." She walks over to my side of the bed and sits down on the edge. "I went in to check on your mother this morning." She bows her head and sniffs. "I'm sorry ..."

I throw the covers off and storm out of my room. Running down the hall, I don't care that I'm wearing a silk tank top with no bra and a pair of matching shorts. I barge into her room and come to a halt. She's not in her bed. People stand by it. One guy has a clipboard. The other turns to face me. He was the one that was in my room a moment ago. His blue eyes look me up and down before he clears his throat. "Ms. York ..."

"Where is my mother?" I demand, taking a step toward the bed.

"Ma'am ..."

"Where in the fuck is my mother?" I shout, fisting my hands.

He lets out a long sigh. "The coroner came and removed her body fifteen minutes ago."

My heart stops. I take a step back at the blow of his words as if they were his fist to my face. Coroner? She's dead? Fifteen minutes ago? Why didn't they wake me? Why didn't I get to say goodbye?

"I have some questions ..."

"Get out," I whisper, tears stinging my eyes.

"Ms. York ..."

"Get the fuck out!" I scream at the top of my lungs.

He just stands there and makes no move to leave. Instead, he pulls his cell out of his pocket and dials a number, turning his back to me.

I can't breathe. My chest is tight, and blood rushes in my ears. I grab my chest and lean up against the wall.

She's dead?

We had more time. I was supposed to get six months. I just buried my father. Now I have to bury my mother. I have no one left. Now it's just me. That thought is crippling.

I had been ignoring her. I had blamed her for everything. But was it really her fault? How much had my father done to her that I didn't know? I feel like he had this other life that he kept from me. Did she feel the same? Now I'll never know.

TITAN

I PULL UP to the York residence and get out of my car. Running up the stairs, I enter without even knocking. It was unlocked.

I rush up the stairs and into the bedroom. I see Emilee sitting on the floor. Her back against the wall, her knees pulled to her chest, and her head down.

I kneel before her. "Em?" I reach out, running my hand through her tangled hair.

She brushes me off.

"Emilee? Look at me." I touch her arm.

She slaps it away with the other. "Go away," she mumbles.

"Emilee …"

Her head snaps up, and her eyes are narrowed on mine. "I said go the fuck away, Titan!" she shouts. "Why the fuck are you even here?" she demands. "Why does everyone call you?" Her voice cracks, and she bows her head.

My heart breaks for her and what she's going through. Both parents in a matter of weeks would be rough on anyone. "I'm here for you."

"I don't need you." Her eyes search the room, but it's just us. "I don't need anyone." She shoves me away and rises to her shaky legs. "I want to be alone."

"I can't do that." I shake my head.

"It's not your decision." Her fisted hands start punching my chest.

I grab her wrists and yank her to me. I wrap my arms around her and hold her shaking body against mine. She buries her head into my chest. "Shh." I run my hand down her back. "It's going to be okay," I lie. "I'm here for you." That's not a lie, but it's also not what she wants to hear right now.

She'll run. I know her well enough to know that she will take off. That's just what she does. What she knows.

She can try to hide all she wants, but I'll find her. No matter where she goes. A King always finds his queen.

I sit next to her at the funeral. Her mother passed three days ago, and she hasn't said anything to me. I don't think she's spoken to anyone. This is the Emilee York I know—completely closed off.

I get up and button my suit jacket and walk to the back of the church, giving her a chance to say goodbye to her mother alone.

"Have you heard anything about George?" Bones asks me the moment I walk through the double doors to stand in the entryway of the funeral home.

I shake my head. "No. You?"

"Same. It's as if he's fallen off the face of the earth."

"Well, he couldn't have gone that far," I whisper, turning to face the glass. I see she's still in the same place I left her, but now Jasmine sits on her right and Haven to her left. "Wherever he is, he'll come back. Especially now that Nancy has passed." He'll want to collect on that trust we found. Legally, he was her husband and is now entitled to everything.

"Do you think this was accidental?" Bones asks.

"She was terminally ill. I think it was just a matter of time." *Very bad timing.* He runs a hand down his face. I turn to look him in the eye. "You think it was intentional?"

"I don't know. It just looks ..." He trails off.

"Suspicious," I finish.

He nods once. "How do we know George wasn't here that night?"

"The detail didn't see anything," I remind him.

"Why wasn't an autopsy done?" he asks.

"Emilee didn't want one." She hasn't spoken to me directly, but she's spent most of her time on the phone making arrangements. She wanted her mother buried as quickly as possible.

"Didn't she learn her lesson with her father?" he growls.

"Titan? Bones?"

We both spin around to see a man standing before us.

"Yes?" I acknowledge him.

"I've been calling Emilee for the past few days now with no answer or return phone calls. Will you have her contact me, please?" He reaches his right hand out, and there's a card in it. Bones takes it.

"Regarding …?" I question.

"I'm Yan. Her mother's attorney. I need to meet with her regarding her will."

Bones and I exchange a look. "Will do."

TWENTY-EIGHT

EMILEE

"Mr. Yan?" I say, walking over to Titan and Bones. I didn't say goodbye. I refuse for it to end this way with me hating her and so many questions unanswered. I was so mad, but now it all seems for nothing. But I can't let it go that she kept secrets from me. I'm an adult, not a child. Why wouldn't she just tell me?

"Ms. York. I was just informing the Kings that I've been calling you."

I say nothing because I've been avoiding him.

"We need to set up a meeting."

"I'm busy," I state.

He nods once. "Yes, but this is important."

"More important than burying my mother?" I arch a brow.

His eyes soften, and he licks his lips nervously. "It's about your mother's will ..."

I hold my hand up to stop him. "I already know she was married to George. And I'm aware of the will. There is nothing for us to discuss."

With that, I walk past them and out of the church. I make my way down the stairs and to the waiting black sedan by the curb.

TITAN

"Em? Em, wait!" I hear Titan behind me.

I ignore him and open the door, but he catches up to me, grabs the door, and shuts it. "Hey …" I spin around to face him.

"How long are we going to do this?" he asks.

I hate how good he looks dressed in his all-black suit. His hair slicked back and sadness in his eyes. How much I miss him. And how there is a hole the size of Texas in my chest. I've never felt more alone. I've never needed someone to hold me before, but I'd give anything for him to. But a part of me just won't let that happen. Now that both of my parents are dead, there's nothing left keeping me here in Vegas. My apartment hasn't sold in Chicago, so I need to go back there. That has been my home. That's where I belong now. "I don't know what you're talking about."

"You. Me. Don't leave like this. Right now. Talk to me."

I remove the sunglasses from the top of my head and place them over my eyes. I don't want him to see me crying. "Don't worry, Titan. I know I'm nothing special." I slap his chest twice, and then yank open the door before falling into the car.

The first tear rolls down my cheek as we drive away, and I hear him calling out my name. I plan on going home and being alone for a few weeks. I've never needed anyone before, and I sure as hell don't need him now.

TITAN

"You have to give her time, Titan," Bones says from behind me. "First, her dad and now, her mom." He sighs. "It's a lot."

"Yeah." I nod in agreement. "I guess not everyone hates their parents like we did."

I was never close with my mom or my dad. My mother was a drunk who loved her addiction more than she could ever love me. My father was married to Kingdom. He lived for it. He also died for it. My mother drank herself into a coma, and my father was killed in his house. The killer was never identified, but I think it was someone in his inner circle. There was no sign of a break-in or a struggle. They found him dead on his living room floor with a single gunshot wound to the head. Whoever did it took pity on him.

The only thing he left me was Kingdom. Twenty-five percent of a multibillion-dollar business.

I didn't want it, but that didn't matter. I was an only child, and I was to carry on the legacy. Just like the rest of the Dark Kings.

Bones, Grave, Cross, and I had our future planned for us before we were even born.

"This is who you are," my father once said. "You were born a king, and you will die a king." It was utter bullshit. But I stepped up and took over his position. As did the others. Mr. Reed is the only remaining original Three Wisemen alive. But he retired years ago, signing over his shares to his sons, Grave and Bones.

"I only hate one of my parents," Bones mumbles.

We don't speak of his mother. She was a saint in a world full of devils. But there's a saying—the good die young.

"Titan?"

I let out a growl at the sound of my name.

"What?" I snap.

"Please give these to Miss York." Mr. Yan holds out a set of papers. "I have tried to reach George, but he's not returning my calls."

"Yeah, well, get in line," Bones growls.

Mr. Yan frowns, shoving his glasses up his pudgy nose. "You're looking for him as well?"

We don't answer.

He runs a hand through his jet-black hair. "I tried to explain to George that Mr. York did not have a will."

Bones and I exchange a look. "What do you mean?" I ask.

"Well, Nick hadn't come to me to set up his arrangements. But George was persistent that Nick had, in fact, a trust. He had seen it."

"So how did you get it?" Bones asks.

"George found it. In the safe at the York residence."

I yank the papers from his hand and shove him away from us. "Hey …"

We ignore him. "So the trust that George presented to Emilee was a fake?" I say.

"Obviously, but it still doesn't make any sense. Why he would use a fake when he was technically already married to Nancy?" Bones adds.

"But ... we spoke to Luca. He said that the trust was legit. So maybe George knew about them, but Yan didn't?" I offer.

"Fuck," Bones hisses.

"He wanted Emilee, but why?" I go on. "Why force her and not just try to seduce her?"

He shrugs. "Maybe he knew she'd see through his bullshit? Or maybe he didn't want to wait the amount of time that would take. In that time, Em could find out that he was married to Nancy. And poof, his plan would be exposed."

I bow my head and run my hand down my face. I have a fucking headache. "We need to find him. We need answers."

TWENTY-NINE

EMILEE

I SIT AT my father's desk. Leaning back in the chair, I have my Jimmy Choo ombre Tartini Swarovski Crystal heels up on the surface. They're my favorite. My mother gave them to me for my birthday a couple of years back. I felt they were fitting to wear to her funeral today. Their divorce papers and my mother's marriage license to George in my hands.

They were fucking married! I can't comprehend it. I can't figure out what I missed. I never saw them flirt or even speak. George was over a lot—in this very room—but my mother never ventured in here. This was my father's space. We spent holidays, birthdays, and vacations with him when I was growing up.

She never smiled at George. Never even looked his way. So why marry him? When did they fall in love? And why the urgency to move so fast? Maybe because of her diagnosis?

I'll never get those answers. Not now. She's dead. George is gone. The house is hauntingly silent. It mocks me. Memories I had inside of these walls were nothing but lies. But it makes me think … Did my father have someone? Was he seeing someone behind my mother's back too? Maybe he was married to someone else. I had gone online and checked. Nevada has public records, but I couldn't find anything regarding his remarrying. But that doesn't mean he didn't go to another state to do it.

I throw the papers onto the desk and grab the fifty-year-old scotch my father kept in his office. He would only drink from it on special occasions. Removing the glass top, I pour it into a tumbler and throw it back. Opening my mouth, I suck in a breath, my mouth burning from the alcohol. Seconds later, I take another.

"Emilee?" I hear Haven call out my name.

I don't respond. Instead, I take another one and remind myself it'll all be over soon. I bought a ticket back to Chicago. I leave at three p.m. tomorrow. And all this shit will be behind me.

It all started with one person—George Wilton. A sorry son of a bitch. A fucking coward. He won't come after me. I have nothing to give him. He ended up with everything. He won.

"Emilee, I've been looking for you," Haven announces as she enters the room.

I look over at her. She has her dark hair up in a tight twist. She wears a black dress that falls to her knees and black Jimmy Choos as well. It's the dress she wore to my mother's funeral earlier. Her amber eyes soften as she exhales and sits across from the desk.

"Why don't you come home with me?" she continues. "Spend a few nights at my house? It'll be like old times."

My eyes drop to her wedding ring. "Nothing will ever be like it was," I find myself saying.

She sighs. "Luca works a lot. All hours of the night. We can have a girls' night. I'll call up Jasmine, and we can—"

"No thanks," I interrupt her, standing.

She stands as well. "You can't do this to yourself."

"Do what?"

"Close yourself off. It's okay to need your friends, Em. I'm here for you. And so is Jasmine. And the Kings ..."

I throw my head back, laughing. "Fuck the Kings." They didn't want to help me in the beginning, not like I wanted. Maybe if they had, my mother would still be alive. Maybe I'd have those three extra months the doctors promised me.

"Emilee, please let me help you," she begs, and her phone starts to ring in her Hermes clutch. Cursing, she digs through it and sighs when she looks down at the number. "Hello?" She turns her back to me. "I'm at Emilee's," she whispers. "I'll be home soon." She hangs up and turns back to face me. She opens her mouth to speak, but I continue.

"Go home to your husband, Haven. I don't need you here." Her face falls, and I look around the study aimlessly. "I see you're here without your security detail. I wouldn't want you to get in trouble."

She lets out a huff, and she lifts her chin. "Now you're just being a bitch."

"Well, it's not hard to do." I lift the bottle and take a drink of it.

"You're just trying to push me away, Emilee. I won't …"

"Fucking leave!" I yell. "Jesus! Why can't you all understand that I want to be left the fuck alone?"

She licks her bottom lip, and I see tears build in her eyes. Without saying another word, she walks out of the study, leaving me alone.

God, Titan was right. I'm a bitch. Grabbing the bottle, I throw it across the room. The glass shatters, and the scotch covers the wall, floor, and bookshelf. I fall into the chair and look at the papers one last time.

I want them gone. I'm leaving all this shit behind me tomorrow, but that doesn't mean I have to leave it how I found it.

TITAN

MY PHONE RINGING has me waking up in the middle of the night. I blink, trying to adjust my eyes to the screen. "Hello?" I ask roughly and clear my throat.

"Titan. We have a problem."

"What is it?" I sit, rubbing a hand down my face.

"It's Emilee."

"Is she okay?" I ask, jumping out of bed, now fully awake and picking up a pair of jeans off my floor.

"She's fine." He sighs. "But you need to come get her. And get in

TITAN

touch with Dr. Lane." They hang up.

I CAN SEE the lights flashing from a mile away. The closer I get, the faster my heart beats. Cop cars line the street, along with fire trucks and ambulances. Flames roar into the dark night.

Pulling into the driveway, I slam it in park and yank on the emergency brake.

"Em?" I shout, running over to the back of the ambulance where she sits on a gurney. A black blanket is wrapped around her shoulders, and she has a mask over her mouth and nose.

What the fuck?

I go to jump up into the ambulance, but a hand grabs my upper arm, holding me up. "I need to speak to you for a second," Jeffrey informs me. Nite stands beside him.

I look up at her and see the medics are still checking her out. Nodding, I turn and follow them both off to the side, out of earshot. "What in the fuck happened?" I ask Jeffrey. I know Nite isn't going to answer me.

"I received a text from Nite. He informed me that my assistance was needed," he begins. "He had removed her from the house, but he couldn't put out the fire."

"Jesus ..."

"I guess when he found her, she was refusing to leave, but he didn't give her a choice. He picked her up and carried her out."

"Fuck!" I look at Nite. "Thank you." I knew placing him as her detail was a good idea. Bones put two guys on the house, but I used him for her personally. Nite is the only guy I trust with this. We wanted to keep this as quiet as possible. The break-in. Her mother's death. We don't want it public knowledge.

Jeffrey steps closer to me and lowers his voice to a whisper, "I need to know what you want me to do here."

My brows pull together at his words before I understand. He thinks the fire was intentional. And if so, she was the one who started it.

This is what she asked Bones and me to do, right? Start a fire and let

George burn to death. Was George here?

I have to protect her. No matter what. "It was an accident," I say.

He nods once. "I'll be in touch."

He goes to walk away, but I ask, "Was there anyone else in the house?"

Nite is the one who answers by shaking his head.

I run a hand through my hair and walk back over to the ambulance. She still sits in the same position. She has ash on her face and black marks on her arms and legs that the blanket isn't covering. "I'm taking her home," I state to the paramedics.

"Sir?"

"I'm taking her home," I repeat with a growl.

"She needs medical attention," the female says to me.

"And she will get it." Dr. Lane is meeting me back at Kingdom. I called him the moment I got off the phone with Jeffrey.

"You want her to sign a waiver stating that she understands she is refusing medical attention?" she asks, verifying.

Emilee shrugs off the blanket and holds out her hand, silently complying to my demands.

Shaking her head in disbelief, the paramedic hands Em a clipboard that she signs and then starts to exit the ambulance. I hold out my hand, and she takes it. I help her over to my car and into the passenger seat.

By the time I'm over in the driver's seat, she has her head back, eyes closed, and is softly snoring.

Thirty

TITAN

"It was arson," Jeffrey states as we stand in the living room of our Royal Suite at Kingdom. He reaches down and picks up his shirt and jeans to start getting dressed. You can never be too careful about who might be wearing a wire. He knows the drill after working with us for so long.

Everyone is here. Bones, Grave, Cross, Luca, and Haven. I guess Nite had messaged Luca. Then Haven called Jasmine. It's one big party. Emilee has been passed out in my bed for the past eight hours. Dr. Lane is here waiting to check on her. He took her vitals while she slept, but he wants to examine her closely for the next twenty-four hours, so Grave has given up his room for him to crash in while we wait for her to wake.

Bones lets out a growl. "What the fuck was she thinking?"

"She's been through a lot," Haven snaps at him. Luca places his hands on his wife's shoulders to calm her down.

Everyone is on edge.

"Is that what your report says?" Cross asks, sitting on the couch.

He turns to look at him. "No."

"Thanks." I reach out to shake his hand. It'll cost me a great deal of money. His help always comes with a price. But it's always been one I'm willing to pay.

"Why did you lie?"

We all turn to see Emilee stepping into the living room. She looks like a victim from a bombing. She's still covered in ash and has black marks all over her skin. Her once perfect makeup is smeared under her eyes.

"Em …?"

"Why did you lie?" she asks, staring at the marshal.

"Why did you start the fire?" Bones asks her.

EMILEE

I DRAG MY eyes to look at Bones when I answer him. "It all needed to burn."

"Jesus," Titan hisses.

Bones steps into me. His eyes narrowing at mine. "Have you lost your goddamn mind?" he snaps.

Jasmine places her hands on his chest and pushes him back. "Let me talk to her." She doesn't allow anyone to protest. She grabs my arm and yanks me back into Titan's bedroom, then closes the door behind us. "Are you out of your goddamn mind?" she hisses, repeating his words.

I don't answer.

"They're going to lock you up in a psych ward," she snaps.

I fall on the end of the bed. "Let them." I could use some time alone. Maybe then I'll get some peace and quiet.

"Emilee, you're talking crazy." She falls to her knees before me.

"Nothing matters anymore."

"Don't do this." She shakes her head, her red hair bouncing around her face. "Don't go insane on me. You're stronger than this."

"Am I?"

"Yes," she barks, jumping to her feet. Reaching down, she grabs my shoulder and yanks me up as well. "You need to get a grip, Emilee! This is your life you're putting in jeopardy. For what? A mom and dad who got divorced?"

"You don't know what it's like!" I shove her off me. It's more than that, isn't it? The lies? The betrayal? I fucked my dad's business partner to save my mother. And he was married to her. I became a fucking escort. I fucked Titan and Bones at the same time. Nothing I have done is sane.

"What? To come from a broken home?" She laughs at that.

"No. To have no one."

Her face hardens, and her green eyes narrow. "I do. I know it more than you do. But there is a difference between you and me. I didn't get the chance to run away from it." And with that, she turns and exits the room, slamming the door behind her.

It opens back up immediately, and Titan enters. "Please go away," I whisper, my voice breaking. "I want to be alone."

"Last time you were alone, you set your house on fire."

"Why is it Cross can do it, but when I do, it's a fucking tragedy?" I say through gritted teeth,

He frowns. "Emilee …"

"Please, just stop, Titan." My shoulders begin to shake with anger. "I'm begging you. Just stop."

"I just want to help you."

I take in a shaky breath. "I don't want you." It's one of the biggest lies I've ever told, but it needed to be said. I've fallen for him, and it was the stupidest thing I could have ever done.

He walks over to a bag on the floor and unzips it. Nite had grabbed it off my floor when he dragged me out of the burning house. He pulls out my boarding pass that I had printed off before I set the fire. "What in the fuck is this?"

"I'm going home," I state.

"This is your home." He points at the floor.

I almost laugh. "What is? Kingdom? Vegas?" I shake my head. "I haven't been here for years."

Walking over to me, he glares down at me. "Let me make myself very clear, Emilee. You are not fucking leaving tomorrow. Or the next day, do you understand me?"

"You can't make me stay." I say and my chest tightens. I feel so lost. Confused. Utterly alone even though he's standing right in front of me.

His jaw tics and his hands fist, wrinkling my ticket. I think he's going to yell at me. But instead he turns his back to me and heads to the bedroom door. He turns the knob but pauses. He turns to face me. And then he's charging me. Before I can move, his hands are in my hair. His lips on mine. And he kisses me. With passion. With fury. It's a mixture of love and hate. His tongue enters my mouth, and he takes my breath away.

When he pulls away, I'm gasping for breath. Opening my heavy eyes, I look up at him. "Titan ..."

"I let you walk away from me once, Em. I won't make that mistake again." Tears sting my eyes at his words. "Did you hear me? I won't let you leave. Not me. Not this time." He runs his thumb over my swollen lips. "Stay here with me. Let me fix it. I promise, I'll get to the bottom of all of it." The first tear runs down my cheek. "Let me take care of you. Let me love you."

THIRTY-ONE

TITAN

I HOLD MY breath as I wait for her to respond to me. I owe Nite fucking everything. He saved her life. I should have been there for her. That's what makes me the maddest. I should have followed her to her house when she left the funeral, but I didn't. I always allowed my pride to get the best of me, but in the end, it's going to cost me everything.

She licks her lips and nods her head once. "I need to go back to Chicago. But I won't stay there."

"Why?"

"Because I still have things there. I haven't been able to return since I got the call about my father. And I just destroyed everything I had here." She gestures to the black dress she's still wearing from the funeral earlier. "I need things …"

"We have *things* here."

"Titan." She stomps her foot.

"I said let me take care of you."

"I don't need—"

"I want to," I interrupt her, cupping her cheek. "Please?" I beg. "Let me show you what you deserve." There's nothing in this world that I can't give her. She just needs to let me.

EMILEE

TITAN HAS KEPT his word. Within two days, all my stuff from my Chicago apartment was delivered to Vegas. We moved it into this house. Most of my parents' house was destroyed. I lost clothes, shoes, essential everyday needs.

I couldn't care less.

I'd been gone for two years and hadn't needed it before, why would I need it now?

Titan spent twenty-four hours straight with me. Which I think was the longest he had taken off work in a while. He had to go back today.

I've been walking through Kingdom for the past two hours, pretending to play machines here and there to get free drinks. I tip the waitresses, and they keep them coming.

Haven has called me three times. I've ignored them all. Embarrassed how I spoke to her that night after the funeral when she reached out to me.

Jasmine hasn't tried reaching out to me once. I feel bad for what I said to her as well. Because out of the three of us, she was the one who came from the most fucked-up family life. Jasmine isn't one to tell her problems, but Haven and I knew they were there. I guess we were just never good enough friends to ask.

I pull my cell out of my pocket and dial her number. She answers on the fourth ring.

"Hello?" She doesn't sound very happy to hear from me.

"Hey," I sit down at a slot machine. It looks like a giant fishbowl. It's called Deal of the Day.

"What do you want, Em?" she asks, letting out an annoyed breath.

"I just …" My eyes drop to the black and gold carpet. "I just wanted to say I'm sorry for what I said to you. For hurting you."

She sighs.

"I know you were just trying to help me." She stays silent. "You of all people should know what that feels like."

Jasmine is by far the most independent out of the three of us, but that's because she's had to be that way.

"Are you gambling?" she asks, changing the subject.

"No." I take a sip of my rum and Coke. "I'm walking around the casino getting free drinks."

"Are you drunk?"

"Maybe a little." I lick my numbing lips.

She chuckles. "Come up to The Palace."

"You're working?"

"Yeah. But I'm done. The guy rented the place for the night and only took twenty minutes." Her laughter grows. "He's in the bathroom getting dressed about to leave. Come up here and we'll raid the minibar together. It'll be like high school all over again."

"I don't know. Nigel won't let me up there. And I'm not doing a job." The room is for paying clients only. And when I mean clients, I mean those who hire a Queen. The casino does not promote the room at all. To all these gamblers that are here on vacation, it does not exist.

She snorts. "I'll send him a text."

"You have his cell number?" Another sip.

"Of course. We're tight like that. Give me ten minutes and head this way." *Click.*

***

"THERE SHE IS." Jasmine gives me a big smile when I enter The Palace. "Told you Nigel would see you up."

"He didn't even question me."

I look around the room. It looks the same from the last time I was up here with Titan. The purple lights give off a glow. The black walls help keep it pretty darkly lit. "Didn't take your client long, huh?" I ask her.

She chuckles, walking over to the bar in the corner. "We didn't have sex."

"What else would you do up in this room?"

"He had me dress as a Dominatrix and spank him." She shrugs. "He has mommy issues."

"This entire room is full of issues."

She throws her arms out wide and spins around in a circle, while saying, "Every queen needs a palace." She quotes the saying on the door.

I laugh and take the drink she made for me and lie down on the floor. The rug in this room is incredibly soft. I guess when everything is meant to cause pain, they decided to make the floor comfortable. She lies down beside me.

"Haven called me."

"What did she want?" I ask.

"She's worried about you. She wanted me to talk to you."

"I'm fine."

"I'm worried about you too, Em. But I was giving you time. I do know what that's like." She sighs.

"How are you doing?" I ask. Everything has been so crazy lately I haven't even thought about asking how she is doing.

"Great," she lies. A softness falls over the room and I sit up to take a drink of my rum and Coke. "Haven was right."

"About what?"

"I have an addictive personality."

I shake my head. "She was just …"

"Correct. I know it. You know it. Everyone knows it." She stands. "Do you think I'm a whore?"

I jump to my feet. "Jasmine, no …"

"You don't have to lie. We've always been honest with one another."

I grab her hand. "I wish I was more like you."

She snorts.

"You're gorgeous." She rolls her eyes. "Sexy and confident. You enter a room, and everyone stops what they're doing to look at you. You're not a whore. Not even close. You know what you want, and you go for it."

"Says the girl in a sex dungeon." She laughs.

I do too. "You didn't sleep with him. And even if you did, so what?" I tuck my hair behind my ear. "Like I said, I wish I was more like you. I was always shy. I had only ever slept with Bones until I moved to Chicago. Even there, I only slept with one guy. Now Titan makes three."

"How is that going?" she asks.

"Good. For now."

She smiles over at me. "He's good for you."

Doesn't mean I'm good for him. I've been thinking about it ever since he begged me to stay. I have nothing to offer him. He owns a Kingdom. I'm homeless, broke, and my current job is being an escort.

"Enough of this. We're going to do shots now." She goes back over to the minibar. "Pick your poison. I have Jim, Jack, and Garth."

"Garth?"

She holds up her phone. "Garth Brooks."

"How about all three?" I offer.

"That's my girl." She punches some keys on her phone, and then "Friends in Low Places," fills the room from her speaker.

THIRTY-TWO

TITAN

I CHECK MY phone for the third time in five minutes. I've become a fucking chick waiting for a call from Em. I'm worried about her. I was able to talk her into staying here, but she's on edge, and George is still MIA. We have no leads at the moment. I shove my phone into my back pocket. "Any word on the guy who broke into her parents' house?" I ask Bones as we walk up the back stairs to Kingdom.

"No. Luca has put the word out and is waiting for info. He'll call the moment he has it."

We walk into the back door of Kingdom and see Nigel standing behind his desk. He is to the Kings like Alfred was to Batman—irreplaceable.

"Hello, Bones. Titan." He nods in greeting.

"Good evening, Nigel," I say, coming to stand in front of the single elevator. I place my card in front of it, and the door slides open.

"Oh, sir. I just wanted to let you know that Emilee has joined Jasmine up in The Palace," he says as the door slides shut.

I look over at Bones, and he shrugs. It's the first he's hearing about this as well. Queens are allowed to join other Queens when doing a job, but it has to be approved through me, and they will both be granted access for their date and each paid accordingly. But I have not done so for tonight.

I place my card to the keypad and press the sixteenth floor. *Looks like we're making a stop.*

We exit the elevator and come up to The Palace door. I punch in the code and enter the room with Bones behind me. We hear their laughter immediately. And I hate how much I missed hearing Emilee's. She hasn't laughed since her mother passed.

We come to the open room and see them lying on the floor. Emilee is on her stomach, her feet kicking her ass while propped up on her elbows. Jasmine lies on her back, staring up at the ceiling. "Porn Star Dancing" by My Darkest Days blasts from a cell phone on the floor lying next to Emilee. Bones and I both do a quick sweep of the room for the client but don't see him. He must have had his service and was done for the night. The thought of Emilee joining them has my teeth grinding. The only person I will share her with is standing beside me at the moment.

"God, remember that time we slashed Trenton's tires and busted out his windows?" Jasmine laughs.

"Of course. You made me take a shot before we went."

"No. No. No." She rolls over onto her stomach as well. "I forced the first one down your throat, but you willingly swallowed the second and third." They both giggle. "Man, he was so mad." Jasmine goes on. "He heard us and ran outside with a bat."

"Yeah, and you held your arms out wide and said *swing, motherfucker*. I'm pretty sure he shit his pants when he saw it was you destroying his precious car." Emilee gets to her feet, and I don't miss how she stumbles. *She's drunk.* And to further prove me right, she walks over to the bar.

EMILEE

"He was pissed." I laugh, adding some vodka to my empty cup.

"Yeah, he was. But the sex we had afterward was off the charts," she adds.

I turn to walk back over to my spot on the floor but come to a halt when I see Titan and Bones standing before me. Side by side, they have their arms crossed over their chests and legs wide. *How long have they been here?*

"Trenton didn't have the biggest dick, but he knew how to use it," Jasmine goes on. "He sucked at oral, though. Fuck, why did I ever like him?"

My eyes go back and forth between Bones and Titan. They both stare at me, giving nothing away. But if I had to guess, I'd say they're pissed we're in here.

"You know that fucker still blames me for getting him kicked off the football team?" she asks, looking up at me from her stomach on the floor. "Like I made him snort cocaine. Em?" she asks when I just stand there. She looks over her shoulder and gets to her feet when she spots the Kings.

Letting out a soft chuckle, she reaches over, grabs my full drink, and smiles. "Now it's a party." She tips my cup back and takes a drink. "Who's gonna strip first?" she asks them.

Bones slides his blue eyes to hers. "Show us what you got." He arches a brow, daring her.

My eyes widen and go to Titan's. I expect him to put a stop to this, but he just stands there. He's pissed. I know it. I've avoided talking to him about what I did for the last three days. I didn't ask him to save me. I stand by what I did. That house was nothing to me. My only regret is that George wasn't here to go up in flames with it.

But I also haven't brought up the fact that he asked me to let him love me. Was that the same as telling me that he loves me? Or that he could if I let him in? I should have told him then how I felt. But I didn't, and now the time has passed.

"I don't think …" I swallow nervously, trying to focus. On top of being surprised by their presence, I'm also drunk as fuck.

Jasmine steps forward, grips the hem of her shirt, and pulls it up over her head before tossing it to the floor. She wasn't wearing a bra. Her paid for tits are on full display. Bones clears his throat, clearly affected by her brazenness. His eyes on her chest. Her hands on her jeans. She has her shoes kicked off and pants undone in a matter of seconds.

Bones drops his arms down to his side as she steps up to him completely naked. She stands up on her tiptoes to kiss him. He slides his hands into her red hair, but the last second, she pulls away, letting out a laugh.

She faces me. My eyes widen as she walks to me. I don't dare look at the Kings. I keep my eyes on her green ones, silently asking what in the hell is she doing? But I don't get to ask out loud. She grabs my arm and pulls me into her. Cupping my face, she presses her lips to mine.

My eyes fall close at her soft lips against mine. With one hand on my face and the other on the small of my back, I open for her. We've kissed before. We once acted like we were lesbian lovers so a group of guys would leave us alone. It worked then, but I have a feeling it's going to have the opposite affect now.

I lift my hands to tangle in her short hair and tilt her head to the side to deepen the kiss. She tastes like vodka and champagne. Her tongue enters my mouth, and I moan. My legs tighten, and my pussy throbs. I didn't realize how horny I was until just now. I don't even know how many days it's been. I'd been too focused on fighting with Titan to think about sex. But now? Now I want it.

I pull away from her lips and remove my shirt. She unbuttons my jeans. I kick them off to the side. Her hands go to my waist, and she pushes me backward. My ass hits the table that Titan had strapped me to last time I was in here.

I pant as I watch her fall to her knees, pulling my underwear with her. She kisses a soft trail down over my stomach and to my thigh. "Oh, God." I throw my head back and close my eyes. My body is on fire. My nipples hard. I'm so fucking wet and very aware that we have an audience, but that has never stopped me before.

THIRTY-THREE

TITAN

I'VE WATCHED GIRLS make out before. I've watched them go down on one another before. I used to have two or three girls in my bed at once. They liked playing with one another, but I've never seen anything sexier than this. My cock is hard in my slacks. And the way Bones is watching them, his is too.

The room is full of Emilee's heavy breathing while Jasmine is on her knees before her.

Neither one of us stops them. Hell, my only thought is to join in. But I stay where I'm at. I'm not sure if they're putting on a show for us or doing it for themselves. At this point, I don't care.

Emilee's breathing picks up, and then she's crying out into the dark room. I want her to do it again, but this time because of me.

Jasmine stands to her feet, and Em sags against the table. Jasmine walks over to us and stops before Bones. She licks her wet lips. "Now kiss me."

She doesn't have to tell him twice. He grips her hair in his hands, yanks her head back, and places his lips on hers. Her arms go around his neck, and he lets go of her hair, grips her thighs, and lifts her off the floor. She wraps her legs around his waist just as he slams her back into a wall.

I go over to Emilee who still sags against the table. For once in my life, I'm not sure what to do. I know what I want, but she's been mad at me. "Em ..."

"Shut up, Titan." She grabs my shirt and pulls me toward her. "And fuck me."

I don't waste a minute either. I'm hard. She's got cum running down her inner thighs. And I want to hear her scream my name.

I shrug off my shirt while she undoes my pants. She pulls out my cock, and I clench my teeth as she begins to stroke it. I shove her hand away, grab it myself, and push inside her, not worrying about foreplay. We can come back to that later.

EMILEE

I FEEL LIKE I'm back in college. That night that Haven and Luca watched Bones and me fuck in the game room. Then I watched Luca fuck Haven on the floor. But it's a different scene now.

Titan is fucking me, but I have a perfect view of Bones and Jasmine over his shoulder.

He has her bent over a small table. Her hands are tied behind her back with his belt. His pants are down around his thighs, and he fucks her from behind. He's bent over her back and has one hand wrapped around her throat while the other is fisted in her hair.

Bones always was a dominant. He never knew how to be soft. He took over you, controlled every inch of you, and any girl wanted that.

He fucks her relentlessly. The sound of their bodies slapping can be heard over Titan and me. She's coming, but you can't hear it because he's cut off her air. Her face is red and slick with sweat. Her mouth is parted, and eyes closed.

Her body thrashes under his as she comes. He stops, pulls out, and yanks her to her feet by her hair. Spinning her around, she falls to her knees. Ripping off the condom, he grabs the base of his pierced dick and orders her to open her mouth. She does, like any other girl in that position, and he fucks her mouth.

Bones always hated wearing condoms, but he'd do it. That's why he preferred to come in your mouth. Didn't need a condom for that.

I see some things haven't changed.

Titan grips my hair and yanks my head back to give him access to my neck. He bites down on my skin, and I close my eyes, whimpering. The goose bumps crawling over my body. "Titan," is the only thing I can get out before I'm coming once again.

THIRTY-FOUR

TITAN

"Ready?" I ask, looking over at Bones.

He nods, chambering a bullet in his 9 mil. "Let's go."

We exit my car, and I see Luca get out of his Bugatti La Voiture Noire with Nite. We left Grave and Cross back at Kingdom with the girls. As soon as we had walked out of The Palace, Bones's phone started blowing up. Luca's source had come through and found out who the guy was that broke into the York's residence.

It turns out, the guy is a fucking dentist. Not what we were expecting.

"We're going in through the back." I tell Luca and Nite. "You guys take the front."

"What if he's not alone?" Luca asks, removing his gun from his slacks.

"No witnesses," Bones says.

Everyone nods in agreement. We came to do a job. And we're going to make sure it gets done.

Bones and I make our way around the back of the one-story brick building. It's a little after midnight, but the informant assured us that he would be here. I guess the guy is going through a divorce and sleeping up at his office.

I shove my elbow into the glass, shattering it. Reaching in, I undo the lock and open the door. I enter first, followed by Bones. We make our way down the dark hallway with our guns raised and ready when we catch sight of Luca entering with Nite in the front.

I enter a room and see a couch facing a TV. Static plays on the screen. Seats wrap around the walls, indicating it's the waiting area. Walking around it to the front, a man lies across it, holding a bottle of rum in his hand. The blanket barely hanging on.

I place my gun in my waistband and look up at Luca. "You got the bag?"

He nods and holds it up. "Just tell me where you want him."

Bones and I grab the guy and gently begin to move him to the nearest room, careful not to wake him just yet. We lie him in a dentist chair. It doesn't have armrests, so I pull his arms behind the chair and Nite duct tapes them together. He shifts a little but doesn't wake.

I sit down at the head of the chair and press the button to lower the headrest so he's lying flat while Bones wraps tape around his legs to secure them to the bottom half of the chair. This bastard isn't going anywhere. He's going to die here.

Luca is over at the mini sink to the right, filling a jug with water. Nite drops the duffel bag at my feet. I reach down and grab the washcloth out of it.

"Everybody ready?" I ask, thankful the guy had some alcohol before he passed out. Otherwise, he would have already woken up.

Everyone nods. I lean over the chair and slap the guy across the face.

"What …?" He opens his heavy eyes. "What's going on?" He starts fighting the restraints. "Who the fuck are you?" His large eyes shoot to each one of us. "What the fuck …?" He fights it harder, making the chair rattle. "Let me go."

"Who sent you to the York's house?" I demand, getting to the point. I want to end this shit tonight.

"Fuck you!" he spits out.

"Wrong answer." I throw the washcloth over his face, and Luca be-

TITAN

gins to pour the water over it. Waterboarding—old yet effective.

His body struggles in the chair, and Luca stops. I pull away the cloth.

"You …" *Cough.* "Son …" Another cough. "Bit…ch." He spits out the last bit.

"We can do this all night," I say. "Now, again, who sent you to the York residence?"

"HELP ME!" he screams, with his struggle.

"Again," I tell Luca. And this time he places the cloth over the guy's face and pours water on it. I count to six before I snap my fingers, and he stops. "I doubt you'll last past ten seconds."

Everything on him is covered in water. It's even splashed on my shirt, and the bottom of my pant legs and shoes are wet.

"I say we just end it now," Bones offers, pulling a knife out of his pocket and pressing it to his throat. Bones has always preferred the bloody side of things. I couldn't care either way as long as it gets done.

"No! No!" the guy cries. "I don't know. It was sent through a text."

I arch a brow. "A text? To what phone?"

"On the floor. By the couch," he rushes out.

Nite exits the room to go look for said phone.

"Please." He begins to sob. "I didn't hurt her."

I grab his throat and squeeze it, taking his air away. "Yes, you fucking did," I say through clenched teeth.

Just then, Nite enters and hands a phone to Luca. He goes through it and then looks at me. I don't like the look in his eyes. "The only number he had contact with that night is a New York number."

"New York?" Bones mimics my thoughts exactly. *Who the hell do we know in New York?*

At least we have a location. That's all we need to know for now. "Thanks for the information." I slap the guy on his wet chest, and water splashes from his soaked shirt. Reaching down into the duffel bag, I grab the other cloth that is in a Ziploc baggie. It's been soaking for the past three hours.

I put gloves on, then open the baggie. Grabbing it, I wad it up and shove it into his mouth, ending his protests. "Bones."

He takes the duct tape and wraps it around the guys mouth and the back of the chair, successfully taping his head to it so he can't get free.

His body begins to convulse as he chokes on the contents of the rag. I smile. "Swallow it up. It's been soaking in poison, it's going to eat you from the inside out."

EMILEE

JASMINE, HAVEN, AND I sit on the couch at the Royal Suite. The guys left us with Grave and Cross.

They've been over in the corner having their own conversations. Grave's cell keeps going off, and I'm pretty sure it's a girl. Every now and then, he smiles and adjusts his pants. She's obviously sending him dirty pictures.

"What is wrong with you two?" Haven asks us.

"Nothing," I answer, tucking a stray piece of hair behind my ear. I showered after we returned from The Palace so at least I don't smell like sex anymore, but I still feel pretty damn drunk. I'm going to have to sleep it off.

"You two are up to something." Haven narrows her amber eyes.

Jasmine goes to speak, but the double doors to the suite open, and the guys enter.

I rise to my feet. "Everything okay?" I ask Titan.

"Yeah." He comes over and kisses my forehead.

We have a lot to discuss, but right now, I'm just glad they returned from wherever they went. And I don't see any blood splattered on their clothes. But ... "Why are you wet?" I ask.

He ignores my question.

"So what did you find?" Grave asks, biting into a banana.

"We're going to New York," Luca announces.

"All of us?" Haven asks.

"Yes," Titan is the one who answers. "Well." He points at Grave and Cross. "You two are staying here."

"Thank God," Grave mumbles with a mouthful. "I hate New York. The city stinks, and I hate how crowded it is."

I'm not sure it's much different than Vegas when it comes to tourists, but I don't voice my opinion.

"Do we even know what we're looking for?" I ask.

"I will by the time we leave," Bones answers me. "I have some contacts that I've already reached out to who are in New York."

"Who do you know there?" I ask.

"He's been fucking a supermodel there for the past few months," Grave answers, winking up at his brother.

"Oh," I say, unable to hide my surprise. I didn't know he was seeing someone. I never thought he'd be unavailable. I mean, I don't want him to myself, but we've had sex. I also don't want to be the other woman.

Bones eyes his brother. "She's not my contact." Then looks at Jasmine. "It's not like that."

She shrugs, shoving M&M's into her mouth.

"Why would Bones think Jasmine cares if he's seeing someone in New York or not?" Haven whispers in my ear.

"Shh," I tell her, trying to cover up this very awkward conversation.

"Have they ...?"

"Hey Jasmine, pass me some of those M&M's," I order, reaching out my hand to avoid what Haven was about to ask me. I don't want to have to explain what we did just a few hours ago in The Palace. It's over. We're moving on.

"I say give it two days. At the most," Bones goes on. "That gives us enough time to get stuff in order before we leave."

"How long will we be gone?" I ask.

"Depends on a few factors," Titan responds but doesn't go into detail about what he means by factors, so I drop it. Not like I have a life here anymore. Both parents dead. Burned down my house. Why do I care how long I'll be gone?

Grave goes off to his room, already calling someone on his cell, and Cross walks over to Bones and starts having a conversation with him. I stand and hug Jasmine bye and then Haven. "I'll see you girls soon."

"Yep, call me later." Jasmine kisses my cheek. "Get some sleep. You need it." She winks at me.

"What's going on?" Haven asks. "I know you guys are keeping something from me."

"Look, we'll have a long flight to New York, okay? I'll tell you then. Right now, I just want to go to bed." I dodge it for tonight.

She gives me a hug and walks out with Luca and Nite. I walk into Titan's room and remove my shirt as he enters.

He locks his doors and turns to face me.

"I'm really tired." I say trying to dodge what I know he wants to talk about. I've been staying with him since I burned down my parents' house, but we haven't spoken. I've ignored him. Until we had sex in The Palace earlier this evening.

He steps into me and lifts his hand. He gently cups my cheek, and I lean into the warmth. "We're not doing this."

"What?" I ask yawning.

"Fighting over something so idiotic. You've played this game long enough." He leans down and kisses my forehead.

"But you lied to me." I dig into my foggy and drunk brain to remember what has kept me standoff-ish toward him for the past week to begin with.

"I never lied to you. I didn't willingly give you information."

"Same thing," I growl.

"No, it's not." He runs a hand down his face. "What do you want, an apology?"

"That would be a good start." I lift my chin.

"Okay." He crosses his tatted arms over his chest. "You go first."

I gasp. "What do I have to apologize for?"

"You put yourself in danger by setting your house on fire." I open my mouth to argue that, but he continues. "And you cost me thirty grand to say it was not arson."

"Thirty grand?" I breathe.

"Yes," he hisses and turns his back to me, entering his bathroom. He slams the glass door shut.

I had set that fire because I didn't want any of it anymore. I did it in hopes that I could move on. And I did it so that piece of shit George wouldn't get the house my father built for my mother. I never meant for it to cost Titan. I didn't expect him to come to my rescue. It's not like I sent him a warning of what I was planning on doing.

I open the bathroom door and step inside, refusing to let him end this conversation like that. I want the last word. Titan stands at the marble counter, rinsing his face in one of the sinks. His clothes are in a pile on the floor next to his feet. All he wears is a pair of black boxer briefs. His ink and muscular body fully on display. "I'm sorry." I swallow my pride, my shoulders falling and my anger fading. "I didn't mean to cost you anything."

His hard eyes meet mine in the mirror. "You think I give a shit about thirty thousand dollars?"

"Yeah?" It comes out more like a question because I thought that was why he was mad. Was I wrong?

He releases a long sigh, grabs a towel off the rack, and wipes his face. He walks over to me. "I don't give a fuck about the money," he says. "I care about you and your safety. And what you did was reckless."

"I ..."

"I'm not trying to start a fight with you, but I also don't want you avoiding me." His eyes roam my face. "This is where you belong." He cups my face again. "With me. I can keep you safe. I can give you what you need."

"And what do I need?" I ask, running my hands up and down his chiseled abs.

A slow and sexy smile spreads across his face. "You tell me."

"You." It's the only answer I can think of. I don't need his money. This Kingdom. Just him.

He lowers his lips to mine and kisses me softly. "I'm right here, Em and I'm not going anywhere."

FRIDAY MORNING, WE'RE pulling up to a remote private airport. It has six hangars. The one on the far right is open, and you can see the pristine jet inside. It's white with a golden K in the middle of a black circle. Same logo that is all over Kingdom. "What is this?" I ask.

"My plane," Titan answers.

He has a fucking jet?

Our Escalade SUV comes to a stop, and we exit and walk into the hangar. He helps me up the stairs, and I see the girls already on it. Jasmine has a pair of black Gucci glasses on and a glass of champagne in her right hand. It has the same logo on it, letting me know it's from the casino. Haven has a bottle of water in hers.

"Do all of the Kings have a plane?" I ask, sitting down across from the girls in the white leather. A black table sets between us with a bowl full of fresh fruit.

"Yes," Bones answers on the other side of the aisle. "Well, everyone except Grave."

"Why doesn't he have one?" I wonder.

"He did. He crashed it," Titan answers, going to sit down next to Bones.

"How do you crash a plane?" Jasmine asks, laughing.

"Funny, I asked him that same question," Bones says typing away on his phone. "But he was too fucked up to remember how it ended up in the Atlantic Ocean."

"I mean, I can see one crashing. But surviving it?" Haven shakes her head. "That would be very low odds." She takes a sip of her water.

"That's why every jet has parachutes on it," Titan adds. He leans over and starts whispering to Bones, ending our conversation regarding Grave and his near-death experiences. I'm not surprised in the least that Grave survived a plane crash. The boy is like a fucking cat, but he has ninety lives.

Haven claps her hands together softly. "So here we are. I'm ready to be filled in."

I look over at Jasmine, and she shrugs. She doesn't give a fuck who knows what we did in The Palace. I take a deep breath. "Okay …"

THIRTY-FIVE

TITAN

We sit in the living room at the Four Seasons in New York. The curtains in front of the floor-to-ceiling windows are pulled back, letting the sun shine in. I can practically hear Bones's skin burning from the light as he sits beside me. He's lucky he naturally has an olive skin tone, or he'd look like a vampire.

"Who are we waiting for?" Emilee asks from behind the couch.

"I have some friends who live here. Well, one of them lives here in New York full-time. The other lives in Vancouver," Bones answers.

"You said they were contacts," Jasmine corrects him. "Do you even have friends?"

"Very few." He tosses back his drink when there's a knock on the door.

He gets up to open the door to greet out guests. I stand as they enter the room. "Avery, Tristan, this is Titan, Luca, Nite. And these are the girls, Haven, Jasmine, and Emilee." They each shake our hands and offer pleasantries.

The Decker brothers are both dressed in black suits. They look like they own a Fortune 500 company and model for *GQ* on the weekends. But I know differently. You don't fuck with them. Their dead body count is higher than ours.

I notice Jasmine lower her sunglasses to introduce herself to them. The girl is always on the lookout for her next victim.

"This is Kayn, head of my security," Avery introduces a third man.

I met the Deckers last year when Bones and I made a trip to Vancouver to look at some property. We've thought about opening up another casino there, but they have too many restrictions. Too much red tape. But we had dinner with them while there.

"May I get you a drink?" Emilee asks, standing from her spot on the couch.

"Scotch, please," Avery answers.

"Same for me." Tristan nods.

"And for you, Kayn?" Em asks.

"Just a water, please."

She goes over into the kitchen, and I lean back in my seat. "Did you guys find anything?"

"Kink," Tristan answers.

"Excuse me?" Jasmine asks with a smirk on her face.

"It's an elite club," he answers her. "Your guy has been spotted in Kink."

"Okay. Where is it?" Bones asks.

"It's not that simple," Avery adds.

"Is it not open to the public?" I ask confused.

"Yes and no," Tristan answers. "Thank you." He takes the offered glass of scotch from Emilee. "It's a two-story club in the heart of Manhattan. The entrance is on the first floor, and it's like any other nightclub. But in the back, there's a door that goes down to the bottom level." He takes a sip. "It is not open to the public. You need a membership."

"What kind of club requires a membership?" Haven asks. "Like an exclusive men's club?"

"One that requires NDAs," Tristan answers, pulling out his wallet. He opens it up and removes a card. He hands it to me. It's a solid black card that reads Kink at the bottom in white letters. I look it over while he goes on. "That card is fifty grand a year."

"What does it get you?" Jasmine asks, looking at it in my hand.

"Anything you want." He winks at her.

"Wait," Emilee starts as I hand the card off to Bones. "I'm confused. What does it actually get you? Why would they make you sign an NDA?" she continues.

Tristan takes a sip and leans forward, placing his elbows on his knees. "Kink is a sex club. You make it downstairs, and it's five thousand square feet of nothing but glass rooms. One after the other. It also has a dance floor, its own bar, and a theater room. All you have to do is sign on the dotted line, and you can do anything you want with anyone you want while down there. Granted you don't have limits. It's a hundred percent consensual. Your NDA covers that as well."

"Oh, I want to join." Jasmine smiles.

Luca looks skeptical. Haven looks terrified, and Jasmine looks like she's found her mothership.

"How do we know he was there, though?" Luca questions. "Do they keep a log of who comes in and when?"

"No." Tristan shakes his head. "The only paper trail they have is the NDA. And no one has access to those. They don't even provide the members with a copy."

"And payment?" I add.

His blue eyes meet mine, and he smiles. "No. Our dues are required on the first of the year. In cash. Large bills. You show up. They run it through their money counter. Once done, they issue you a new card, and you're on your way. No proof of payment. And they can suspend your membership at any given time for whatever reason."

"Fuck. Can I buy into this franchise?" Jasmine asks with a whistle. "This sounds like my kind of business."

Everyone laughs at her.

"But there's the cards," I say, trying to figure this out. "That's how they keep track of everyone."

"The card is just a tool to get you in. As if you were wearing a wristband to show you're over twenty-one at a fair. It doesn't have my name on it anywhere. She could take it." He points at Jasmine. "And use it for entry and they wouldn't question her. I would have been out fifty grand and that's that. It doesn't actually keep track of their members."

"But they would be allowing her to enter without an NDA. So, there's a flaw," I observe.

"Essentially. But you have to be invited. Now, they don't scan the cards to make sure that you are, in fact, the cardholder. You find a member card, and you're in. But not many know about the bottom floor of Kink. The top floor of the club has a different name. So the odds of a stranger picking one up on the streets and knowing its significance is unlikely." Tristan takes a drink.

"Let me see your card." Jasmine holds her hand out to Avery.

He shakes his head. "I'm no longer a member. I prefer not to parade my sexual desires around in front of others."

"In front of others," Haven repeats. "Like they watch each other down there?" Her amber eyes are wide.

My eyes go to Emilee, and she blushes. My dirty girl would like that.

"Yes. As I said, all the rooms are glass. You can watch all of it. Or you can choose the one room they offer for privates. They accommodate all tastes," Tristan adds.

"And what are your tastes?" Jasmine asks him with a raised brow.

"We're getting off track," Luca says, running a hand down his face before Tristan can answer her. "But you can confirm he's been there?"

Tristan goes to speak, but Emilee interrupts him. "This is George we're talking about. How in the hell did he find fifty thousand dollars to join a sex club?" she asks skeptically. "And how does that work anyway?" She looks back and forth between Avery and Tristan. "This is September. The year is almost over."

We're assuming our contact is George. When we looked up the number, it was not available. So, it has to be a burner phone of some sort. But he is the only guy we can think of who would send someone to the York's house who would know about a safe in the office. No one else makes sense. But she has a point. Where would George find that kind of money for a sex club? But I'm also not an idiot. He's had money this entire time. He refused to pay us because he didn't want to. Not because his funds were unavailable.

"Doesn't matter." Tristan shakes his head once at her question. "You pay full price no matter when you want to join. So, say you just have to join in December. Come January, you're paying again."

"Seriously, this is my dream job." Jasmine nods to herself. "Sex. Money. Exclusive clubs."

"Here, I have a picture for you." Tristan reaches into his pocket and removes his cell. He scrolls through it for a few seconds and then hands it to me.

I stare down at it. My blood running cold.

"Titan?" Bones calls out.

I blink, bringing the picture closer to my face. "Uh …" I clear my throat. "When was this taken?"

"Two nights ago."

I start shaking my head. "That's impossible."

"I was there. I took it," Tristan announces. "You gave us the number. As you said, it was not in any database. But we were able to ping it to Kink. Then we had a woman reach out to that number. She made contact, and I took the picture. That's what took us so long. He wasn't responding at first. It took him a couple of days to take the bait."

Fuck! I hand him back the phone. Standing, I start to head to the door of our suite. "Bones!" I snap before walking out.

"What the hell is going on?" he demands, entering the hallway and shutting the door behind him.

I begin to pace.

"You look like you've seen a ghost."

"We were wrong," I say.

"About?"

"We thought this was George. It had to have been George who sent the guy to collect the money from the York's residence."

"Yeah. So why do you seem so confused now?"

"He was the only plausible answer," I ramble.

"I agree," he goes on.

"But …" Fuck! This is worse than I thought.

"But what?" he demands.

I continue to pace. My mind trying to piece together what I know and what I saw.

"Titan, but what?" He grips my shoulders and yanks me to a stop.

My wide eyes search his. "We were wrong."

EMILEE

"What do you think they're talking about?" I ask, biting on my nails as I stare at the door. Whatever was on that phone, Titan did not like.

"Who cares?" Jasmine answers, gawking at Avery and Tristan. They've vacated the couch and now stand over by the floor-to-ceiling windows talking to Luca. Avery stands with his arms crossed over his chest while Tristan leans his shoulder onto the window with his hands in the front pockets of his black slacks. The fabric pulling across his bubble ass. Even I can't deny that they are both hot. Chiseled jawlines. Blue eyes and dark hair. They could almost pass as twins. But I heard Titan talking about them earlier. I know that Avery is the oldest, and he has facial hair where Tristan is clean shaven.

They wear expensive suits and Rolex watches. They look like pretty boys. They remind me of the boys in college who drove Teslas and spent Daddy's money on vacations to the Hamptons and weekends in Paris. But something tells me that's not what they do or how they make their income. They may be nice to look at, but they have this air about them that screams dangerous.

Maybe mafia like Luca? That could be the connection, but Bones was the one who said he knew them.

I can't figure it out.

Jasmine is sitting beside me drooling thinking about being the center of a Decker sandwich. And even Haven looks a little interested. "Calm down, bitches. You're panting like you're in heat."

"What? I can look." Haven shrugs.

"I can fucking play. I'm single," Jasmine states.

"What do you think they do for a living?" I ask softly.

"I imagine they both run a sex club. And I'm their newest toy." Jasmine all but moans her answer.

I roll my eyes.

"I think they work on Wall Street. If not, definitely finance," Haven answers.

I snort.

"No fucking way," Jasmine protests. "Those two gorgeous faces are not wasted by sitting behind a desk on the phone all day. No. They work with their hands."

"Yeah, but what do they do with them?" I add.

"Smear chocolate all over me," Jasmine replies.

Haven and I burst out laughing. God, the girl really is a sex addict, and she needs rehab.

My eyes go to Nite. He stands beside them as well. He never says a word, but Tristan is talking to him. Nite just nods and shakes his head. It's like Tristan knows he's a mute and is only asking questions that require a yes or no answer.

A phone rings and Tristan pulls his out of his pocket. Straightening his stance, he holds up a finger to the guys and walks away from the window to take the call. "Hey, babe?" he answers, before walking into a bedroom off the living room.

"They're both probably taken." Jasmine throws her hands up, leaning back into the couch.

"Maybe his girl is into lesbian love," Haven suggests, and I snicker. "I mean, we all know you are."

"Bitch," Jasmine teases before throwing a pillow from the couch into her face. "We should have never told you."

Haven is laughing. "I'm just jealous I haven't received that kind of attention from you." She throws it back in Jasmine's face, and Jasmine tosses it to the floor.

The door to the suite opens, and I jump to my feet. "Hey." Titan's eyes find mine, and he looks mad. Bones runs a tatted hand through his hair. "What's wrong?" I ask.

"Nothing," Titan growls. "But our plans have changed."

"To what?" Luca asks just as Tristan exits the bedroom, pocketing his phone.

"The girls aren't going tonight."

"What?" Jasmine jumps up from the couch. "I wanna see all the sex."

"Why not?" Haven asks.

Titan looks at me. "Because we no longer need you there."

"But—"

"You're not going, Emilee," he snaps, interrupting me. "You girls will stay behind at the hotel tonight. The guys and I will go and find him on our own."

"This is bullshit!" Haven sighs from the couch. She's lying upside down with her head hanging off the cushion and her legs dangling over the back.

We're all on our third margarita. The sun set hours ago, and we've closed the curtains to the outside world.

"Luca wouldn't even tell me what the hell was going on," she adds.

After Titan and Bones entered the hotel suite in a pissy mood, the guys had a meeting. And after that, things were weird. Titan didn't have much to say to me other than don't wait up for him as they left the suite.

"What if we go out anyway?" I offer.

"I'm down for that," Jasmine says, hopping off the kitchen counter that she's been perched on eating flaming hot Funyuns.

"It's only eleven o'clock. We can be ready and at the club by one." I'm not sure where exactly the club is located or what New York traffic is like, but I think we could make it there by then.

"I'm in." Haven rolls off the couch and onto the floor.

"You do know that the guys will be mad at you for going out, right?" Jasmine asks.

I wave her off. "I'll deal with Titan later."

"Where should we go?" I ask. Kink is out of the question since we don't have memberships. I guess Tristan has connections, and he's taking the Kings, Luca, and Nite to show them around as potential members. If Titan comes back saying he signed an NDA and paid fifty grand, I won't get mad. I'm a Queen, for fuck's sake. But since we didn't go with the guys, we can't get access.

"You know what is in New York, don't you?" Haven asks.

Jasmine and I exchange a look and then shake our heads. "What?" I ask.

"Seven Deadly Sins. They opened one up a couple of years back."

"Oh, yeah." I nod. "I remember Josh mentioning it a few times. Jet runs the New York location."

Haven is on her phone scrolling when she holds it out to Jasmine and me. "And look who is in town for the weekend working."

"It's Josh," I say, taking the phone from her. She had pulled up his Facebook page. She became friends with him back when she visited me in Chicago. I never get on it anymore.

It's a picture of him standing behind a bar making a drink. He's looking up at the camera. He's got his bleach-blond tips standing straight up. A barbell in his right brow and he's licking his upper lip. The status says *let me serve you.*

"Fuck!" Jasmine takes the phone from me. "He's hot as fuck. I'll take one for the team."

Haven and I laugh. "We don't need you to sleep with him," I say.

THIRTY-SIX

EMILEE

An hour later, we're walking into Seven Deadly Sins. The music is pounding, and the place is packed. I'm not surprised. The one in Chicago was always the same. It was in an industrial part of town, with nothing but abandoned warehouses surrounding it, but everyone knew what it was and where it was located. Sometimes I'd have to text Josh and tell him that I was there, and he would let me in through the back because of the long line around the building.

Grabbing Jasmine's hand, I drag her to the bar. She hangs on to Haven. Pushing our way through, I come up to the bar and see Josh over in the far corner with his back to me. He's bent over pouring alcohol into a glass.

I lean over the bar and scream as loud as I can. "JOSH!" Hoping he hears me.

He straightens and spins around. His green eyes meet mine, and a huge smile spreads across his face. "Lee!" He shouts my nickname. He pushes up the door at the end of the bar, comes around, and wraps his arms around me, picking my feet up off the floor. "Oh my God." He places me back down. "What in the fuck are you doing in New York?" he asks loudly over the music.

"I could ask you the same thing." I laugh. It's nice to see him. He was more of a friend than a fuck. We hung out all the time. We'd go shopping, to dinner, movies. He was my best friend. My only friend in Chicago. Seeing him now reminds me of how much I miss him.

"I'm here for the weekend. But may be moving here," he answers.

"That's awesome," I say not really sure what to do now or how to act. I never told him I was leaving. Or about my mother. I just quit answering his calls, and he quit reaching out.

"Did you move here?" he asks.

I shake my head. "Just here with some friends." I gesture to Jasmine and Haven.

He introduces himself and then he asks us what we'd like to drink before returning back behind the bar. Moments later, he's placing three shots of Crown in front of me. Apparently, we're here to get fucked up if you ask Jasmine. She had placed our order.

We each down ours, and she's ordering more.

TITAN

I STAND IN the middle of this freak show. When it comes to sex, I'll try anything on a woman, but I draw a line when it comes to one wanting to parade me around like a dog on a leash with a gag in my mouth. I can't say that for the others who are at Kink tonight.

We've been here for over three hours and gotten nowhere.

Nite, Luca, and Avery are upstairs at the nightclub keeping lookout. Bones, Tristan, and I are downstairs. He was able to get us down here. We had to act interested. Well, I did. I think Bones is into this scene. I can't say I'd bring Emilee here because I don't like the idea of strangers watching us. That's why we have The Palace back at Kingdom. It gives the client and their queen privacy. Here, you have a lot of eyes on you.

Like right now, we stand in a room. The silver plaque above the door we entered said the Gallery. We stand in the back, up against the wall. There are five rows of seats in front of us, ten seats in each row. A glass is all that separates us from a room. A woman enters a door in the back.

She comes to the center and removes her black robe. She's completely naked underneath. She looks to be early thirties. Her black hair is down and over her shoulders, hiding her rather small tits. She comes to the center of the room and spreads her legs wide. There are ropes secured to the silver rings on the floor. She places each ankle in one and pulls them tight. Then she looks up at the two ropes that hang from the ceiling. One by one, she secures her own wrists in them. Once she accomplished what she wants, she stares at us through the glass.

"Can she see us?" Bones asks softly.

"No," Tristan answers. "The glass is a two-way mirror."

"Why is she just standing there?" I wonder.

"She is waiting for someone to come play with her."

I look over at him. "You're joking?"

He shakes his head, watching her. "Nope."

"What if no one goes in there?" Bones asks.

"Oh, that is never a problem here in Kink. That's why the members show up every night. There is always someone willing to play when a toy is offered."

And sure enough, the back door opens, and two guys enter. The woman tries to look over her shoulder to see, but she isn't able to see them due to how her arms are secured above her head.

The guys begin to undress … "I'm out," I say and push off the wall. I exit the room and into the hallway. It's very dim in Kink. There's music playing but nothing like a club. It's soft. I'm guessing they want you to hear the men and women moaning more than the songs. It's a part of the appeal.

The door opens behind me as Bones and Tristan exit.

"Your guy spent most of his time in the Gallery a few nights ago," Tristan says. "If he shows, he'll go there first."

"I'll wait out here in the hall to see if he goes in there," I say, not in the mood to look at dicks tonight.

"Why don't we ping the number?" Bones offers. "He may already be here. We haven't checked all the rooms."

"We did earlier today," Tristan answers, signaling to a bartender.

TITAN

"There was no activity. He's either thrown it away or had it off."

A cute blonde behind the bar begins to pour three glasses of scotch.

"I still think something is fishy about this," I say through clenched teeth.

"There has to be an explanation," Bones agrees. "And we'll figure it out. We just need to find him. And fast."

Tristan walks up to the bar and takes the glasses of scotch the blonde made for him. She gives him a big smile and her white teeth glow from the blacklights around the bar. She winks at him.

"Thanks, love," he tells her.

"Anytime, T."

"I can't believe I've been coming to New York forever and didn't know this place existed," Bones says, taking a sip of his scotch. Then he looks at me. "Do you think Mr. Bianchi is a member here?"

I shrug. "Not sure why he wouldn't be. The guy runs the fucking mafia." Luca's dad is what you would consider any member of the mafia. A ruthless motherfucker. He's been fucking around on Luca's mother for years. He's always had a side piece. They don't marry for love in the mafia. Well, most don't. Luca just happened to marry a woman he loved. But there were other reasons to that as well. "At least now you know about it. You can bring Lola here when you come visit her."

He shakes his head. "She wouldn't come here. Plus, I ended that."

"When?" I ask.

"About an hour ago." He takes a drink of his scotch.

"Does that have to do with Jasmine?" I ask.

He snorts. "No. Lola called me and informed me she had planned us a trip for next weekend. We were going to England. She wanted me to meet her parents."

Tristan whistles. "How long were you two fucking?"

"Three months," Bones answers. "Two months too long."

Tristan pulls his cell out of his pocket and unlocks his screen. After reading a text, he puts it back. "No sign of your guy upstairs."

I run my free hand through my hair. "Maybe we should go back to the suite and regroup. Try to ping his cell." We still have the phone of the bastard who we killed a few days ago. We can dig through it to see

253

what else we can find. Plus, as much as I don't care for this place, it has made me horny for my girl.

"Can you get us back in tomorrow night if we need it?" I ask.

He nods.

"I'm buying a membership," Bones says before throwing back what's left of his scotch.

THIRTY-SEVEN

EMILEE

T**HE GIRLS AND** I sit at a round booth right off the dance floor. I have sweat covering my boobs and my back. We've been dancing for three songs straight and finally decided to take a breather. I'm in the middle of them with a drink in my hands. They're laughing and joking about who Jasmine is going to go home with when I feel my phone vibrate the table.

I pick it up in front of me and open the text.
Titan: We're headed back. Be naked in bed for me.

"The guys are on their way back to the hotel," I call out over "Lollipop" by Framing Hanley.

Haven shuts up and gulps down her drink, acting like she spent her last eight dollars on it. And begins to scoot out of the booth.

"You can't be serious?" Jasmine protest. "They message you, and you run back to them like a lost puppy?" She arches a dark brow.

"When you fall in love with someone, you'll be the same way," Haven tells her.

She shakes her head viciously. Her short red hair slapping her in the face. "Nope. You can love someone and still not be at their beck and call."

"Oh, really?" Haven places her hands on her hips. "Like you are with Trenton?"

Jasmine opens her mouth but then shuts it. "I know. It sucks being addicted to dick." She pouts, making us laugh.

"Yeah, well …." My voice trails off as I spot a guy at the bar from across the dance floor. He has his back to us, dressed in a black leather jacket with dark jeans and black boots.

"What is it?" Jasmine asks, but I ignore her.

I can't take my eyes off him. He turns to the side, giving me a profile view, and my breath gets caught in my lungs. He leans his arm up against the bar and smiles at the brunette who looks half his age. Reaching his left hand out, he takes a lock of her hair in his fingers and twirls it around like he's flirting.

"What are you looking at?" I hear Haven ask.

"I think she's off in la-la land," I hear Jasmine speak.

I ignore them both even though she's not far off. I think I'm in the twilight zone. It can't be …

I get out of the booth and ignore them as they call out my name. Making my way across the dance floor, I'm bumping into bodies. Some even cuss at me, but I ignore them.

Walking up to the man, I shove the girl out of my way into a guy who stands behind her. Placing myself in front of the man, his eyes meet mine. My heart begins to pound as recognition shows in his.

"Emilee?" He gasps.

I blink. Trying to count the drinks I've had in my head. I have to be imagining this. "Dad?" I choke out.

I expect him to hug me. To show some kind of excitement that I'm standing in front of him. My mind is racing as fast as my heart, trying to process what I'm seeing. The lights are flashing and the music is so loud the floor shakes with the bass. I blink again, thinking he'll disappear. That maybe someone had slipped something into my drink. I lick my numbing lips. "What are you …?"

He grabs my upper arm. His fingers dig into my skin as he drags me through the crowd. I don't try to stop him. Soon, we're barging through an exit door, and he's yanking me through a parking lot. The night air hot on my sweaty skin.

I see a red Ferrari. He opens the passenger side door and shoves me into it, then runs around the front, gets in, and starts it.

"Dad?" My voice breaks with emotion. "I don't understand. What are you …?"

"Not right now." He throws it into gear and takes off, squealing the tires.

I sit back and take in the red interior and lit up dash. My hands are sweaty, and I rub them on my bare legs, regretting the mini dress I wore out tonight.

Looking over my shoulder, I realize he's getting on the highway. "Dad, where are we going?" I ask, getting nervous. I was in shock that he was there. Alive. "You're dead," I tell myself more than him. "I'm hallucinating. Dreaming," I say more to myself. I've fallen asleep, and the girls and I never even left the hotel suite.

"I'm very much alive," he growls. He's mad at me.

"I don't understand. What …?"

"We will not discuss this right now!" he snaps.

"Where are we going?" I ask again, digging in my clutch for my phone.

"To the airport. I have a jet there. It will take you back to Vegas."

"What?" I shriek. "I can't go back. Everyone is here."

He quickly slides his eyes over to mine before going back to the road. "Who the fuck is everyone?"

I lick my lips nervously but answer. "The Kings." Then I remember that only two of them are here. Not all of them.

"Fuck," he hisses.

"They can help you," I add quickly. "Whatever is going on." I remember that he had owed a million dollars to someone. I don't know if they ever told me who it was. A loan shark or something. Fuck, my mind is too foggy right now. What was that guy's name? Didn't he have like six weeks to pay it back? How long ago was that?

"No they can't," he argues.

"They can. I promise they will."

"The Kings don't help anyone but themselves."

I don't like how he spits out his words. Or the fact that he's lied to me. "You don't know them!" I shout.

"You're going back to Vegas to be with your mother," he grinds out, switching lanes.

My heart skips a beat. Now I know I'm dreaming. "My mother is dead," I say, looking out the small window. "George is gone. And I burned down the house you built her." Might as well tell the ghost of my dad everything. Dead loved ones do that, right? Visit you in your dreams?

"You did what?" he barks out.

"It's all gone. All I have is Titan."

"What do you mean all you have is Titan?" he asks slowly.

I turn to look at him. The lights from the dash showing his five o'clock shadow. I always thought my father was handsome with his deep-set brown eyes, square jaw, and dark hair. From the photos my mother had shown me, he was a pretty boy in high school. All the girls wanted him. My mother was the one who landed him.

"We're dating," I say.

He slams his fists into the steering wheel. "No. No." He's in denial. Just like I am that I'm really sitting next to him.

He's not real.

"Yep," I answer. My phone vibrates in my lap, and I look down at the screen. "And this is him now. Hey, baby?" I slur.

"Where in the fuck are you?" he snaps in my ear.

TITAN

I PACE THE hotel suite. Luca sits on the couch with Tristan. Bones and Avery stand by the window with glasses of scotch in their hands. Nite and Kayn are perched on the other leather couch.

I look up when the door opens, and I see Emilee enter. My hands shake with the anger I feel toward her right now. She wears a black mini dress and her hair down. She can barely walk in her heels, but I expected that. Haven filled us in when we arrived back here, and the girls were missing. Luca called her, and she answered, telling us that she and Jasmine were on their way back to the hotel, but Emilee had left the club with a man. They didn't get a look at who he was. Just saw her walk up to him and then they left together.

To say I'm furious is an understatement. "Where in the fuck have you been?" I snap.

She raises both of her hands in surrender. Like I'm a cop accusing her of a crime. "I told him you could help him." She manages to get out.

"What are you talking about?" Bones demands, also standing. "Help who?"

Instead of answering him, she turns, giving us her back and stares at the door she left wide open.

And in steps the very man we've been searching for all night. Silence falls over the room as he walks over to her. He places a protective hand on her shoulder and pulls her into his side.

I see fucking red. Removing my gun from my waistband, I point it right at his motherfucking head. "Get the fuck away from her."

"Titan." She gasps.

He shoves her away from him and into Bones's arms. He secures them around her, holding her in place. It's the same scenario she was in when we went to George's house and Grave brought her to his office. But this time, Bones has her, not me.

A cruel smile spreads across his face. "I told you, Emilee. The Kings don't give a fuck about anyone."

I look at him down my barrel as I hear the others get up from their seats. I hear someone cocking their gun behind me. I'm guessing Luca.

"What are you doing, Titan?" Emilee wails. "Please stop. He needs help."

I snort. "Where was he when you needed help?" I ask.

His eyes go from mine to his daughter's. She's hysterical at this point. Bones has her arms pinned behind her back as she frantically tries to get to her piece of shit father. "Need help with what?" he asks.

I snort. "Like you give a fuck."

He takes a step toward me, pressing the barrel of my gun into his chest. "You better answer me, son. You're not the only one carrying a loaded weapon," he warns.

I pull my lip back with disgust as he calls me son. I may love his daughter, but I hate this man. What he's put her through. Now this—the fucker never was dead. She thought she had lost her father, then mother. Only she didn't lose him. She'd be better off if she had. Because now we know he's carrying a very big secret around. And it could put her life in danger.

"Please ..." I hear Emilee sob. "Don't do this, Titan. Don't take him from me again," she begs.

My chest tightens at her words. That she would want to save his sorry ass. So easily forgive him.

A cruel smile spreads across his face. As if this was a setup. He's testing me. To see what she means to me. Do I kill her father and lose her forever? Or let him live and possibly take her from me? Either way, I lose because she will pick him. He's her father that her mother cheated on and left. He has her sympathy. I'm just the guy she's been fucking for the last month.

Making up my mind, I click my safety on and lower my gun, and say, "Yeah, babe." His dark eyes narrow on me calling his daughter by a pet name. I've never done it until now. On purpose. "Tell your father how George forced you to fuck him after your father died to help pay your mother's medical bills." I may not be the person she loves in this room, but he let her down. She needs to remember that.

His eyes widen, and they go to her. "He what?"

She's sobbing in Bones's arms. But he's no longer restraining her. Instead, she has her head in his chest. She's so trashed that she'll be passing out soon.

"You died. Left him everything," I fill him in. "He shut off her cards and told her that he would pay for Nancy's medical bills if she fucked him." His wide eyes come back to mine. "Spoiler alert. She did. More than once."

"Emilee?" He snaps her name like she did something wrong. He begins to walk over to her, but I slam my fist into his chest, stopping him. "Bones, put Emilee in bed. We have some shit to discuss with Nick."

THIRTY-EIGHT

TITAN

Bones exits the bedroom I'm staying in with Emilee and nods once at me, letting me know she is already passed out.

I sit on the couch next to Luca, and her father sits across from us on the other one. Tristan sits in the chair to my left next to Avery. Nite and Kayn lean against the floor-to-ceiling windows.

"We're waiting," I growl, glaring at her father.

He runs a hand through his hair. He has looked physically shaken ever since I announced his best friend and business partner fucked his daughter. But I don't buy it. He faked his own death. He'll do anything.

"I …" He lifts his head and swallows. "I was in trouble. And needed money. George suggested I fake my death. I had life insurance. He suggested we write up new papers that had me handing over everything to him."

Bones snorts.

Nick ignores him. "I was to lay low while he waited for the payout. Then he was going to pay off what I owed, and I'd be in the clear."

"When was the last time you spoke to him?" Luca asks.

"A couple of weeks," he answers. "He called and told me that there were some issues with the insurance …" He stands from the couch and begins to pace the large open space between the couch and glass coffee table. "Said that his attorney informed him it could take a few months. But that it was handled."

"And you believed him?" I question.

"I had no reason not to," he snaps, getting angry. "I gave him access to my accounts in order to take care of Nancy."

My eyes slide over to Bones for a quick second and then back to him. "For Nancy? Why?"

"Because she was on the company policy up until we divorced. She didn't own any shares of the company. I was paying out of pocket."

"Wait." Bones lifts his hand. "You were continuing to pay for her health care out of pocket after you divorced two years ago?"

He nods. "Why do you sound surprised by that?"

I sit back in the seat. "Because three months ago, she remarried." His eyes widen. "To your pal, George."

"That motherfucker!" he shouts.

"Which he lied to Emilee about. Used her for sex …"

Nick picks up a glass bowl that sits on the end table and throws it across the room, breaking it into a million pieces and bringing Bones's words to a halt. "I'm going to murder him," he growls, fisting his hands.

"Get in line," I say.

"Where is he?" Tristan is the one who asks. I'm pretty sure he and Avery are up to speed by now. They're smart guys.

"He was here in New York."

"You sure?" I ask. Last we heard, he was in Paris.

He nods. "I saw him. He was at Kink with me."

"He has a membership?" Avery questions.

He nods, shoving his hands through his dark hair. "The next morning, he boarded a private plane back to Vegas."

I sigh. "I doubt he's still there. Even if that is where he went."

"He's probably long gone by now," Bones says. "Nancy left him everything in her will. That was why Emilee set the house on fire. Even if she won't admit it, I know why she did it."

Nick falls back down onto the couch. "She'll never forgive me. Not like I deserve it."

I stand, done with this conversation. I'm tired. It's almost four a.m. I want to curl up in bed with her and get some rest. "She will, but you're right, you don't deserve it." I walk past the couch and toward the bedroom.

A hand grips my upper arm and pulls me to a stop. I turn to face her father. "Thanks." He sighs. "For taking care of her." Letting go of me, he takes a step back. "When she told me that you and her …" He clears his throat. "I thought—"

"I know what you thought," I interrupt him and lower my voice. "Just know that you were wrong."

EMILEE

I WAKE WITH a pounding headache. My eyes are sensitive to the sunlight streaming through the floor-to-ceiling windows. I moan, burying my face into my pillow.

"Here. Take these," I hear Titan say from beside the bed.

I lift my head and crack my eyes to see him standing there with two aspirin in one hand and a bottle of water in the other.

I sit up and take them from him. "Fuck." I toss them into my mouth and gulp down the water. "You would not believe the dream I had last night," I say.

"Try me." He crosses his arms over his chest and glares down at me.

I frown. "Were we fighting when I passed out?" He doesn't answer. I sigh. "Look, I wanted to go out. I'm not going to apologize for going to a club with my friends."

"That's not the part that pisses me off," he states. "It's who you ran into while there."

I frown, trying to think back on what … "Oh. Josh?" I ask, and his brows rise to his hairline. "Haven met him when she came to visit me in Chicago. When we decided to go out, she saw he was in town for the weekend working at the Seven Deadly Sins here in New York. We were never serious. We were just friends who fucked."

"Seems like a common occurrence for you."

My jaw tightens at his words. "Hey, that's not—"

"Fair?" he interrupts me.

I throw off the covers. "Fuck you, Titan," I growl, getting out of bed. I wrap a towel around me that was lying on a chair and yank open the bedroom door. I come to a halt when I see Bones and Luca sitting at the kitchen table with Haven and Jasmine. Nite is standing in the kitchen, and a man is standing next to him. "Dad?" I breathe.

"Hey, sweetie," he says softly, setting down his cup of coffee.

I stand frozen in my spot. "It was a dream," I whisper.

"No, it wasn't." He comes closer to me.

"You're alive?" I choke out, tears stinging my eyes.

He nods once. "Yeah, I am."

He reaches me and holds his arms out wide, waiting to see what I do.

"But you're ... I saw you ..." I never saw his body. He had been cremated, and we had a memorial service in remembrance.

"I'm so sorry, Emilee. Please forgive me."

The first tear runs down my cheek. "Of course." I choke. "Of course." I run into his open arms, and he wraps them around me. I never thought I'd get this again. His love. His smell.

I don't dare close my eyes, afraid he may disappear. "I don't understand. How are you here?" I pull away and look up at him.

He wipes the tears from my cheeks. "It's okay. We have plenty of time to talk about it."

"We do?" I ask surprised.

He nods. "Yeah. We're going back to Vegas. Together."

"We are?" I can't believe it. "When?"

"Whenever you want. I have a jet fueled and on standby."

My face falls. "I burned down your house," I say, and my bottom lip begins to tremble at what I've done.

"Don't worry about that." He cups my face. "Luca has a penthouse downtown that he has offered me. No one will know that we are there."

I take a step back from him and nod. "Okay."

"Go pack your things and I'll inform them we are ready."

I turn and walk back into our bedroom. I'm throwing things into my suitcase when the door opens, and Titan enters. "You can't be serious?" he growls. "You're going to go with him?"

"Yes," I say and stop what I'm doing. "He's my father. I thought he was dead ..."

"Yes, because he tricked you. He tricked everyone."

"He was in trouble." I don't know the full story, but obviously, he faked his death and needed the insurance money.

"God, you can't be that fucking stupid," he snaps.

My chest tightens at his words. How cold they were said. As if he believes I really am stupid if I go with my father. "Titan ..."

"No!" he shouts. "He could have come clean to you. Or filled you in on his plan. But he didn't, Em. He didn't trust you."

His words hurt because they're true. But I swallow the knot in my throat. "He's here now."

"To use you," he snaps. "Just like George did. Just like ..."

"Like you did!" I shout.

His eyes darken and his chest bows out.

"You fucking used me too, Titan. Don't pretend you didn't."

He says nothing. Just stands there like a fucking statue.

"Get on your knees, Em! You want your phone? Get. On. Your. Knees. That sound familiar?"

He steps into me, pressing his chest into me. "You wanted me as much as I wanted you."

I shake my head. "Not like that. I didn't want to be your whore."

He tilts his head to the side. "You didn't do it for your phone. You did it because you wanted to be a Queen. You had no problem whoring yourself out for money then."

I slap him across the face, and my palm instantly stings from my force on his cheek. "Fuck you, Titan," I growl as his murderous eyes glare down at me. His face now red from my hand.

I grab my things while he just stands there watching. And once I'm done, he doesn't follow me out of the bedroom.

THIRTY-NINE

TITAN

I SIT UP in my office with the blinds closed. It's a little after nine a.m., and it feels like it's midnight. I've been pissy ever since Emilee walked out of our hotel in New York a week ago.

The Kings have stayed clear of me. Grave is out doing what Grave always does—getting high and in trouble. Cross is right there with him. Bones has been burying his head into Kingdom. He's picking up the slack for his brother.

I haven't seen Luca or heard anything about George. At this point, it's no longer my problem. She's gone. Her father can figure it out now. I've written off the five hundred thousand he owes us.

My door opens, and Nigel enters. "Sir, we have a problem in the high stakes room."

"What is it?" I growl.

"Robert Jenkins is back. He's currently up ninety thousand."

"Thank you, Nigel," I say and stand. Ninety thousand isn't fucking nothing, but I've been itching to beat the shit out of someone since I left New York. I've already threatened the kid with his life, and he obviously didn't take me seriously.

I pick up my cell from my desk and exit my office. I make my way down in the elevator to the second floor. Then across tower one to tower two. Each one holds a high stakes room, but tower two is the biggest. That's where all the whales play. It's where big spenders lose their beach homes and others win their private jets. Some tables start buy-ins at a hundred grand.

I approach the black columns that are on either side of the high stakes room entrance with gold lights wrapped around them. Entering the room, I scan the tables for him. I find him at the very last one, tucked in the back. He has his head down and a black hat on his head. He thinks he's hiding from my security cameras.

This is why we pay Nigel so much. He is always looking out for our casino. He can spot a needle in a haystack.

I march my way back to him, and without any warning, I knock his hat off his head.

"What the ...?"

I grip the back of his neck and slam his head into the green felt as hard as I can, then let go.

He falls out of his chair and onto the black and gold carpet.

The room falls silent. I look up, and everyone quickly resumes what they were doing. "Call for Nigel," I tell the poker dealer. He nods quickly. "Tell him to deliver the son of a bitch to tower one." With that, I walk back through the room.

Just as I get back to tower one, my cell beeps in my pocket. I pull it out to see it's an email. I pull it up and my teeth grind.

It's a client requesting a Queen. And guess who it is? Fucking Em.

Thankfully, I have a guy to take my frustration out on.

EMILEE

I SIT ON the end of the bed, and my heart is heavy. My father and I returned to Las Vegas a week ago. I thought coming back with him that things would be like old times. They're not.

He's on edge. He hasn't said it, but I can tell. He's always on his phone trying to get ahold of George, but there's no answer. I overheard him a couple of days ago speaking to someone, I think it was Luca. He has him doing some kind of search for a phone number, but I don't think any information has been found yet.

Titan is always on my mind. I feel bad for what I said to him. I was mad, and in the heat of the moment, but I never thought of him to be anything remotely like George. I was attracted to Titan and had wanted him for a long time. I'm not sure if it would have happened any other way. But even so, I shouldn't have slapped him or walked out on him.

He had a point. My father had lied to me. The question is why? Even now, he won't tell me that. I don't know the specifics of why he faked his death, or how long he was going to pretend to be dead. Would he have ever come clean to me?

Every time I try to talk to him, he pushes me away. He says he has it taken care of and not to worry. He's treating me like a child. Like I can't handle the truth.

It's making me nervous. He has something planned, but I just don't know what it is. And I have a feeling I won't like it.

My cell beeps on my bed, and I pick it up to check it. I figure it's Haven or Jasmine. We haven't seen each other since we returned. I miss them so much.

Opening up the email, it's from my Queens app. It's a date for tonight with the same guy I had last time.

I bite my bottom lip, looking it over. He wants to take me to dinner again. Same place. Same time. And wants to pay me five thousand dollars. He's requesting I wear a red dress and my hair down. No limit on drinks this time. Maybe he realized I can handle my liquor.

I shouldn't …

"What are you doing, sweetie?" My father enters my room.

I look up at him and sigh. "I just got a request for a date tonight."

He frowns, confused.

"I'm a Queen," I remind him. He knows what I've done ever since he decided to fake his death. Even though he won't talk to me, I laid everything out to him on our flight back to Vegas from New York.

"How much?" he surprises me by asking.

"Five thousand," I answer. "But I'm not going to do it." I exit out of the app.

He runs a hand through his hair nervously.

"What's wrong?" I ask.

"Well …" He comes to sit down beside me. "I … just … It's …"

"Just spit it out, Dad." I say, tired of his rambling. We're both adults here.

"I got myself into trouble, Emilee. And I need help getting out."

"How much do you owe?" I ask, ducking my head. It can't be easy for him to admit this.

"A million dollars."

"What?" I gasp like I'm surprised. I just wanted to see if he would lie to me again.

"It wasn't all my fault." He gets defensive. "George made a deal. But my name was on that contract too. Now he's skipped town, and I'm stuck with nothing."

"Why didn't they go after him? Why didn't he fake his death?" I ask.

"Because he didn't have the life insurance policies that I did. And it would look suspicious for him to get them, and he turn up dead. We needed to avoid any investigation."

I nod in understanding.

"I had money hidden in the houses," he says softly.

My chest tightens. "No?"

He nods once. "It was in the master suite. I had a hidden safe in the closet …"

"I didn't know." Tears prick my eyes. "Maybe it's still there …"

"No. The night we returned from New York, I snuck off to the house once you went to sleep, and there was nothing left of it."

I burned it all. In order to keep it from George, I destroyed something that my father needed. "How much?" I clear my throat.

"Five hundred thousand."

My stomach knots. "I'm so sorry," I cry.

"Hey." He pulls me into his side. "You didn't know. No one did. Not even your mother or George. It was my secret stash." He kisses my forehead. "Don't worry, sweetie. We'll get through this. I'll figure something out." With that, he stands and exits my room.

I wipe my teary eyes and pick up my phone. I accept the date, knowing I have to help my father. Without knowing it, I've managed to ruin everything.

FORTY

TITAN

My phone beeps, and I look at it. Emilee has accepted the date.

Of course she fucking has! She's a Queen and bows to no one. Why would I be any different? She's not going to consider how I feel about that right now. I allowed it because she really wasn't doing it. Now things have changed. I could fire her, but that would show that I care, and my plan is to try my hardest not to give a fuck about what she does or who she sees.

"I told you what would happen if I saw you again," I tell the kid, putting my phone away.

If she wants to do this, it's her choice.

He spits blood onto the table that I have him seated at in the meat locker. "Fuck you, man."

I busted his face up pretty good with the one hit to the poker table. Now he's about to see what I can really do.

I punch him in the nose, knocking his head back. He cries out as blood goes flying from my skull ring making contact. "You know, I'm doing others a service by getting rid of you."

His head falls forward, and he moans while the blood drips from his face.

I grip his hair and yank his head back. "Look at me when I'm talking to you."

His eyes are barely open due to how swollen they are. "I was offered twenty grand just to kill you," I tell him. "I said no, he's young. He won't come around here anymore. He won't steal from us anymore. But lo and behold, here you are. And guess what?" I shake his head with my fist still in his hair. "I'm going to do it for free." Then I slam his face into the table once again.

EXITING THE ROOM, I wipe my bloody hands off with a towel and enter the elevator. After scanning my card, I go up a level and step off. I walk over to Nigel's desk in the corner. "I need a cleanup crew," I tell him.

He nods and picks up his phone.

I turn to walk to the elevator to go upstairs when I see her walking up the steps outside. She wears a red dress that stops mid-thigh. Black heels and her hair is down, curled and lies over one shoulder. Her lips match her dress and so does her small purse in her hand.

Nigel hangs up his call and goes to open the door for her.

She enters the door and gives him a big smile. "Thank you, Nigel." Her voice alone makes my breath pick up.

I miss that woman more than I'll ever admit. A king never shows his weakness. Not even to his queen.

"Miss York, it's been too long," he tells her.

"It has." She looks up, and the smile drops off her face when her eyes meet mine. She gasps softly when they drop to my blood-stained clothes. "Titan," she whispers my name and takes a step toward me.

I step back, and she stops.

Her face instantly falls.

What was she expecting? That I would drop to my knees the moment I see her? I refuse to do that no matter how much they shake.

"Are you okay?" she asks, biting her perfectly painted red lip.

I look at her body. Her legs look as ravishing as ever. Her thighs soft and inviting. I can tell she's lost weight by the way the dress hugs her small frame, and I wonder if she's even eating. Do they have any money? Is that why she's doing this? Pimping herself out?

Her face is slimmer, and her eyes look darker, sadder—like she's lost sleep—but that's just wishful thinking on my end, right? I want her to miss me like I miss her. I wish to see her in a bad mood and pissed at the world. Instead, she looks amazingly gorgeous and sad at the same time.

Like a broken doll that hasn't been played with in years. Her eyes beg for attention while her body screams take me.

My fingers itch to rip her dress off like I did that first night up in my room. To throw her on my bed and kiss her, fuck her. Make her fucking mine like she was. But Emilee York will never belong to me. I got everything I was going to get out of her, so I turn to the elevator, hold up my key card, and enter once the doors open.

But as it stops on the Royal Suite, I pull out my cell and make a call.

He answers on the first ring. I start the conversation, knowing I'll be the only one speaking. "Hey, I need a favor …"

EMILEE

THIS DINNER IS going about as good as the last one. *Boring as fuck!*

It's all business talk. But thankfully, I'm able to drink without any limits. I just keep telling myself that five grand is a lot to just be arm candy, and that I can do this for a few hours. It's not going to last all night.

Then I think of Titan. I can't get the look on his face out of my mind. Pure hatred. Just like he was in high school and college.

How had we gone from enemies, to lovers, to enemies again? At what point did I want more? At what part did it all fall apart?

"There you are. A little late, huh?" Jacob says.

I look up to see who he's talking to, and I mentally sigh. It's fuckface again. The business partner's son who stopped me in the hallway to the ladies' restroom last time.

Wonderful!

His eyes meet mine, and he smiles as if he can hear my inner thoughts. He knows I hate him. His presence alone makes my skin crawl, and the fucker gets off on it.

"Another one," I say, lifting my half full drink of champagne. Might as well down this one and get to the next. Maybe the time will fly by if I'm hammered.

Three more glasses and an hour later, I'm starting to see double of everything. My mind is foggy and my lips numbing. Champagne always gets me fucked up faster than anything else.

Jacob reaches over and places his hand on my thigh. I tense. Is this why he's allowing me to drink? To loosen me up to go all the way with me.

He notices and leans into my face. "You okay?"

"Yeah." I clear my throat and nod. Fuck, I need to sober up. "May I get a water?" I ask the waiter as he picks up the plates.

"Sure—"

"No need," Jacob interrupts him. "We're on our way out, and I have some in the limo."

I swallow, and all of a sudden, my tongue feels like sandpaper. *Shit.* This isn't good. He takes my hand and lifts me to stand. I can already tell I'm wobbly on my heels.

Closing my eyes, I take a deep breath. It's not that far. I just have to make it to the elevator where I can lean against the back wall. Then the short distance to the limo. I have this.

We all pile into the elevator, and it starts to descend. The last drink I had begins to hit me harder. I'm blinking rapidly, unable to keep my heavy eyes open. My ankles give, and I fall to my right.

"Whoa. Be careful." *It's the kid.* I can smell his breath on my face, and it reeks of vodka.

"I'm fine." I push him off me.

Jacob sees me out of the corner of his eye and wraps his arm around my shoulders, pinning me into his side. I allow it. I'd rather be close to him than the young pervert.

When the elevator dings and comes to a stop, the door opens, and we all step off into the hot summer night. "Wait right here. I'm going to walk Mr. Links to his car," Jacob tells me.

"What?" I ask confused as to why he would walk the man we had dinner with to his car, but they're already walking away.

The elevator is in the alley. And you can either go left or right. We came from the right, I think. The limo is parked out on the street nearby. I begin to walk in that direction.

"Hey, wait up," the kid calls out.

"Go away," I say over my shoulder.

"You don't really mean that," he says. Coming up behind me, he wraps his arms around me, pinning my arms to my sides.

"Get off me," I growl, trying to free myself but unsuccessful.

"I'll pay you double if you let me fuck you without a rubber," he whispers.

"I'm not going to …"

He buries his head into my neck and sucks on it. Hard. I cry out when his teeth bite into my skin.

He's ripped from me, the momentum knocking me to the ground, scraping my legs and hands on the asphalt. I scramble backward until my back hits the concrete wall. "Nite?" I gasp, looking at him standing over the kid in front of me.

His eyes meet mine for a brief second before he kicks the kid, knocking him onto his stomach.

"Where did you come from?" I ask, looking around quickly. "What are you doing here?" I ask as if the mute will answer me.

"I sent him."

I look to my right and see Titan walking toward us. I use the side of the building to push myself up. "Titan …"

"Save it, Em. You can yell at me later." He comes up to me and cups my cheeks. "Are you okay?" he asks.

"I … I think." I'm breathing heavy, my knees are skinned, and my hands burn from catching myself when I fell, but other than that, I'm physically okay.

He tilts my head to the side and lets out a growl when he sees my neck. My hands instantly go to the tender area. "What did he say to you?" Titan demands.

I swallow but don't make him wait. "That he would pay me double if I let him fuck me without a rubber."

He lets go of me, steps back, and spins around. Just as the kid makes it to his feet, Titan nails him in the face with his fist. The guy stumbles back, and Titan hits him again before he can recover.

I stand back and watch Titan put all those fights I watched Grave do in the ring to shame. Titan is a force like nothing I've ever seen. The kid never even gets a shot in.

"What the fuck is going on?" Jacob snaps, walking up to us.

Titan turns to face him, and Jacob stops when he sees the blood splattered all over his clothes and an unconscious kid on the ground.

"What the fuck, Titan?" he demands. "Do you have any idea who that is?"

"I don't give a fuck who he is," Titan growls.

"You can't do that." He shakes his head. His eyes still on the guy lying at an odd angle. I'm not even sure he's still alive.

"I can." Titan drops to his knees and holds out his hand to Nite who has been standing there quiet this entire time just watching. He places a knife in Titan's hand.

He grips the kid's hair and pulls his head up and stretches the back of it across Titan's leg. He takes the knife and slices it across the kid's throat. I cover my mouth as the blood pours from the open wound and all over Titan's jeans.

Jacob just stands there, his body shaking, eyes wide. I think he's in shock. "What …? What did you do?" he whispers in horror.

Titan closes the knife and hands it back to Nite, who puts it in his pocket. He immediately pulls out his cell and starts typing away on it.

Titan steps up to Jacob. "You left Emilee unattended. He pinned her arms down to her side and bit her." He points at me. "Told her he'd pay double if she'd fuck him raw." His voice rises.

"I'm … sorry," he adds quickly, clearly terrified of Titan. Jacob takes a step back.

"You know the rules, and you broke them," Titan growls.

As a Queen, I don't know what the clients are allowed to do. I just know what the Queens can and can't do.

"I didn't know he ..."

"Bullshit!" he snaps. "You know he came on to her at your last dinner."

My eyes widen. *He knew that?* How did Titan know that?

"Yes. Yes. I told you." He nods quickly. "I didn't keep it from you." Snapping, Jacob takes a step toward me, and I press my back into the wall. Not like I'm afraid of him. I feel safe that Titan is here. But still, I don't want him touching me.

"You're out," Titan says.

Jacob squares his shoulders. "Out? Do you know how much money I've spent at Kingdom?" he demands through gritted teeth. Clearly pissed at these turn of events.

"That was your choice." He waves a hand in the air, dismissing him.

"My choice?" he snaps at Titan. "If he wanted to fuck her, he can fuck her!" he shouts. Jacob reaches for my arm and yanks me from the wall. I try to pull away from him, but he's got a grip on my arm while he drags me to the center of the alleyway.

"Stop!" I shout, trying to shove him away from me as Titan reaches into the back of his jeans.

"They're just fucking whores!" Jacob yells, shaking me. His fingers digging into my forearm.

Bang!

I scream in surprise as the gun goes off. My heart stops, and my breath gets stuck in my throat as I watch Jacob fall to his knees and then to his chest in a puddle of his own blood in a back alleyway.

Oh, my God. Oh, my God. I'm chanting in my head as I feel blood on my face, chest, and arms. I stumble backward into the wall once again as I quickly try to rub it off.

FORTY-ONE

TITAN

I PLACE MY gun in my waistband and turn toward Nite. "Tell the cleanup crew two bodies."

Nite nods and goes back to texting on his cell.

I turn to face her. She stands against the wall in a state of shock, staring down at the blood smeared across her hands and arms.

"Em?" I ask her.

She doesn't acknowledge me.

"Em?" I take her face in my hands. "Emilee, look at me."

Wide blue eyes meet mine.

"Breathe," I order. Her face is pale. "Take in a breath, Em. Come on." Her skin is covered with his blood from the shot, and her body shakes. I don't think she notices. "Emilee?" I bark this time, giving her a little shake. Her lips part, and she sucks in a deep breath. "That's right," I say gently.

"You ... killed them."

"Yes." *And I'd do it again.* No one is going to put her in any situation that could cause her harm.

TITAN

I had an idea of how tonight would go. That's why I called Nite to watch her. He had informed me the minute the kid arrived. If he wouldn't have, then she would have never known I had surveillance on her. But he made a very bad mistake and paid for it with his life.

"You killed them," she repeats again.

"Em ...?"

"For me?" she asks, blinking rapidly. Not only is she in shock but she's also quite drunk.

"Of course, it was for you." I know the rumors that are told about the Kings and me, but we don't kill for sport. You won't have any clients, if you kill them all off. But for her? I'd kill them all. "He hurt you." It's the only reason I have.

Her bottom lip begins to quiver, and tears fill her pretty eyes. "But why?" she whispers. "Why would you do that?"

I open my mouth to tell her I love her, but now is not the right time. She's covered in blood, and two dead bodies lay literally at our feet.

I've waited twenty-six years to tell her how I feel, so what's another day? "Come on. Let's go to Kingdom. We need to wash off." Then I look at Nite. "Make sure to get their phones."

I PULL UP to the back of Kingdom and get out of the car. I run around the front and open her door. After I help her out, I remove my shirt and wrap it around her and take her hand to help her up the stairs. Nigel is already there waiting for us.

We enter the Royal Suite and go straight to my bedroom. I know that Bones is at Glass with Luca, but I'm not sure where in the fuck Grave and Cross are.

I undress her and start the shower. We get in, and I place her under the sprayer. The blood runs off her skin and down into the drain, washing away any evidence of what I did.

"I don't want to anymore." It's the first thing she's said to me since we've left the alleyway. She sat in my car silent and shaking uncontrollably, rocking back and forth. I was afraid to say anything to her. She

279

needed time to process it all. What happened to her, and what I did in order to protect her.

"Want to what?" I ask, running the soap up and down her cold arms, cleaning her skin.

"Be a Queen anymore," she whispers.

I want to smile but refrain. The only way she was doing that again was over my dead body. "Okay. You don't have to do it anymore."

"But ... I burned my parents' house down."

"That's okay." That house is the least of my worries.

"No." She shakes her head. "I burned my father's money."

My hands stop moving. "What do you mean?"

She licks her lips. "He told me that he had money hidden in the walk-in closet. But now it's all ash."

"What makes him think that?" Most of the house was destroyed, but there are parts that managed to go untouched. The neighbors had called the fire department before it all burned.

"He told me he went back the night we returned to Vegas." She bows her head. "I had burned it. He needed it. That's why I took the job to-night."

I grip her chin and lift her head, so she has to look at me. "Don't ever do anything other than for yourself, Em."

FORTY-TWO

TITAN

T HE SUN HAS been up for a few hours. We all sit around the conference table silently. I twirl a pen in my hands as Cross flips his Zippo. Grave's hungover ass drinks Pedialyte out of the bottle. And Bones types away on his phone when the door opens.

Nigel shows Nick York to his seat across from me. I thank him, and he exits, leaving us alone with him.

"What is this about?" he demands, straightening his tie. "I was informed I had to attend a meeting with the Kings?"

I sent Nigel out to retrieve him an hour ago. I half expected him to already be on the run.

"I remember a time when you begged to meet with us," Bones states, referring to when we loaned him money.

He swallows but squares his shoulders. "What does this pertain to?"

I almost laugh. This fuckface thinks he has leverage here, but he doesn't. "We know you lied to Em," I state, and his face drains of what color it had. "You see, we placed surveillance on the outside after the break-in. It was mainly to see if George came back, but it worked in our favor nonetheless."

"I don't know …"

"You told Emilee that you went back to the house to get the money you had hidden in your *secret stash*. You lied." The guys and I watched it this morning after I filled them in on everything that happened last night and what Em told me. And just as I expected, he had lied to her. We kept it running in case George ever decided to show his face again. Now I'm glad we did.

"I'm guessing you were hoping that she wouldn't share that information," Bones adds.

He dips his head and starts breathing heavily. "What do you want?"

I ignore that question and ask my own. "Worried she may realize what a piece of shit you are and disown you?"

He picks his head up and glares at me.

"She will once we tell her how you set her up," Bones growls.

"I didn't—"

"You did." I Interrupt him. "And I have proof." I state, placing two cell phones on the table.

He pulls on his collar. "What is this?" he demands.

"Evidence," I state. "You see, you owe several people money. One of them being Jacob. And when he saw that your daughter was a Queen, he wanted to go after her to get to you." I press play on a video on Jacob's phone. It's of Emilee walking into the back of Kingdom the night of their first date. Jacob was already there, parked around the corner, watching her. Recording it. Then he sent it to Nick's old number. But he didn't send a message. The video comes to a stop, and I sit back in my chair.

"You can't prove that," he growls.

"But I can." I open the phone once more and go back to the text messages. "She can work off my debt." My eyes meet his. "Is what you replied to his video."

"Is that true?"

He jumps to his feet as Nigel holds the door for Emilee to enter.

"Emilee …" he starts.

"Is that true?" she demands, tears in her eyes.

TITAN

"What are you ...?" He spins around to glare at me. "You set this up."

I sit back and cross my arms over my chest. "She deserves to know." Emilee has a big heart. She wants to see the good in people. I mean, look at the type of people she has surrounded herself with. Bones, me, the rest of the Kings. She believes in second chances, and I love her for that. Without her forgiveness, I would have never had my chance with her. But her father? Enough is enough. She needs to see that he betrayed her. And it could have cost her, her life.

"You were willing to let him sleep with me because you owed him money?" she goes on, and her voice cracks.

He opens his mouth, but nothing comes out.

"You set her up," I say, filling the silence.

He turns around to face me.

"Just like you did with George. You knew what he wanted. What'd he do to her if you walked away." I'm fishing. I don't have confirmation yet, but I'll get it.

He pulls his lips back. "You think you're better than me?" He shakes his head. "She is a fucking Queen. Call girl. Escort. Whore! She fucks men for money." He points at her.

I grind my teeth and fists my hands. "The only guy she fucked for money was your business partner because you left her with nothing," I snap. How could he only think of himself? I went through all the documents that Yan had shown Emilee after her mother had passed. And they were legit. Except for the will he left her. That money did not exist. It was something that Nick and George had come up with to buy him time while he was pretending to be dead. He had it written where Emilee had to be thirty-five in order to inherit three million. By the time that rolled around, he'd risen from his grave and taken every cent he had and would be in another country.

"It's not like George raped her," he spits out, and I stand. "She willingly ..."

I storm over to him, grab his shirt, and drag him over to me. I slam him face-first into the floor-to-ceiling windows that overlooks Las Vegas. "You knew, didn't you?" I growl and yank his head back. "What he would do to her. Was that part of the agreement?"

283

"Titan, we had an agreement," I hear Bones say.

"You fucking knew the entire time." I shove his face into it one last time, ignoring him. Then I push him away from me where he falls to the floor.

Blood covers the window where I slammed his face into it. "He promised ... to take care of her."

"How could you?" Emilee whispers, watching him.

"I did what I had to do," he says, rolling onto his side and sitting up.

"At the expense of me?" She sniffs.

"They were going to kill me," he growls, hugging his side.

"And he fucking used me!" she shouts, walking around the table. "For Mom. She needed me ..."

"She was a whore too," he spits up at her.

Bones jumps to his feet and grabs her arms, stopping her. The door to the conference room opens, and Luca enters, followed by Nite. Nick hangs his head and sighs.

"It's a party." Grave snorts, downing more Pedialyte.

"Thought you would want to see this." Luca throws a stack of papers on the table.

I walk over and pick them up, skimming over them. I begin to laugh. "Boy, did you fuck yourself. Five point two million dollars." I whistle. "That's a lot of money to have stashed away when you owe a couple of million." I throw the documents in front of him on the floor. "You couldn't touch it, though, because you put it in your wife's name. But she didn't know about it, did she?" I quirk a brow.

He just stares at the papers while blood drips from his busted lip.

The dates show the account was opened six months ago. "You knew that she and George were sleeping together, and you needed a way to hide money. From your ex-wife and your business partner. But then you had to go into hiding when you faked your death. Meaning no contact with the world. Not even Nancy. So you had no clue that she had died. You were too busy in New York living the single life. And why would George inform you of her death? He was getting everything you ever had."

"Stop!" He slams his fists down on the papers.

TITAN

"Am I warm?" I ask

"Where did you find these?" Bones asks Luca.

"We caught a break. Titan had found an account number when going through his study after the break-in. I found that they belonged to an offshore bank account. It took me a while because I was looking for his name, not Nancy's."

"Is there anyone that you haven't used?" Emilee asks softly. Pure defeat in her blue eyes. I hate that he's hurt her so much.

He looks up at her but doesn't answer.

She yanks her arms in Bones's hold, and he lets her go. Her watery eyes look from his to mine. And without another word, she exits the conference room, choosing to walk away from him.

I kneel next to him. "You'll never hurt her again, Nick." I can't take the chance of him harming her. Em is mine. We will start a family of our own someday, and I won't allow this sorry son of a bitch to put my children in harm's way. He has to go. Bones was right, he and I have an agreement on that situation. I slap Nick on the shoulder. "Be careful what you wish for." And then walk out and after my future wife.

EMILEE

I GET OFF the elevator and march into the Royal Suite.

"Em?" I hear the door shut behind me.

I ignore Titan and make my way to his room. My eyes catch site of his balcony, and I shove open the sliding glass door and walk out onto it. I suck in a deep breath of fresh air.

"Emilee?" Titan sighs.

I spin around to face him. When we woke up this morning, he asked me if I trusted him. After what he did for me last night, there was no way for me to say no. He then informed me that he had a meeting today, and he wanted me to attend it. I had no idea that it was going to be with my father. "What, Titan?" I ask, angrily wiping the tear from my cheek.

"I'm sorry."

I chuckle at that. "You did nothing wrong."

"I'm sorry you had to hear that." He walks over to me and pushes a strand of dark hair behind my ear.

"No, you're not," I say.

"You're right. I wanted you to see what he did to you. How he put himself first. You needed to know what kind of person he truly is."

I always thought he was a saint. A man who had everything in the world. A reputable business. A loving wife. How many people had he used? How far would he have gone if Titan wouldn't have intervened last night? "Thank you."

"Don't thank me, Em." He cups my face. "I hate to see that look on your face. And I hate that he wasn't the man you thought he was."

I reach out, grip his shirt, and pull him toward me. "Titan …"

"Yeah, Em?" His eyes search mine.

"I love you." I say the words that I've never told another man. I have no regrets or second thoughts. This man is the one for me. And I hold my breath, hoping that he feels the same about me.

He brings his lips to mine. "I love you too." Then he's kissing me.

EPILOGUE

EMILEE

I STAND IN front of Titan's bathroom mirror, wringing my hair out with my towel. He messaged me earlier that he wanted to have dinner tonight. After everything went down with my father in the conference room last week, he took a couple of days off. We spent them in bed with room service. It was nice. But things quickly went back to normal, and he had to return to Kingdom. I've spent every day with the girls, trying to get back to our routine and let go of everything else.

I want to move on. I want to be happy with Titan and let go of my father and everything that has happened since I returned from Chicago. I'm going to enjoy every second I have with this man. I saw him at his worst. He killed not only one, but two men. In brutal fashion. But he did so for me. He protected me. He cared about my well-being. Who else can I say has done that lately? *No one.*

I haven't heard from my father. Honestly, I don't want to see him. I feel betrayed. I was excited and caught up when I realized he was truly alive to see how much he had lied to me. He should have come to me. Told me. I would have kept his secret. Now I just want to forget his betrayal. What I did when I thought I had no way to help my mother other than fuck his business partner.

I exit the bathroom and enter Titan's bedroom. The sun set an hour ago. The dark curtains that cover the floor-to-ceiling windows are pulled back and open, showcasing the lit-up city.

My eyes fall to his king-size bed and see a box sitting on it. "Titan?" I call out but get nothing in return. His bedroom door is shut, and he had told me earlier that he had to work late tonight.

Walking over to it, I look over the black box. It has a yellow ribbon wrapped around that ties into a bow in the middle. A card is sitting on top.

My Em,

You deserved something special. Get ready and meet me upstairs.

I place the card on the white comforter and read **GUCCI** in white letters across the box. I pull the lid off and push back the yellow tissue paper. I gasp when I see the black sequin dress. It's one shoulder, ankle length with a slit up the side to the thigh. I hold it up to my body and run back into the bathroom, looking at myself in the mirror.

He's up to something, and I can't wait to see what it is.

TITAN

I sit at my desk in my office when Bones enters. I look at the clock, and say, "Make it quick. I have plans tonight."

He smirks, falling down into his seat. "I know. You've reminded me ten times today."

I'm taking Emilee to dinner on the rooftop of Kingdom. I've had staff members up there for the past three hours getting it ready. A table for two, champagne, twinkling lights, and a rolled-out black carpet. The works. And not to mention, the fireworks show that is set to go off after I get down on one knee and propose.

Emilee has never needed an audience. She would prefer a quiet proposal—just us one on one in an intimate moment over a huge show in front of hundreds of strangers. And I want to give her that. I want to give her everything. But I'm going to start with offering her my life. I just pray that she accepts it.

"Stop worrying." He waves me off as if he can read my mind.

I hold up my hand, ignoring him. "What did you want?"

"I just wanted to let you know that Nick has been taken care of."

Bones had reminded me that we had an agreement when I wanted to fucking kill Nick in the conference room. Earlier before the meeting, we had decided that Bones was going to get rid of him, and I wasn't going to ask any questions.

I know Emilee is hurt over what her father had done, but Bones thought it would be best if he took care of him on his own. Keep my hands clean, sort of thing. She can't hate me for something that I didn't take part in. I nod. "Thank you."

"Don't mention it." He smiles, letting me know that he enjoyed whatever he did to the fucker. "Oh, and I wanted to let you know that I'm taking some days off." He looks at his watch as though he has somewhere to be.

I frown. *That's unlike him.* "Everything okay?"

"Yep." He slaps his hands on his jeans-clad thighs before standing from his seat. He makes his way over to my office door and stops, turning back to face me. "Congratulations, Titan. You deserve to get what you've always wanted."

I run a hand over my hair nervously. "She hasn't said yes, yet."

"She will," he assures me before he exits.

EPILOGUE TWO

BONES

I FEEL MY phone vibrate in my pocket, and I pull it out to see I have a picture from Emilee. I open it up. It's of her and Titan standing on the rooftop of Kingdom a couple of nights ago. He's holding her up off her feet, his hands on her hips. Her head bent down, kissing him. Fireworks are going off in the background, lighting up the Vegas skyline. With the caption that says, *I said yes.*

I smile and type back "Congratulations." I couldn't be happier for my best friend and the love of his life. I could never love Emilee like she deserved. Or any woman for that matter. Kingdom will always come first, and I know that's not how love should be. I've accepted it.

That's why I've flown halfway around the world. I tell myself this is about Kingdom. But it's also about the woman in that photo.

"They're getting married." I hold up my phone to the man's face before me. He sits tied to a chair in the middle of the cold and damp room. A single light bulb hangs above his head from a chain.

"Argghh," he mumbles around the gag in his mouth.

"I'll make sure to give them your wishes." I tap his face a couple of

TITAN

times with my open palm.

He pulls away the best he can, which isn't far. I pocket my cell and pick up the knife that sits on the table next to him. It's stained with his blood. We've been in here for over eight hours.

"It's been a while since I got to carve a man." I tell him, running the blade gently down the side of his face, just letting him feel the cold steel while I fuck with his mind.

He throws his head back and fights the restraints, but he's not going anywhere. "See, George, five hundred thousand dollars isn't that much money. I could have let it go, but then you fucked with Emilee."

He shakes his head quickly. His teary eyes begging me not to kill him. To spare his sorry, fucking pathetic life.

"And that sealed your fate."

I run the tip of the blade down his bare chest, splitting the skin like butter. He screams out as the blood flows like a steady rain.

I once told Titan that if I ever found this fucker, I was going to make him pay in pounds of flesh. And I'm a man of my word.

ACKNOWLEDGMENTS

Thank you to my PA, Christina Santos. This woman is amazing! She deserves a metal for how hard she works. I love her to pieces and can't imagine life without her.

Thank you to my author bestie, Siobhan Davis. I am constantly in awe of her. She's always there for me no matter what time of day or night with words of encouragement. Thank you for not only being my inspiration, but for being a best friend.

Thanks to my editor, Jenny. I know half the time, I make up words that probably have her laughing. But I'm thankful for our friendship. Seven years together, and I love you.

Thanks to my cover designer, Shannon, Shanoff Reads. I had a great time working with you on this cover and swag for Titan. I can't wait to see what you do for the rest of the books in the Dark Kings series.

Thanks to my formatter, CP Smith. As always, she blows my mind.

And a big thank you to my proofreaders, Elizabeth Clinton, Amanda Marie, Brenda Parsons, Shaley Clements, Lauren Lascola-Lesczynsk, Sarah Piechuta, and Rita Rees. Thank you to these amazing ladies who took their time to read over my story with very little notice.

I want to thank my lovely betas, Rita Rees, Fay Moore, Amanda Anderson, Whitney West, and Heather Brown.

I want to thank my Sinners. They are amazing! Christina Santos, Fay Moore, Lauren Lascola-Lesczynksi, Sarah Piechuta, Sophie Ruthven, Heather Brown, Tara Hartnett, Rita Rees, Karen McVino, Elizabeth Clinton,Kat Strack, Brandi Zelenka, Michelle McLellan, Amanda Marie, Brenda Parsons, Ashley Estep, Tiffany Johnson Mauer, Jenny Dicks, Mary Dbo, Catherine J Lawrence, Book Bre, Luetta Lyons, Heather Hopkins-Kirby, Shonna Mccabe, Whitney West, Melinda Benn, Paramita Patra, Eliette Alonso, Kerri Elizabeth, Amanda Anderson, Wendy Leach Charron, Laura Peterson, Melissa Cunningham,

Mercedez Potts, Melissa Sagastume Gil, Ashley Carver, Jasmina Ceha, Natasha Bartholomew, and Katie Friend.

I want to thank Sarah Ferguson with Social Butterfly for everything that she did to help me get Titan to the readers.

And last but not least, my readers. Thank you for taking a chance and wanting to read my books. I hope that you all love them as much as I do.

TITLES BY SHANTEL TESSIER

The UN Series
Undescribable
Unbearable
Uncontrollable
Unforgettable
Unchangeable
AUnforeseen
Unpredictable

Seven Deadly Sins Series
Addiction
Obsession
Confession- Coming soon

The Selfish Series
Selfish
Myself
Selfless

Standalones
DASH
Donut Overthink It
Just A Kiss
Slaughter
Champagne Wishes – Wild in the Windy City anthology
Make You Beg – Bully Me: Class of 202 anthology

The Dare Series
I Dare You
I Promise You
If You Dare

Printed in Great Britain
by Amazon